That Time

May

Cease

MORE BY THIS AUTHOR

Historical Fiction

The Testament of Mariam

This Rough Ocean

The Chronicles of Christoval Alvarez

The Secret World of Christoval Alvarez
The Enterprise of England
The Portuguese Affair
Bartholomew Fair
Suffer the Little Children
Voyage to Muscovy
The Play's the Thing

Oxford Medieval Mysteries

The Bookseller's Tale
The Novice's Tale

The Fenland Series

Flood
Betrayal

Contemporary Fiction

The Anniversary
The Travellers
A Running Tide

That Time

May

Cease

Ann Swinfen

Shakenoak Press

Cover design by JD Smith www.jdsmith-design.co.uk

For

Carol Patterson

Dear friend since childhood

Chapter One

*A*t first, when I woke, I thought I was back in Muscovy. The moisture from my breath had frozen in a rim of ice along the edge of the bedclothes, and despite my dog Rikki, curled up against my back and providing a hint of warmth, I was shivering. Although I had recently taken to wearing over my night shift the curious knitted garment Goodwife Maynard of St Thomas's had given me when I journeyed to that remote northern land of the Russians, I knew that I would soon need to spend some of my limited resources on more blankets. At the moment I possessed two, together with a thin secondhand feather quilt. These, plus my cloak laid over them, plus the company of Rikki, failed to provide enough warmth to stop me waking early, once the last of the previous night's fire had died away to nothing.

It had begun snowing early in November, and the snow had never melted in the weeks since. Every few days, more snow fell, and yesterday there had been a mighty blizzard. Older folk said that the winter was nearly as cold as the famous one in 1564, when the Thames had frozen over and a great Frost Fair had been held on the ice, with fairground booths set up upon the very river. Nobles had driven their carriages or ridden on horseback down river from Westminster to Greenwich. There had been market stalls and dancing bears on the ice, and everyone who could find a pair of shinbones to strap to his feet had learned to skate. The Queen herself, with the courtiers, had made sport upon the ice.

The sick children in our wards talked excitedly of all they would do when they were better and the river froze. I think their eager anticipation helped many of them to recover sooner than expected. Although thick ice was forming along both banks, north and south of the Thames, making the work of the river watermen almost impossible, this year it had not yet met in the centre, where the current running down from Oxford and beyond, and the strong tides flowing back and forth to the sea, kept the water clear, except near the pillars of the Bridge, where clumps of ice gathered and then broke away, making the navigation of all ships hazardous, even the great merchantmen.

There was one great blessing of the cold weather. It put an end, for a time, to the plague, which had been claiming victims all the previous year. For some reason that no man could understand, the plague abated in cold weather, and returned again when the weather grew warm. Some said the plague bred in the warmer air. Others believed it to be carried by rats, dogs, and cats, though, to tell truth, I have seen a whole household die of the plague where there was no animal to infect them.

London was never altogether free of the plague, and, when it struck, all places of entertainment, including the playhouses, were closed down by order of the Lord Mayor and Common Council, so the players dreaded the plague both for itself and for the damage it did to their trade. The Council, on the other hand, was always glad of an excuse to close the playhouses, which they regarded as nurseries of sin and debauchery. There were writers of pamphlets, mostly of a Puritan persuasion, who could become very eloquent on the subject.

Although the river had not yet frozen right across during this winter, those fringes of ever growing layers of ice along both banks made embarking and landing from wherries both difficult and dangerous, which meant that the wherrymen suffered yet again from lack of fares. It seemed almost impossible to trust one's memories of the heat and drought of the summer, when the river had been so low that men could walk or ride across it through the sludge and shallow water. The problem then with using the wherries had been the unpleasant scramble across muddy boards to reach the boats, which had not depth enough of water to moor at the landing stages.

A difficult summer had now been followed by a difficult winter for the wherrymen, so that some had been forced to sell their boats – if they could find a buyer – or lay them up in hopes that better times might come. Meantime, the men themselves joined the ever-growing ranks of London's poor, some of them begging on the streets, some seeking paupers' lodgings at St Thomas's or Bartholomew's for themselves and their families, some (the less fortunate ones) finding themselves sent to Bridewell as beggars fit for work and so set to hard labour. Least fortunate of all joined the dead discovered frozen every dawn on the streets of London and Westminster and Southwark.

For every day now there were beggars found perished in the street, where they had tried to shelter in the doorways of houses and shops or in the porches of London's many churches. Since the Queen's father had abolished the monasteries, which once cared for the poor and homeless, the problem of poverty had grown worse year by year, despite legislation to put those deemed sturdy beggars to work in Bridewell and provide limited shelter for the rest. The children, at least, went to Christ's Hospital, where they were fed and clothed and taught lessons, but their elders were still a blemish on the city.

Everyone gave thanks to God that there had been a good harvest, but people eat more when the cold is severe, so that already there had begun to be murmurings about food running short before the next year's crops could be gathered. Moreover, a winter as severe as this, if it continued, meant a delay to the spring ploughing and planting, which in turn meant a likely meagre harvest to come.

It was no use brooding upon such worries, I would have to get up.

As I threw the bedclothes aside with a pretence of grim determination, the icy crust from my breathing shattered and slid to the ground. I lowered my feet gingerly to the bare boards and gasped as the cold penetrated through the old pair of hose I had worn in bed as comfort for my feet. Rikki opened his eyes, gave me one disbelieving look, then closed them again.

'Be grateful,' I admonished him, 'that you do not need to strip, wash and dress, but carry a warm coat with you everywhere.'

He ignored me, merely huddling closer into the tumbled bedclothes.

Each morning when I rose this winter, I found the water in my washing ewer frozen solid and the inside of the window so thickly coated with ice that the grudging light of pre-dawn was little better than night. Darkness lingered late, so that I went to my work at the hospital by starlight. The very stars seemed frosted, glittering with an alien cold, against which the few candlelit windows made a pitiful defence. In the evening when I returned, the stars had taken possession of the world again, their blue light casting a ghostly pallor over faces in the street.

Today was no different. The water in the bowl I had used for washing the night before was frozen and I looked at it in disgust. I paid Howard, the water carrier who rented one of the attics above my room, to fetch me water every day, but he would not bring today's supply until later, after I had left for the hospital. I decided to give washing a miss this morning. Instead I hopped about on the cold floor, stripping out of my nightshift and dressing for the day ahead. I decided to wear Mistress Maynard's knitted tunic under my doublet and breeches, despite the fact that it gave me the appearance of a bulging and badly made cloth doll.

However, with my physician's gown over the top I would look only a little bulkier and I would certainly be warmer.

When I drew aside my thin curtains and opened the ill-fitting shutters, I found that the irregular glass of my window was adorned with a delicate tracery of ice flowers, which made it difficult to see out, although it was still so dark that there was little enough to see in any case, apart from the torches flaming at the gateway to the Bridge, and, across the river in the City, a handful of lit windows. Even so, here in Southwark a few people were already abroad, dim figures moving blurrily along the street below. The labourers of Southwark are early abroad, willy-nilly.

The house itself was very quiet. No sound could be expected from the room below mine. Simon Hetherington, like all players, would have slept in, had he been there, though of late he had been sharing lodgings in the City. The Atkins family, who kept the lodging house, would not have risen yet, while the water carrier could set his own hours, being his own man and not working for a master. The other previous inhabitant of the attics was gone, the quiet old woman, she who had earned a few pence by spinning white stuff and otherwise lived on poor relief.

Secretive and shy as a mouse, she rarely mixed with the other tenants, so she had been dead several days when Howard – not having heard or seen anything of her – thought to knock on her door. There seemed no mystery about her dying. There was neither food nor fuel left in her room. She had merely lain down one night and never risen to another bitter day.

The attic room being empty and no new tenant offering for it, I had suggested to Goodwife Atkins that I might find someone. The group of beggar children I had befriended some while before needed better lodgings than their usual abandoned houses or neglected outbuildings. The eldest boy, Matthew, was now employed at St Thomas's as one of the lads who ran errands or did any odd task about the hospital – scrubbing floors, turning the spit in the kitchen, or mucking out the stables. I had suggested him to Eddi, one of the older hospital lads I knew, and Matthew had been taken on trial some while before. He was eager and hard-working, which had won him permanent employment, so that he could provide in some measure for the other three.

Early in December I was able to recommend Katerina for a post as a laundry maid, her usual occupation of selling nuts and fruit to playgoers having come to an end when the winter weather closed the playhouses. The twins Jonno and Maggie trailed after the older two, lending a hand when they might, though earning nothing, bar the odd farthing when someone was feeling generous. However, working at the hospital they were entitled to food in the refectory. With Matthew's and Katerina's earnings paying for lodgings, the children would be safely provided for. The youngest child, Jamey, was now cared for amongst the orphans at Christ's Hospital, where he had begun at last to talk and to catch up with other children of his age.

Goodwife Atkins had, understandably, voiced some doubts when I suggested the children as tenants.

'I misdoubt me, doctor,' she said. 'We've never rented to children before. Who's to say they will pay their rent and behave themselves like decent Christian folk? And all four in the one room? They are not kin, are they?'

'Two of them are,' I assured her. 'As for the two older ones, I think they have come to regard themselves as one family, brothers and sisters all. They have been together for as much as five years, I believe, looking out for one another. That speaks something of loyalty and decency, I would say.'

Eventually she had agreed, albeit reluctantly. I had warned the children that they must behave as model tenants if they wished to remain, and they were so taken with their lodgings that they had promised fervently that they would. They had once visited my room and could hardly believe their good fortune in finding what Katerina called 'a real home' – a room with a fireplace, a bed she could share with Maggie, and a couple of straw palliasses on the floor for the boys. Since they had moved in, a fortnight before, she had been scavenging amongst the hospital's cast-offs to furnish the small room up under the roof beams, bringing back cups with broken handles, a torn and ragged rug, and a rusty old cooking pot which she spent every evening rubbing with sand until it would be fit to hold food.

I could hear no sound of the children stirring yet, but they would soon be about, for they were eager to show themselves promptly for work. In their desperate young lives they had never before had both paid employment and a permanent roof over their heads.

As I picked up my cloak from amongst the tangle of bedclothes, Rikki came alert at once. Recognising the signs, he leapt down from the bed and waited, tail wagging, beside the door. I straightened the bed roughly, then pulled a woollen hood over my physician's cap, caught up my satchel of medical supplies and pulled on the wolf skin gloves I had brought back from Muscovy last spring. At the time I had thought I should never have need of them in an English winter, but I had misjudged the unpredictability of English weather.

I was grateful for my fur-lined cloak, a gift from one of my wealthy patients. I had cured him of the stone, without his needing to endure the risk of the surgeon's knife, by prescribing a course of infusions made with *vaccinium myrtillus*, *galium aparine*, *taraxacum officinale*, and *althea officinalis* to dissolve the gravel, together with *matricaria recutita*, *melissa officinalis*, and *foeniculum vulgare* to counteract the spasms of pain.

Rikki and I descended the stairs as quietly as possible, for the sake of the other tenants, but ice which had formed around the frame of the front door meant that I had to pull it closed more loudly than I would have liked. Outside, the air was so cold it was painful to inhale. Whereas in my room the breath from my lungs had merely made a cloud before my face, now it began, almost at once, to form crystals of ice around the edge of my hood. I set off as briskly as I could, though the settled and packed snow underfoot was treacherous. I was grateful I had such a short way to walk to my work, casting a sympathetic glance at those who were making their way to the Bridge. Many who worked in the City could not afford to live there. Southwark lodgings were cheaper, but you paid for them in the long walk every day through the snow.

My lack of regular wages during the summer had left me short of the chinks and even though I had been back at the hospital for some three months now, I needed to count my pennies. With the coming of the snow, however, I had ordered a pair of stout winter boots from William Baker, the former soldier who was now a shoemaker. I was glad of them in this deep snow, but it meant I was short of coin for fuel and food, so that I had taken up my entitlement to hot, simple food in the hospital refectory. This meant that I lit my fire only at night, and Simon would often visit in the evenings to share its warmth. It made for cold mornings, but I was looking forward now to breaking my fast at St Thomas's.

As we neared the hospital, Rikki ran ahead, and he was already scratching at the door of the gatekeeper's lodging when I reached it. The door opened just wide enough to admit a person shuffling sideways.

'Come in quickly, doctor,' Tom Read said, 'I dasn't let the cold air in.'

I squeezed through the gap and he slammed the door behind me. He had a good fug built up in here, compounded of smoke from his fire, the elderly dog smell from his wolfhound Swifty, and a certain ripe aroma of his own. He was cleanly in his habits, but I suspected he did not bathe often in this bitter weather.

'Come you to the fire,' Tom said.

'I see Rikki has not waited to be asked,' I said with a laugh, as I held out my hands to the warmth.

Swifty had eased a little to one side and the two dogs were curled up together so close to the fire I was afraid their fur would singe.

'They'll do,' Tom said, 'will you take some hot ale?'

8

'Nay, I thank you, Tom. I'm off to the refectory.'

'Porridge and maslin bread again today, I'm afraid.'

'Warm and sustaining. We cannot expect to feast like courtiers on singing birds and sugar banquets. Superintendent Ailmer must watch the hospital's pennies.'

'Aye, true enough. But here, take a pot of this honey. Stir it in your porridge or spread it on your bread. 'Twill make either taste better.'

He handed me an earthenware pot, its cork tied down with a scrap of cloth and a length of twine.

'How is it you always have honey, Tom? You do not keep bees yourself. Is this St Thomas's honey?'

He winked and tapped the side of his nose. 'Edwina Brockhurst as works with the hospital bees is somewhat sweet on me. She hopes to make me the sweeter with her regular gifts of honey.'

I laughed. 'You old rogue! She's young enough to be your daughter, though I'm glad of the honey.'

'Granddaughter, more like. But who am I to refuse such acceptable gifts? I fear I may have a rival, though. One of the journeymen who works in the printing shop has his eye on her, I'm thinking. He may win her away from me.'

With my hand on the latch of the door, I turned back.

'Were there many brought in, this night?'

He grimaced. 'Aye. Mebbe a score. Some still living, though they may have died since. You'll find some in your children's ward.'

As the Watch patrolled the streets of Southwark by night, they regularly encountered the poor lying in doorways and by a kind of selective blindness would ignore those they knew as regular street dwellers who gave no trouble. But if they came across the dead and dying, they would have them carried to St Thomas's. The dead were deposited in the chapel, to await a brief funeral and burial in an unmarked pauper's grave. Those who were merely dying were passed to the care of the hospital. Some lived. Some did not.

I nodded. There was nothing to say. A score of victims laid low by winter and poverty was not the worst, by any means, of this sorry nocturnal harvest. I slipped through the door, sealing in as much of Tom's precious warmth as possible, and crossed the courtyard.

The refectory, lying adjacent to the hospital kitchen, benefitted from some of its warmth, though not so much as to persuade me to remove my cloak. I accepted my bowl of porridge from one of the serving dames, several chunks of rough bread from another, and found a seat on the dais amongst the physicians, surgeons and apothecaries. On the lower tables, set at right angles to the dais, groups of hospital servants and nursing sisters were also spooning up porridge. It was lumpy, but hot. No one was inclined to talk. Breakfast was a hurried meal, quickly eaten before beginning the long hard day of work in the wards and stillroom, and for others in the many workshops attached to the hospital. I allowed myself a little of Tom's honey on my bread, but returned the rest of the jar to my satchel to augment my stores of food at home.

In the Whittington lying-in ward, I was glad to see that a good fire was burning and the women had already been fed and washed.

'Two new births in the night, Dr Alvarez,' said Goodwife Appledean, who had charge of the midwives. 'No difficulties, and no need to call you in.'

I smiled at her as I removed my cloak and hood and hung them on a peg beside the door. She was skilled at her work and would only send for me at night when there was a particularly difficult birth.

'That is good to hear,' I said. 'I will just see to them, then go to the children. I hear some were brought in from the streets.'

I walked over to the basins of soap and water to wash my hands, and she went with me.

'Aye.' She shook her head sadly. 'I saw them go past. 'Tis a disgrace that so many are dying on the streets this winter.'

I began my round of the ward with my most serious case, a woman past the usual age for child bearing, who had given birth to twins three days earlier. She had a history of stillbirths and infant deaths, with five older children still surviving, none of whose fathers were known for certain. Formerly one of the Winchester geese of Southwark, her whoring days were over, and she now lived with one of those out-of-work wherrymen. Their union had not received the blessing of the church, though by declaration before witnesses they had a kind of common law marriage, which did not bar her from this ward, endowed by a former mayor, Richard Whittington, for the lying-in of unmarried mothers.

Nell and her man must both have been past fifty, but here she was with two tiny scraps of sons, neither of them as large as a ha'penny loaf. I looked to the babes first. One looked a better colour than on the previous day, the other was still greenish white, like grass cut off from the sun. Nell was asleep, her mouth open.

'Have they been feeding?' I asked Goodwife Appledean.

'That one has.' She indicated the better seeming one. 'The other? He makes a start, then it seems too much effort for him, and he gives up. I doubt he'll live.'

I lifted the smaller baby out of the wicker cradle and laid him on the end of the bed. As I examined him, he opened eyes of a brilliant dark blue which wandered vaguely at first, then fixed on my face.

'I'd not say that he has quite given up yet,' I said, wrapping him again. 'At her age, perhaps Nell has not enough to feed two. I would like you to try this one with goat's milk, sweetened with a little honey.' It was an old remedy of my father's, for newborns whose mothers had died. 'Not much at a time. And often. Every hour at first.'

She nodded. 'I'll see to it at once, doctor.'

'We'll look over the night's new births first, then you may make an assay of it.'

As she had said, the two babies born during the night presented no problem, and I finished my examination of the rest of the ward while she prepared the feed for the weaker twin.

The children's ward was crowded, with scarce enough room to move between the ranks of truckle beds, cots, and even mattresses on the floor. Although we were temporarily spared the plague, the cruel weather, which particularly besets the poor, had brought a wave of chest and lung infections, and very nasty ulcerated throats. The beds in all of the wards at St Thomas's were pushed together to make room for more, hastily knocked together by the hospital carpenter and his boy.

At some times of the year the children's ward was noisy, the less seriously ill tending to climb from their beds and run about, barely under the control of the more inexperienced of the sisters, who were apt to be assigned to this ward, those with more experience being needed on the wards which dealt with the kind of serious injuries often suffered by the labouring men of Southwark.

When my place here at St Thomas's had been given to another during the previous year, matters in my two wards had fallen into a sad shambles which I was gradually setting to rights. I now had two reliable women here in the children's ward. One was Goodwife Watson, a middle-aged widow who had no great experience of nursing, but a lifetime's experience of child rearing. She was kind and motherly, a great comfort to distressed and sickly children.

The other was unusual amongst St Thomas's sisters, who were rarely less than forty years of age, and married or widowed. Alice Meadows was not above one and twenty, born into a yeoman's family in Kent. Left an orphan the previous year, she had come to London and sought work in the hospital not merely because she needed employment but because she had a true interest in healing the sick. She had once let slip that her grandmother's sister had been a wise woman, skilled in herbs, and her first interest had arisen from watching this great-aunt at work.

As a woman she could never become a physician – unless she took on such a disguise as mine – but she might aspire to rise to such a position as that of Mistress Maynard, in charge of all the sisters in the hospital. While some of the women were able for not much more than changing sheets and feeding the sick patients, a few, like Alice or Goodwife Appledean, aspired to true medical knowledge. Neither the medical schools of the universities nor the Royal College of Physicians would have recognised their worth, but in the everyday treatment of patients in a hospital like ours such women made possible their successful care.

'More of the destitute brought in last night, I understand,' I said to Goodwife Watson. 'How many?'

'Seven, Dr Alvarez. Two are but cold and hungry. One, I think, will not live. The others?' She shrugged. 'I cannot be sure. Perhaps, if we are not too late . . .'

'I will look at the worst case first,' I said.

It was a boy who might have been seven or eight, but by all the signs of a lifetime of poverty, he could be older, stunted by lack of food and those common scourges of pauper children, scurvy and rickets. He was restless and feverish, barely conscious. I wished that they had sent for me to this case during the night. As Goodwife Watson feared, we might already be too late.

Alice was sitting beside his truckle bed on a low stool, bathing his burning face with water. As I approached, his whole body jerked in spasmodic coughing.

'Has he been given anything to eat or drink?' I asked.

'I tried to give him to drink of swish water,' she said, 'but he swallowed very little.'

'That was right, but now I will try something stronger. Fetch me the tincture of febrifuge herbs and a small spoon. We will see if we can get a little of it down him.'

While she fetched the tincture, I forced open the child's mouth and studied his throat. It was badly ulcerated. The swish water would help, and the tincture might reduce his fever, if it had not already too strong a hold, but the real problem was the child's wasted body, which had no strength in itself to fight the illness.

With Alice holding the boy's head firmly I did manage to administer the tincture, although he writhed and groaned the while. I followed it with more of the swish water, slowly, small spoonful by small spoonful. Gradually as his half conscious body became aware of the pleasant taste, he took it more readily, and then greedily.

'Keep up with this,' I said to Alice. 'As much as he will take. It can do him nothing but good. I doubt we shall be able to give him food today, but perhaps tomorrow a little broth.'

'Will he live, doctor?' she whispered.

I saw how tired she looked.

'You have been caring for him all night?'

'Nay, only since he was brought in. After midnight, it was. Perhaps two o' the clock. I slept till then.'

'Then you have been his best hope. I cannot say for sure if he will live, but if the fever breaks in the next day or two, and if we can persuade him to eat, then there is a chance.'

I left Alice caring for the boy, while Goodwife Watson and I saw to the rest of the children. There was no running about in the ward today, and a great deal of painful coughing. Most of the children had some form of throat or chest problem, and once I had completed my rounds, I sought the sisters who worked in the stillroom, and ordered a fresh batch of swish water.

During the winter I seemed to spend a good deal of my time, when I was not on the wards, supervising the preparation of gallons of swish water by the sisters. We make this by simmering honeycomb gently in water (Coventry water is best, if you can get it), together with peppercorns, bruised root of ginger, pieces of lemon, and sticks of the rolled bark of the cinnamon tree. It is then strained and given as a warm drink to patients with throat infections. The mixture, though hardly more than a country wife's remedy, is remarkable efficacious and comforting for the patients. Even the children enjoy it.

After I had stayed in the stillroom, making sure the spices were not skimped, my very clothes began to smell of the mixture, which was not unpleasant, and seemed almost to warm the air around me with spices, as I picked my way carefully along the street with Rikki, back to my lodgings that evening. It had snowed repeatedly during the day, then frozen, then snowed again, so that the ground under foot was ever more perilous. I saw that Simon was waiting outside my lodgings, his hands tucked under his armpits for warmth. He was stamping like a horse to keep his feet from freezing, and his breath rose up in the still, cold air and hung about his head like smoke. Rikki ran to him, tail waving, and leapt up to greet him. I have tried to break him of this habit, for it is apt to bowl over the unwary, but Simon was guilty of encouraging it, as he did now, mock wrestling with Rikki and allowing him to lick his face.

'How long have you been waiting?' I asked.

'Long enough to turn into a man of ice,' he said, 'though probably not above ten minutes.'

'You should have come to the hospital and waited there in the warm. Or asked Goodwife Atkins to let you in. Come, and I will make us some hippocras as soon as I have the fire lit.'

We climbed the stairs to my room, Rikki bounding ahead of us, and at once I set about making a fire, while Simon found the bottle where I kept the mixture of spices steeped in wine for the making of hippocras. When the flames had caught I poured a flagon of inexpensive wine into a pan and warmed it on the trivet at the side of the fire, adding the drops of spiced cordial until I was satisfied with the strength. My home might be no more than a tiny room, but I took pleasure and even a certain pride in being able to entertain him there. Rikki pushed his empty dish across the floor in a suggestive manner, but I knew that Tom always fed him with scraps from the hospital kitchen before I collected him in the evening, and I refused to be taken in by this performance.

When Simon and I were settled with our tankards of the warm spiced wine and a couple of pies I had bought from a stall beside the hospital, I smiled across at him and raised my glass.

'Your health!'

'And yours.'

'Is it still too cold for Master Burbage to open the Theatre?'

'Much too cold,' Simon said gloomily. 'He talked of hiring Blackfriars, the indoor playhouse where the children's companies sometimes perform. He has tried before, but nothing comes of it. Neighbours, it seems, complain to the Council that the audiences would be rowdy and mischievous.'

'I expect they would.'

He grunted. ''Tis all very well for you to say that, Kit, with your salary at the hospital, whatever the weather. And no doubt your private patients need you more than ever. We players, when the playhouses are closed, we are not paid and do not eat.'

This happened every winter, but the playhouses had been forced to close earlier than usual this year, with the snow coming so soon. The London crowds are sturdy, but standing in a playhouse open to the sky had been too much for them with the early onset of the cold weather.

I leaned forward. 'Are things that bad? Shall I lend you some money to tide you over?'

'Nay, it's not yet come to that.' He kicked glumly at a cushion lying on the floor and sent it sailing across the room. 'I shall manage well enough for another two or three weeks. After that, I might come begging.'

'Do you still lodge with Kyd and Marlowe?'

'Marlowe was sent away to the Low Countries some weeks ago, so only Kyd and I share at the moment.'

I made no reply to that. Like me, Marlowe had been employed by Sir Francis Walsingham on intelligence work.

Unlike me, he had never worked at code breaking, and I could only guess at his missions – sometimes carrying secret despatches, I suppose, and also (so I had heard it whispered) insinuating himself amongst the Catholic exiles to foment trouble. This last was a favourite activity of Robert Poley, the man who had first entangled me in the secret service and who was a constant threat to my safety. Now that I was no longer employed by Walsingham, I knew only that Poley had begun working for the Cecils, Lord Burghley and his son Sir Robert Cecil. As for Marlowe, I had no idea. It might be the Cecils who had sent him abroad, or he might be employed, like Thomas Phelippes, in the network of intelligencers funded by the Earl of Essex.

Simon took a deep drink of his wine and set the tankard down on the floor beside his chair. 'I am thinking of returning to Southwark.'

My heart gave a joyous leap and I smiled at him.

'Your room here is still empty,' I said. 'Are you not content in the company of those clever playmakers?'

He fidgeted and looked somewhat embarrassed.

'I find that I prefer having my own room. Kyd is good company, but he never stops talking. When he is working on one of his plays, he has to try everything out, reading it out loud, and pacing about. You know that he was one of the first to write our new kind of drama, but now, with Kit Marlowe and Will Shakespeare gaining so much success, he doubts himself. He is forever wanting me to play the parts as he writes them, before he is convinced they will serve.'

'I can see that might be tedious,' I said, hiding my smile. Simon was in love with the playhouse, but perhaps not of an evening, when he wanted a quiet hour or two with a tankard of ale and his feet up. No wonder he visited me so often, despite the long walk.

'But is not Marlowe entertaining, when he is there? I thought he was a great friend of yours.'

Simon pulled a face. 'He's a quarrelsome fellow. Difficult to share lodgings with. Takes offence where none is meant, or chooses to do so. Sometimes, I think he is not quite honest. Some of his friends assuredly are not.'

'When he was in service with Sir Francis,' I said slowly, 'I know that Phelippes was never quite sure of him. Marlowe was not so dubious as Poley, but I think Phelippes was not certain where his loyalties lay. Nor whether he was a good Protestant.'

Before this I would never have said so much, not until Simon raised his own doubts of the man.

'Now here is a curious thing,' he said. 'Marlowe seems to have gone abroad on some business for the government, as he has done before.'

I nodded. During my time in Walsingham's service I had encountered Marlowe on the stairs at the Seething Lane house from time to time. I had even deciphered one of his coded reports, but we had never worked together, as I had worked with Phelippes and Nick Berden and Francis Mylles. For which I was grateful. Whenever I had met him elsewhere, he had always provoked and insulted me.

'What is curious about that?'

'He has been in Flushing,' said Simon. 'You know that it is an English cautionary town, and Philip Sidney's brother Robert its governor?'

'I know.'

'Well, Marlowe was staying there with two other men, a goldsmith – a respectable craftsman – and another man who used to work for Walsingham. It seems they have been making counterfeit coins, and have been arrested trying to pass a false Dutch shilling off as genuine. The two men (not the goldsmith, who seems simply to have been employed by them) each accused the other of being the forger. Marlowe has sent word to Kyd for help, though how he expects Kyd to help him, I cannot fathom. Kyd is a timid creature, like his animal namesake.'

A strange tale indeed. What could be the purpose of it? Marlowe might spend more money than he ought, and be often short of funds in consequence, but I did not think him stupid. Counterfeiting coin, unless done with great skill, is the act of a stupid man. Somehow, it had the sound of a Walsingham projection, with some hidden purpose behind it, but Walsingham was gone. Could Phelippes have originated such a scheme involving false coinage, perhaps to undermine the Spanish in the Low Countries? Possibly. But not without the backing of a powerful man, and Phelippes worked for Essex. Or was it a projection of the Cecils? Or had Marlowe – who was ever breaking beyond the bounds of the law as well as discreet behaviour – taken it into his head to devise some wild scheme of his own? It would not surprise me.

'What has become of Marlowe?'

'He is to be shipped back to England under guard, a prisoner.'

'He's coming back to your lodgings? Be careful, Simon. These could be dangerous matters indeed. Forging coin counts as petty treason, and the penalty is death.'

'Nay, he has taken other lodgings now. Or so he said in his letter to Kyd.'

I swirled the hippocras in my tankard, watching the patterns it made, the grains of the spices dancing in circles, looping around each other, their movements seemingly random, and yet underneath it all was a pattern.

'Now that Walsingham is dead,' I said, 'and when he is not making plays for Burbage and Henslowe, who does Marlowe work for?'

Simon shrugged. 'That I couldn't say for sure, but I think it must be Burghley and Cecil. It is they who are to question him once he is back here, or so he believes. He is sometimes also in attendance on Thomas Walsingham, Sir Francis's nephew, as a kind of household poet.'

'The son of Sir Francis's cousin,' I said absently. 'Thomas Walsingham. Not Sir Francis's nephew.'

Our talk turned to other things – my work at the hospital, how soon it would be warm enough for the playhouses to reopen, and what parts Simon hoped to play when they did.

'There is to be a new piece by Marlowe's played at the Rose, as soon as the warmer weather comes,' said Simon. 'I shall hope to take a part in that, though I haven't seen the play yet.'

Marlowe again.

'A talented man,' I said dryly. 'Making both false coins and plays. At the Rose, did you say?'

'Aye. The snow has damaged the roof of the Theatre and it cannot be repaired until the snow is gone and the weather improves. Master Burbage has been in conference with Henslowe. It seems Henslowe's Admiral's Men are much depleted by some players leaving and others ill or dead. They are talking of taking the Admiral's Men into our company. Master Burbage is insisting that we shall stay under Lord Strange's patronage and remain Lord Strange's Men.'

This was surprising news indeed.

'And this combined company will perform here in Southwark, at the Rose?'

'Aye. So it makes all the more sense for me to move back here.'

'One player who will not leave Master Henslowe,' I said, 'is Ned Alleyn, for he is married to Henslowe's daughter.'

'Aye, and has an interest in some of Henslowe's other businesses – bear baiting, whore houses, and the like.'

'Richard Burbage had best watch out, then,' I said, 'for Ned will want all the great dramatic roles for himself.'

'He will. Dick will not be pleased.'

Later, as Simon was leaving, a sudden thought came to me.

'The other man with Marlowe in Flushing,' I said. 'Not the goldsmith. The other man, who was he?'

'His name was Richard Baines.'

Richard Baines. I knew him. He was indeed one of Walsingham's former agents. I did not like him, a sneaking, treacherous fellow.

Simon paused in the doorway.

'It seems there was another man of your acquaintance in Flushing. Robert Poley.'

Chapter Two

Slowly the winter began to ease its grip a little and from every side the dripping of icicles could be heard. Roofs which had groaned under their burden of snow sighed, sagged, and leaked freely onto the heads of householders. Howard, in the tiny garret above my room, woke in the middle of the night to find himself awash in bed. In fury he tipped the water on to the floor, whence it found its way between his floorboards and the joists to form a lake in the middle of my floor. I cursed it soundly, but was glad my bed was on the other side of the room.

Simon had returned to his Southwark lodgings by then. I took care not to let him see how glad I was to see him back, though the children made no secret of their excitement at his return. They had always thought of themselves as honorary members of Burbage's company from their long association with the playhouse.

Work at the hospital continued to demand most of my time until the winter ills began to ease off a little. Nell's twins survived, despite their chancy start, even the weaker one, who thrived on the diet of goat's milk and honey. By the time we had nourished both mother and sons up to strength, he had nearly caught up with his stronger brother. I had ensured that St Thomas's would continue to supply him with milk from our herd of goats even after they returned home, for there would have been little chance of that poor family obtaining it elsewhere in London. As the ice in the river began to thaw there was some chance that Nell's man might begin to earn fares again with his wherry.

The very sick boy brought in from the street by the Watch lingered a long time, hovering on the threshold of death, but the young sister Alice had taken a fierce interest in him, sitting up night after night until at long last his fever broke and he began to recover. Although the worst of the lung fever was over, he was as weak – so the saying goes – as a newborn kitten, and would need weeks of nursing yet. Once he was strong enough I had hopes that a place might be found for him at Christ's Hospital. He told us his name was Robert, but if he had any other name, he did not know it. Nor had he any family that he knew of. For as long as he could remember he had been one of those lost children who live by scavenging and begging in the streets, until at last death overtakes them. It was Robert's good fortune that the Watch had found him and brought him to us before it was too late.

Marlowe was returned to London a prisoner, in company with the goldsmith Gifford Gilbert, with whom he had worked in Flushing to make a bag full of false coins. Despite the apparent quantity of forged coins, Marlowe had the opportunity to put just one Dutch shilling into circulation before he was arrested, betrayed to the governor of the town by his fellow lodger and false coiner, Richard Baines. And Baines, it seems, had sailed across the Channel on the same pinnace, the informer going free, while Marlowe and Gilbert were manacled. I wondered how the arrogant and fastidious Marlowe had cared for that. Though, of course, he had been in prison before, after that killing in Hog Lane.

'It is very curious,' I said to Simon, when he relayed all this to me. 'There was a man called Gilbert Gifford who was employed by Sir Francis during the Babington affair, yet this Gifford Gilbert cannot be the same man, for he died two years ago in Paris. My guess is that this fellow, this goldsmith working with Marlowe, has taken a false name to cover his employment as a false coiner. Is it meant as some kind of jest? Thumbing the nose at those in authority? Marlowe knew Gilbert Gifford and such an insolent jest would be like him.'

'All I know of the goldsmith,' Simon said, 'is that it seems Sir Robert Sidney reckoned he was no way guilty, merely a craftsman employed by Kit Marlowe and Richard Baines. After questioning by Lord Burghley, he was released and has disappeared, no doubt anxious to save his skin.'

'How do you come by so much knowledge?'

I was truly curious, for in Sir Francis's day such matters would have been kept strictly *sub rosa*.

'Oh, Marlowe told us about the whole affair,' Simon said carelessly. 'He is furious with Baines, for he says the striking of counterfeit coins was all Baines's idea, with some plan of circulating them among the Catholic exiles in the Low Countries, or among the occupying Spanish forces, in order to cause confusion and distrust.'

The plan had a sort of authentic sound to it, like some of the wilder projections which used to be discussed – though rarely implemented – back in the Seething Lane days.

'So which of them was responsible?' I asked.

Both men were devious, untrustworthy, and of doubtful loyalty to England. Both had been in serious trouble before. And both were now probably working for the Cecils. As well as for others?

Simon shrugged. 'Who can say which of them was the perpetrator? Each accuses the other, but from the sound of it, both were in it together. They shared lodgings. They employed the goldsmith together. They joined in the making of the coins together. But it was Baines who betrayed Marlowe to Sir Robert, not t'other way about.'

'But why?' I shook my head in bafflement.

The task of such projectors as these men was to undermine and entrap England's enemies, not their fellow agents. The betrayal might have arisen merely from personal spite or animosity, but if this had existed beforehand, why were they living and working together in Flushing?

Before Simon could answer, I answered for him, at least after a fashion.

'It seems to me that someone wished to do Marlowe serious harm, or else to discredit him. Baines is a blaggard for hire. Pay him enough and he will betray his own mother into the hands of the torturer Topcliffe.'

Simon nodded. 'You may have the right of it. Marlowe has the gift of offending people. The whole affair, or at any rate the part Baines played, all perhaps arise from some private slight.'

I did not pursue the subject further, though I suspected that this public and serious attack on Marlowe, for an offence which can carry the death penalty, was no private affair. Instead of Marlowe, the real intended victim might have been the new intelligence service created by the Cecils. Or more particularly, Sir Robert Cecil himself. Could my lord Essex be behind it? He hated Cecil, and no doubt he also hated the more substantial intelligence network the Cecils were creating, which seemed to be proving more effective than his own, even though he had managed to employ Phelippes, formerly Sir Francis's most senior man.

As we discussed the curious affair of the counterfeit coinage, Simon and I were picking our way over half-melted banks of snow and slush in Shoreditch, heading for the Theatre. I had promised to lend a hand this evening as the players packed up their costumes and properties at the playhouse and conveyed them across the river, where they were to be appearing, for a time at least, at Henslowe's Rose playhouse, once the weather improved enough to draw an audience.

'Here is Marlowe now,' Simon said, as we joined the throng of players carrying the large baskets of costumes out from the Theatre to two waiting carts. 'You may ask him yourself.'

I shook my head. I had no intention of initiating a conversation with Marlowe. In any case, I knew very well that I would get nothing from him but prevarication and lies amidst the insults.

'I would not dream of hampering his assistance to Master Burbage,' I said smoothly.

There was no way Simon could mistake my sarcasm. Marlowe? Sully his costly, dandified clothes, by lending a hand here? Pigs, as the saying goes, might sprout wings and take to the skies.

However, no one could avoid overhearing Marlowe as the rest of us worked and he watched us, perched on the front of one of the carts.

'Why, 'tis no great matter, to create coinage,' he announced, in his usual swaggering, boastful way. 'Any man of moderate skill may accomplish it. I learnt of it first from a fellow called John Poole, some years ago now. He was a man with much knowledge of the mysteries of metal working, and I pumped him dry, with a mind to trying it myself one day. For why should a man slave to earn the grudging pennies bestowed by some parsimonious lord, when he may strike his own shillings and nobles, as many as he could wish?'

John Poole, I thought. *That name is familiar.* Then I placed it. The man had been held in Newgate for several years. That must be where Marlowe had met him, when he was himself imprisoned after the stabbing of William Bradley not far from here. Walsingham had John Poole under watch for a long time – a Catholic known to smuggle priests and treasonous books into the country, and a man who had defamed the Earl of Leicester. His knowledge of metals had led to his imprisonment for false coining on that occasion, but it was not his only crime. I was unsure what had eventually become of him.

'Striking illegal coin bearing Her Majesty's image,' Guy said mildly, as he tucked his musical instruments carefully amongst soft drapery, 'that is an act of treason against the Queen, just as issuing false coinage is treason against the State.'

'Aye,' Dick Burbage said, 'so how is it that you are here, Marlowe, idly watching us work, and not kicking your heels in some miserable prison?'

Marlowe smirked. 'My value is well known to the great men of this country, not least the Privy Council itself. They know that devil Baines's accusation arose from pure malice, and dismissed it out of hand.'

At this I could not resist speaking, though I should have done better to have kept my tongue behind my teeth.

'I am somewhat puzzled, Marlowe,' I said, with an innocent smile. 'On the one hand you boast of *your* knowledge and skill in producing counterfeit coins, yet on the other you say that Baines's report of your . . . activities . . . to Governor Sidney is pure malice, the scheme having originated with him, not you. Where, I wonder, does the truth lie?'

He turned on me, suddenly savage.

'Keep a respectful tongue in your mouth, Jew boy, or I am sure there are plenty of reasons to have it cut out.'

There was a shocked silence at this. Marlowe had often insulted me before, but he had never made such an overt threat. Guy laid a hand on my arm, as if to restrain me, but there was no need. I did not intend to allow myself to be provoked into a violent quarrel with Marlowe. He was known for vicious brawling and never hesitated to draw steel.

'That is enough.' Master Burbage had come out of the Theatre unnoticed, and must have heard the last exchanges. He locked the outer door of the playhouse and turned toward the loaded carts. 'Best we set off before full dark and unload at the Rose. Philip Henslowe is expecting us and we will not keep him waiting.'

Marlowe leapt down from the cart. At first I was afraid he might tackle me, but instead he fell into deep conversation with Master Burbage, indicating by his back turned to me that I mattered no more to him than a dog's turd beneath his heel.

'Come, Kit,' Guy said, 'will you walk over to Southwark with us?'

I realised that I was shaking, more from fury than from fear.

'Aye,' I said. 'I should not have spoken.'

'It needed to be said.' Guy smiled. 'But perhaps it had been better had someone else had the wit to say it. A curious business altogether.'

'Not really,' I said. 'Not the false coining. Not Marlowe mixed up in some dirty underhand plot. Nay, the only point that puzzles me is whether Baines did betray him out of personal malice, or whether he was acting on orders from someone higher up. And if so, who?'

Moving all Lord Strange's Men's costumes and properties across the river and into the Rose took us several hours. I had been behind the stage here before, when Henslowe's copyist had been attacked and injured, but otherwise I knew the playhouse only from the front. Now I saw that the Rose, being the newest built of the playhouses, was in some ways better provided than the Theatre or the Curtain. The tiring house was more spacious, with ample room for storage, and there were a number of devices to provide excitement for the playgoers. A trap door in the apron stage was standard in all the playhouses (a handy entrance to Hell), but the Rose had several mechanical hoists for raising and lowering players to and from the projecting roof of the balcony which extended over the back of the stage. Thus a god or spirit might be lowered to earth, or some saintly character raised to Heaven. A fairylike creature could almost appear to fly. I noticed that Will and Cuthbert had their heads together as they examined the machinery, and Cuthbert (as usual) was taking notes.

For all the hurry to move the players' properties to the Rose, it was not yet spring. The melting snow up river caused the Thames to rise, so that low-lying properties on both sides of the river were flooded. What with that and the prevailing damp air, we had a new outbreak of chest infections amongst Southwark poor. At least with this miserable weather there was no sign yet of the plague. Parliament returned nervously from exile in healthier Hertfordshire to sit in Westminster on the nineteenth of February, having retreated to the country during the fairly minor outbreak of the previous year. It was well for some, like the Court and Parliament, who could afford to flee the crowded streets of London during the plague, though most of us could not.

In February also, Master Henslowe had decided to brave the shivering weather and reopened the Rose early for several performances of Robert Greene's *Friar Bungay and Friar Bacon.* Simon was taking only a minor part and I had seen it before, so I did not join the small, frozen crowd.

'Not worth opening the playhouse for that,' Simon said crossly, warming his hands before my fire. He was blue and shivering with cold. 'Four performances and barely a full house even if you added all the audiences together. We'll not open again until the weather improves.'

'Bear in mind it is an old play,' I said, handing him a mug of hot spiced ale. He took it gratefully and cupped his hands around it. 'Everyone in London must have seen it at least twice. Why should they stand in the cold to watch it again?'

He shrugged. 'We have nothing else ready. It was a way of giving the two companies a chance to grow accustomed to working together. Not that there are many of the Admiral's Men left.'

He threw himself down on a chair and stretched out his wet boots to steam before the fire.

'Those who are left of Henslowe's company reckon that the Rose is *their* playhouse, so they should have all the best parts, though we have the better players by far.'

'And Ned Alleyn?' I asked, somewhat provocatively, I admit.

'Oh, Ned is a fine actor,' he agreed. 'I've no quarrel with Ned. I shall never forget his Tamburlaine. But it's the tupenny-ha'penny jobbing players who are most of what is left of the Admiral's men, trying to set themselves above Dick Burbage and Guy Bingham.'

'And Simon Hetherington?'

He grinned. 'Aye, and above Simon Hetherington. I have not the experience of Ned or Guy, nor have I trod the stage since I could first walk, like Dick, but I *am* better than these fellows. It is no boasting to say so.'

'Well, I expect matters will settle down, and Master Burbage and Master Henslowe between them will solve the problem. What shall you play next, once it is worth opening again?'

He held out his tankard for more ale.

'Will's play of the sixth Henry was such a success last year, that we will play that again, though no doubt Ned will be given the part of Talbot in place of Dick. Dick will not be pleased at that. In the meantime, Will is hard at work, scribbling away at parts two and three of the sixth Henry. It was such a long reign and the disputing factions so complicated, he says that he needs three plays to do justice to the subject.'

'I can see that he might. And has not the errant Marlowe a new play? Now that he has been warned off coining his own riches, I assume he must work like the rest of us.'

'Aye, he's at work on something, but as usual he is keeping it very close to his chest, so we do not know what it is about.'

'I wonder whether he is still in Burghley's employ,' I said thoughtfully, 'if he ever was. When I worked briefly for Phelippes last year, there was never any mention of him in the service of my lord Essex and the brothers Bacon.'

'If the business in Flushing was somehow related to Lord Burghley's intelligence service,' Simon said, 'do you suppose the Lord Treasurer Burghley would still want to employ him? Things seem to have gone very awry.'

'They often do. And you must remember that Marlowe suffered no punishment whatsoever for counterfeiting, which is a serious crime. After he was questioned by my lord Burghley. Why was that? To me that suggests that he is being protected, and by someone very powerful. Probably Burghley himself.'

'The man Baines seems to have vanished.'

'No doubt he will surface again, making trouble.'

'And your friend Robert Poley is very busy.'

I grimaced, not appreciating his jest. 'How do you know that?'

'Ah, you know that Guy is a great gatherer of London gossip. With such a talent, he should have worked for Walsingham. He has a cousin in the service of Sir Thomas Heneage, Treasurer of the Queen's Chamber, who is part of the Cecil establishment, if we may call it that. It seems Poley is very well in with Sir Thomas, sent hither and thither on Sir Thomas's affairs. That, it seems, was why he was in Flushing when Marlowe and Baines were there. Poley travels more than your great merchants, and even in winter. Denmark. The Low Countries. France. Scotland. All of them have had the pleasure of a visit from Robert Poley. It seems he holds a high position these days.'

'Something of a change from his days as a prisoner-informer in the Marshalsea, and the two years he spent in the Tower after the Babington affair,' I said dryly. 'Denmark and the rest are heartily welcome to him. I am surprised a man of Sir Thomas Heneage's distinction can bring himself to trust such a slippery, dangerous fellow. Walsingham always mistrusted him, as did everyone who worked at Seething Lane, like Phelippes and Mylles and Berden and Gregory. He is much more dangerous than a man like Baines, because he can be charming and plausible, unless you are able to glimpse the villain behind the mask.'

While Simon and the rest of Lord Strange's Men kicked their heels in their lodgings or at the Rose, Master Burbage had set his builders to work on the repairs to the Theatre. Like a number of buildings in London during the winter, the playhouse had suffered considerable damage to its roof as a result of months of snow and ice. Even the thaw had led to further damage, as the melting snow had penetrated the narrow spaces between the roof timbers. As well as the immediate damage there was the fear of future rot.

'Everything must be stripped down,' Cuthbert explained, when I asked why the work could not be completed before the playhouses opened for the summer season. 'In truth, it means we must rebuild the whole roof. It will take weeks, probably into the autumn. Hence this collaboration with Master Henslowe.'

'Then it is fortunate that your father is a builder as well as the manager of a players' company,' I said.

He grinned. 'Aye. When he built the Theatre and the Curtain, all the world was amazed, but now the Rose has some devices we would like to bring to the Theatre.'

'And shall you?'

He shrugged. 'There are problems. When he first built the playhouses, my father had a business partner, John Brayne, my mother's brother, and there were some difficulties between them. Now Brayne is dead but his widow is trying to seize a larger share than her husband ever had a right too. She is a shrewish, litigious woman, trying to take us to court at every opportunity.'

I nodded. 'Guy mentioned something of this to me once.'

'Then there is the problem of the land lease.'

I raised my eyebrows in query.

'The lease on the land where the Theatre is built runs out in a few years' time and there have been some suspicious dealings over ownership of the land. We think the present landlord will try to drive us away, for he could earn far more by building houses on the site, now that part of Shoreditch is becoming respectable, not just a sprawling overflow from the City.'

'But surely–' I was shocked. 'He would not pull down the Theatre!'

'It is quite clearly stated in the lease that anything we build on the land belongs to us. He has no right to the building.'

'I cannot see what good that can do you, if he can turn you off the land.'

'Buildings can be dismantled,' Cuthbert said.

'That would be a desperate measure. And besides, what good would a dismantled Theatre do you?'

'What indeed? In the meantime, we repair the roof of the Theatre and share Master Henslowe's playhouse here in Southwark. For a time, at any rate. But we will not undertake the unnecessary expense of new devices until all these disputed matters are settled.'

According to what I heard from Simon, when we shared a fire in the evening, the two companies of players were learning to work together. Master Burbage's company being the larger, with most of the experienced players, the combined company would indeed be known as Lord Strange's Men. I never heard what Lord Howard, the Lord Admiral, thought of this, but perhaps he no longer wished to be patron of a players' company.

Although there were many jobbing play makers in London – from the so-called 'University Wits' (though many of them were now dead) to anonymous hacks who could scramble together some foolery from a penny pamphlet – the two great heroes of the day were Kit Marlowe and Will Shakespeare, two men of the same age but very different characters. Marlowe had shot across the world of the playhouse when barely more than a student, with his violent and frightening play *Tamburlaine*. Will had made a later and more hesitant start. Lacking Marlowe's arrogance and self-assurance, Will had taken longer to find his voice and his confidence, but I believed that his subtlety and his deeper and warmer understanding of his fellow men would prove him the better play maker than Marlowe with his dark and cruel vision of humankind.

Not everyone agreed with me – and perhaps I was somewhat biased by Marlowe's open dislike of me. However that might be, it was Marlowe's new play that was to be the next one to be staged, Will not yet having completed his two additional Harry Six plays. Simon had persuaded me to attend the Marlowe play, as he was playing one of the better roles, but I did not care for the title, *The Jew of Malta*. I could hardly forget Marlowe's constant jeering comments about Jews, and knew for certain that this would be no flattering portrayal.

Simon and I had never seriously discussed questions of faith and belief. The very first time we had met, six years ago now, he had called me a 'Portingall', though he had never done so since. To an Englishman, the term 'Portingall' does not merely mean a citizen of Portugal. It means those particular Portuguese who had been fetching up in England since the Inquisition had moved into our country and the forced conversions had begun. 'Portingall' meant New Christian, *converso*, *novo cristão*, Marrano. In other words, secret Jew, false Christian, deceiver, trickster, usurer, unbeliever, slayer of Christ. I knew that in the old mystery plays – slipped into disuse since Henry divorced the English church from Rome – the Jews had always been portrayed as villains. I had little doubt what kind of Jew Marlowe would put upon the stage.

So although we had never probed each other's religious beliefs, I think that by now Simon thought of me – if he ever shaped such thoughts coherently – as being very little different from himself. Like everyone else he knew, I attended a Christian church every Sunday and took communion at the most sacred times of year, certainly as Easter and Christmas. I spoke as if I were native born English, and although he knew of my Portuguese past, I think he no longer *felt* it, if that makes any kind of sense at all. Certainly he must have heard Marlowe's favourite form of insult, calling me 'Jew boy', but somehow I think it passed over his head as easily as when Marlowe called Guy a 'scurvy knave', or Dick a 'pale faced milksop'. All were equally meaningless, so the title of the new play must have not awakened in Simon the resonances of alarm and distaste that it awoke in me.

At Simon's insistence, I attended the first performance on the six and twentieth day of February, at the Rose. It says much of what I experienced there that I could not remember afterwards what part Simon played, or how well he played it. All I remember was Barabas, the Jew, a rich merchant and villain living in Malta. As the most important part, Barabas was played by Ned Alleyn, all Dick Burbage's complaints being set aside. In truth, despite his talent, I do not think Dick could have played the part, not yet. He was only a little older than I, so the character of a vicious middle-aged man would have been beyond him. Most actors relish the chance to play a villain. It affords them the opportunity to act out the kind of villainies and sins that they would never attempt in real life. I can understand that. But the character of Barabas was something more than your usual stage villain. Into him Marlowe had poured all his powerful sense of evil, violence, hatred and betrayal.

Of course, Marlowe *would* call his Jewish villain Barabas. By naming the character after the criminal pardoned and released at Passover, instead of Jesus – against the wishes of Pontius Pilate but at the insistence of the Jewish crowd – he was reviving the old justification for hatred of the Jews by all right-thinking Christians, who could reason that even the Roman governor would have released Our Lord, but it was his fellow countrymen who chose to have him killed.

Add to that, the fact that Marlowe makes the wealthy Jewish merchant a living, breathing embodiment of the theories of Niccolo Machiavelli, whose political ideas were then being hotly debated in London. Could such heartless, villainous, self-seeking practices be justified as a means to good government and a peaceful state? Except that, in Barabas Marlowe portrays a man who uses Machiavellian theories for his own personal ends. The fact

35

that he is exceptionally rich is emphasised, for there was an undercurrent of hostility amongst the solid English citizenry that somehow the foreigners who had come to settle here were making themselves wealthy at the expense of Englishmen. It was an attitude which had been familiar to me almost from the time I had come to England. Of late, with greater numbers of refugees fleeing here from persecution in Europe, the grumbling and the hostility had become more vocal. I was certain that this play of Marlowe's would serve to fan the flames of that particular fire, and as it turned out, that is exactly what it did.

Throughout the play there is a bitter sense of betrayal – Barabas betrays his own daughter, amongst other crimes. I wondered whether Marlowe was pouring out his own anger and sense of betrayal after Richard Baines's activities in Flushing.

An evil, wealthy Jew. A very Machiavel. A betrayer. The play was ripe with some of the worst of Marlowe's dark view of the world.

I did not think the play was even very skilfully written, apart from the passages of Marlowe's usual flowery versifying. The story was confusing and absurd, involving plots and counter-plots (familiar ground here) in which Barabas's escalating villainy grew from individual vengeance to a plan to poison a whole convent, the whole island of Malta, the whole Christian world, as far as I could gather. The details of the story are blurred in my mind. What remains clear was the mood of my fellow playgoers which grew perceptibly more frightening as the play continued.

The first performance of a new play by Marlowe – and they had come streaming across the river on foot and by wherry to see it. Looking down on the groundlings from above, you could not see a square inch between their packed bodies. On the benches in the galleries it was little better. Once we were in place, we were held immobile by our neighbours' shoulders, hips, and elbows. It was difficult to breathe. To move was impossible. As the play progressed through its tortuous plot, as Barabas's villainies grew more and more evil, the crowd grew tense. I could feel it in the bodies pressed against mine. Every time the player taking the part of Barabas came on stage (I had almost forgotten it was Ned Alleyn, a man I liked), an angry mutter began to swell, from groundlings to upper gallery. The player wore a long, straggling false beard, and a wig down to his shoulders, with an enveloping gown and a hooded cloak, to add to his sinister appearance. The costume would also serve the purpose of disguising him sufficiently that the audience would not recognise him afterwards in the street, else I think he would have been lynched.

Ned was a popular player and famed for his enacting of the great dramatic roles Marlowe had been creating, but I thought that in this case, things might be different. Many of the simpler sort amongst the playgoers found it difficult to separate the player from the part he played. Therefore, in Will's Harry Six play, when Ned had recently portrayed the great English hero of the French wars, their adoration of Talbot had transferred itself to Ned Alleyn. The danger was that this growing hatred of Barabas and all he stood for might also be supposed the true character of the man who played the part. To these unsophisticated citizens, it must seem that Ned could not act out such villainies on stage unless he truly desired them in his heart.

As the play drew towards its conclusion, the hatred became almost palpable in the air around me. And when Barabas met his gruesome and humiliating end, there was a roar of vicious approval that could have been heard across the river, and which filled me with terror. I was thankful I had worn a plain doublet and breeches to the playhouse and not my medical garments. They might have identified me as a possible Portingall, though not all the physicians in London were Portuguese by any means. Indeed, now that my father and Dr Nuñez were gone, I believe Ruy Lopez and I were the only ones left. In my workaday clothes, however, I could pass for any ordinary young Londoner.

Nevertheless, as soon as the play was over I fought my way out through those ugly crowds who hung about the Rose, and ran for my life through the back alleys to my lodgings. The playgoers had included a fair number of apprentices, who always enjoyed the violence and danger in Marlowe's plays, and today I had seen how the matter of *The Jew of Malta* had aroused their lust for some violence of their own. London is full of these youths, mostly come from elsewhere, without the restraint of families to keep them in check. It takes very little to set them off, with their cry of 'Clubs!' summoning their fellows to the latest trouble-making. And indeed there might be those amongst the crowd who had seen me either at St Bartholomew's or St Thomas's and would know I was a Marrano.

Although the weather made attendance at the playhouse just bearable, these narrow alleys through which I stumbled were so overhung with buildings nearly touching overhead that heaps of befouled snow still lingered unmelted and unseen. And in these dirty nests of poverty, no one had the means to hang a lantern or flaming torch beside their door, as was demanded in the better parts of the town. Twice I stumbled and fell headlong into the snow piles, contaminated with who knew what filth.

By the time I broke free of the maze and reached the waterside street of Bankside, I was soaking and shaking with the cold. Here there were lights before the doors of private dwellings like our lodging house, while the places of entertainment like the bear pit and Bessie Travis's whorehouse shone their welcome out in the early dark. I could even hear the cheerful sound of Bessie's recently acquired hurdy-gurdy. The river ran dark and swift on the other side of the Bankside, reflecting here and there the lanterns bobbing in the sterns of wherries. Just upriver a cluster of them near Molestrand Dock and Falcon Stairs had clearly just collected playgoers from the Rose who were returning to the City, but I could also make out a crowd heading toward me on their way to the Bridge.

I scrambled up the steps to the house and closed the door firmly behind me, although that was no protection. It was not kept locked, so that lodgers might come and go as they pleased. Once in the sanctuary of my little room, however, I locked and bolted the door and flung myself down on the bed, my heart pounding, like a hare closely pursued by hounds. Rikki, startled by my violent entrance, jumped up beside me and licked my chin reassuringly, but it was a long while before my heart steadied.

Marlowe's play ran for many days, always to packed audiences, and hatred of Jews began to be whispered in the streets and painted up on walls. Since childhood I had known about the massacres in Spain and Portugal. Some eighty or ninety years before, more than two thousand New Christians had been butchered in Lisbon. I had heard that similar widespread slaughter had also taken place centuries ago in England, before the Jews were driven out, but I had never thought to experience it myself. Not here. Not in England. Not now when I had thought myself safe, regarded as English and Christian.

I slipped to and from my work, watching over my shoulder, avoiding dark corners and crowds of noisy apprentices, still the ones most likely to start a brawl. I kept away from Simon and I was sure he avoided me. Perhaps he was shamed by what had been set on foot in the playhouse.

Chapter Three

In time, matters became easier again between Simon and me, but during the weeks first following the playing of *The Jew of Malta*, when we were still avoiding each other, I noticed that he was spending more time with Marlowe, as he had done once in the past. I know not how it happened, but Marlowe was like the candle flame that draws the moth. Dangerous. Fatal, even. Does the moth know, as it begins its *danse macabre* about the flame that it is dancing with death? Did the young men drawn to Marlowe's fatal glimmer even glimpse into what danger it might lead them? Men who were drawn in by him had died before now, others had suffered prison or exile. A man with a honeyed tongue and a ready sword, was Marlowe.

Surely, I thought, Simon must see him for what he was, under the glamour. In some ways Marlowe reminded me of Poley, or rather Poley was a crude imitation of Marlowe, his cruelty and treacherousness hiding behind a slick surface charm, but without Marlowe's formidable intelligence and smooth poetic tongue.

One of the things I loved about Simon was the fact that he possessed qualities that I lacked. His gentleness, his readiness to trust all he met, were in strong contrast to my own innate fear of others, at least until long familiarity could make me sure of them. I suppose I owed this to the terrors of my childhood and to my continuing deception in disguising myself as a man. And though I loved him for it, I could see that Simon's trustfulness made him vulnerable to such as Marlowe.

As once before when he had kept company with Marlowe, Simon began to dress like him in finery far out of the reach of a mere player. Once I might have thought he borrowed from the players' stock of costumes, but by now I knew those costumes pretty well. So when I saw Simon sporting a doublet of heavy bronze velvet, slashed with a lining of scarlet silk, I knew it did not come from the costume basket. And a garment like that was far beyond a player's means, unless it were given him by a noble patron, but Simon had no such patron. The agate buttons alone would have cost him a month's earnings from Master Burbage. I did not like to ask him how he had come by it, nor the silk hose that had replaced his woollen ones.

Now that Burbage's company were playing at the Rose, they had taken to eating and drinking at the Lion, a substantial inn which stood a little way up river from my lodgings and not far from the Rose. Several of the players had now taken lodgings on this side of the river, so during the spring they often gathered there after the play. The food and ale were good, and there was even French wine for those who had the chinks.

One evening, dining at the Lion with Simon at his expense (the warm weather had returned, and the playhouses were filled with citizens eager for entertainment after the long, dull winter), I found myself leaning back in my seat and laughing at some tale he was telling about a back-stage disaster. I thought, *I am happy. At this moment, I am truly happy. I wish that this moment could last forever.* It was a kind of wonder to me, for normally I did not stop to consider my feelings, or my state of mind. Since my father's death and the terrible expedition to Portugal, I had been so preoccupied with making some new kind of life for myself, that I had lived more than ever from day to day. Last year, when I had lost my position at St Thomas's for several months, had forced me to concentrate on mere

41

survival, never pausing to probe my own soul, nor often to think ahead to what the future might hold for me.

As we walked home after our meal, I know I was more silent than usual. *Where shall we be*, I wondered, *Simon and I, in ten years' time? Will he take a wife? Will he want me as a companion then?*

'Why do you frown?' he asked. 'Have I offended you?'

The awkwardness we had experienced after the Malta play seemed to have crept back between us.

'Offended me? Of course not! Why do you say such a thing?'

He propped his shoulder against the door frame of the lodging house.

'You have scarce spoken a word this half hour.'

'I have been wondering what will become of us, with the passing of the years.'

'Why do you think that now?'

'I don't know. Perhaps because so many of the older people I knew have died or grown frail and aged. Perhaps because I cannot see much for me in the future. I will never be a great physician, a Fellow of the Royal College, only a licensed practitioner, for I have not taken my degree. I will never be anything more than I am now.'

He looked at me keenly, leaning close to make out my face in the dim light cast by a flaming torch outside the whorehouse three doors away.

'Do you want more?'

I did not answer him at once. Then I looked up at his face. He was a good six inches taller than I now, and I had to tilt my head back.

'Simon, do you think you will ever marry?'

He gave me a curious look. Then he smiled and did something he had never done before. He touched my cheek with the tip of his finger.

'Let us make a pact, Kit. I will only marry if you do likewise.'

I felt the blood rushing to my face, and I was glad I was not so fair-skinned as he, and that the light was poor. I laughed, then.

'Very well. It is a pact. I will only marry if you do likewise.'

A few weeks later I was again sitting at a table outside the Lion on the riverbank, with Simon and others of the company. They had come straight from a full house and an enthusiastic audience, and were more cheerful than I had seen them since the hard times during the winter. They were doing well at the Rose, and any problems with the former members of the Admiral's Men seemed to have been solved. I would have been quite content, save that Marlowe had joined us and was making a great business of monopolising Simon. He had his arm around Simon's shoulders, sitting close beside him on the bench, and was urging him to drink wine, not ale. Simon was wearing yet another new doublet. Will pulled out a joint stool and sat down beside me, listening to the chatter but not joining in.

'You are quiet tonight, Will,' I said, raising my tankard of small ale and viewing him over the brim.

He seemed far away, but then he pulled his thoughts back from wherever they were wandering and fixed me with that terrible penetrating look he sometimes wore. I found it disconcerting, and lowered my eyes to my ale.

'I learn more by listening than by speaking, as I have observed you do also, Ganymede,' he said.

Ganymede. Cup-bearer to Jove. Some said Ganymede was a beautiful youth and Jove's catamite. But other versions of the legend told that Ganymede was a girl, disguised as a boy. I realised suddenly from what I read in Will's eyes that he had seen through my long-practised disguise, and knew me for what I was. I felt myself first frozen cold, then engulfed by a wave of heat, as my heart seemed to stop beating and then rush like a galloping horse.

'Have no fear,' he said, touching my hand lightly, so that no one saw in the summer twilight. 'I have no wish to lay open the secrets of your heart. I reserve that for my plays.'

My worries over Marlowe's influence on Simon, who was clearly spending much beyond his means on wine and costly garments, came to a head a few days later. I had taken Rikki for a walk on our return from the hospital. Instead of going directly back to my lodgings we followed the river along Bankside, past the bear baiting and Paris Garden. Had we continued to Lambeth, as I had first intended, I would have missed an encounter which was to have profound consequences, though I did not know it at the time. Our walk was curtailed when one of the laces of my shoe broke. I managed to tie it together, but the shoe was awkward and uncomfortable, so I turned back, Rikki running on ahead.

As I neared the Atkins house, I saw that Simon was standing just beyond it, arguing with two men. Even from a distance, I had the sense that they were somehow threatening him. Rikki came to a stand a few yards away, and I saw the hairs on his neck rise. He growled low, once, in his throat, and the muscles of his shoulders tensed.

I hurried forward. I had never known my dog attack anyone unprovoked before, but he had certainly shown himself fearless in protecting me that time in the Low Countries. If he took it into his head to attack these men now, I did not like his chances. Both wore long daggers and looked as though they would not hesitate to use them. I stooped and caught hold of Rikki's collar.

Our arrival put an end to whatever the three of them had been arguing about. One of the men, who seemed to me faintly familiar, merely said, 'Take heed, Hetherington. Time is growing short.'

With that they both turned and strode away, without the courtesy of a bow to Simon and ignoring me completely. I saw that Simon had gone very white, but pretended I had noticed nothing.

'I have an excellent flagon of ale from the Lion waiting for me upstairs,' I said. 'Will you join me?'

Then without waiting for him to answer I opened the house door and started up the stairs. I could hear him following me. As I set about fetching out the flagon and two tankards, Simon sank on to the end of my bed and began running Rikki's ears through his fingers. Out of the corner of my eye, I saw that his hand was shaking.

'Who were your friends?' I asked casually.

He gave a bitter laugh. 'No friends of mine.'

'Nay, it did not seem a friendly conversation.' I paused. I was determined to know. 'So who were they, these no friends of yours?'

'Their names are Nicholas Skeres and Ingram Frizer.'

'So those are their *names*,' I said, 'Nicholas Skeres and Ingram Frizer. But *what* are they?' I realised that I knew a little of Skeres, who had been one of Walsingham's agents, but an obscure one. That was why he seemed familiar. I must have seen him occasionally about Seething Lane.

Simon looked at me wildly, something besides distress in his eyes. It almost seemed like fear.

'What are they? A fine pair of gentlemen, Skeres and Frizer. They lend money to foolish young men, and tangle them in the birdnets of debt with their lime of sweet promises. Oh, yes, a fine pair of gentlemen!'

I sat down abruptly next to him on the bed and grabbed him by the shoulders.

'What are you saying, Simon? Have they entrapped you?'

He would not look me in the eye until I shook him hard.

'Simon, for sweet Jesu's sake! Be honest with me!'

He jerked himself free and passed his hand over his face. I realised then how exhausted he looked and got up to hand him the tankard of ale, which was all the drink I had in my lodgings. He drank it thirstily. I had little enough to

45

eat about the place, but I found some bread and some cold cooked bacon, which we ate in silence.

'Last winter,' he said wearily, at last, 'when that bitter weather kept the audiences low and then closed the playhouse for months . . . well, you know that. I was very short of the chinks.'

I opened my mouth to say, 'But why did you not come to me?' then shut it again. I thought I knew why. Pride. Delicacy about presuming on our friendship.

'But now?' I said. 'Everything is going well at the Rose, is it not? With the Theatre closed, the Rose is packed full every day. You are all earning beyond the usual.'

He shifted uneasily. 'I have had unexpected expenses.'

'You mean your fine new clothes? And wine to drink instead of ale? I know who is behind it,' I said bitterly. 'Marlowe has urged you on to the same heedless extravagances as he is known for.'

He would not look me in the eye.

'Oh, Simon, how could you be so foolish!' I was truly angry with him. 'You have borrowed money from those men? How did you meet them?'

'I met Skeres through one of the members of our company – not one of the players, the fellow who looks after our properties, buys what's needed, or makes them. A throne. A blunt player's sword. Wooden shields for soldiers.'

I nodded. 'I know the man you mean..'

'He had borrowed money from Skeres. Indeed, he said that Kit Marlowe had recommended him. I thought if Marlowe had found him safe to deal with, there could be no risk in it. I was introduced to Skeres in a tavern – oh, several months ago. About the time we played *Friar Bungay*, and it looked as though we would never have an audience, or earn another penny. I was already in debt then. Skeres said he had no ready coin at the moment, but he knew a gentleman called Frizer who dealt in loans.'

46

'A moneylender,' I said. 'I thought none but Jews might lend money. I would guess that he did not lend it to you out of kindness and without interest.'

'The law says that ten per cent is the most that may be charged,' said Simon. 'But I had no security for my bond – no property, you see, or plate or jewels. Their practice is to lend you part of the sum in coin and part in commodity. I needed ten pounds.'

I gasped. Ten pounds! Without my realising it, Simon must have been living even more above his income than I had guessed. I blamed Marlowe for that. Ten pounds must be about what Simon would earn in a year. A good year. And last winter and spring had not been good.

'Frizer loaned me ten pounds in coin and ten in lute-strings, which I could sell for twenty, and so repay the debt. The bond is due on the last day of June.'

I frowned. I could not quite understand this. Why would Frizer give Simon ten pounds worth of lute-strings if he could sell them himself for twenty? It sounded like a swindle to me.

'So?' I said.

'So I signed a bond for twenty pounds, took the ten pounds in coin to pay several debts I owed and to live off while the playhouses were closed down.'

'And the lute-strings?'

His mouth twisted in a bitter smile.

'Ah, it seems the market is flooded with lute-strings at present. I could not sell them, not for twenty pounds, not even for the ten pounds I had been told they were worth. In the end Skeres was kind enough to take them back off my hands for two pounds and ten shillings. No doubt by now they are in the possession of some other fool.'

So Skeres and Frizer were working this trap together.

'That means,' I said slowly, 'altogether you had twelve pounds and ten shillings, but you are in debt to Frizer for twenty pounds.'

'Yes.'

'So what that really means is that he has charged you interest of seven pounds and ten shillings on twelve pounds and ten shillings. That's sixty per cent, instead of the legal maximum of ten per cent. Sixty per cent!'

I gasped. It was inconceivable.

'And over a period of a few months!'

'I do not have your ability for figures, Kit, but you probably have the right of it.' He buried his head in his hands.

I sprang to my feet and began to walk about the room.

'I can help you with about ten pounds,' I said. It was the sum total of my savings since I had returned to work, together with fees from several of my private patients over the bad weather of the winter. Worried for the future I had been putting aside every penny I could spare. 'But I cannot possibly find twenty.'

'Nay! I would not ask it! I do not know what to do.'

'I see.' I did indeed. There was a very bad stink about this whole affair.

'And you see,' he said, his voice tense, 'if Frizer can kill one of his victims, he can very likely kill another.'

'What do you say? He has killed a man?'

'Aye, so Skeres says. One who could not repay his debt. Frizer escaped with a verdict of self-defence. They claimed it was a brawl, begun by the other man. As he was dead, the man could not speak for himself.'

Simon looked at me steadily. He truly believed that Frizer would come in pursuit of him next.

'That makes no sense,' I said. 'Those who owe him money are far more valuable to him alive than dead. Why should he kill you?'

'As a warning to others, I'm thinking. This is what happens if you do not pay.'

I concealed my shudder at this and assumed a brisk air.

'It is my belief that Frizer must be a fool or at least a poor businessman, if he kills off those in debt to him, but I agree that you should try to raise the money to pay off the loan and its monstrous interest as soon as possible.'

I did not add: 'for fear of what might happen if Frizer chooses to pursue you with violence.'

After a lengthy argument, I made him promise to use my ten pounds towards the debt. Since the Rose had begun to draw good audiences, he had been able to set aside two pounds himself. If he could raise the remaining eight, he could free himself of his bond. I suggested the pawnbroker de Barros out at Shoreditch, but Simon had nothing worth pawning except his costumes, and those he needed for his profession. Shamefaced, he admitted that he was still paying off the tailor who had made the doublets, and so could neither pawn nor sell them yet. I was no better off, I had nothing but the tools of my trade. I possessed only one spare suit of clothes and my best physician's gown which I wore when visiting my private patients in the City, for I had lived frugally for months, putting every spare penny aside into those savings I now offered Simon. He hated the thought of taking my money, that I could see, but he swore that he would pay it all back.

'Not by taking out another loan!' I said with a wry laugh.

'Nay,' he said soberly. 'I'll not be so foolish again. Our earnings look to be good this summer. I shall pay you back from those.'

Nevertheless, there remained another eight pounds to find.

Then, after no more was heard from Skeres or Frizer, I was lulled into a mistaken sense of safety, especially after we learned that Frizer had gone down into Kent to his patron, young Walsingham, Sir Francis's cousin. However, he would soon be back in London, so the word was. By giving up his room in the Atkins house to one of the other players, Christopher Haigh, and sleeping on my floor, and eating less than a church mouse, and calling in some small debts owed to him, Simon had managed to gather together another pound, while I had received fees amounting to two pounds from two of my private patients. He needed five pounds more to free himself of his bond to Frizer.

'I am going to appeal to Sara,' I said, as we parted one morning, Simon heading for the Rose and I for the hospital. 'I will have no opportunity today, but I will call in tomorrow when I go over the river to see a patient of mine in Goldsmiths' Row.'

'I cannot borrow from Sara,' he objected.

'We have run out of time. Frizer will be back in London in a day or two. Your bond is due at the end of this month. I do not see what else we can do.'

'No!'

He slammed his fist into his hand.

'This has gone far enough. I didn't want to borrow from you. I certainly will not borrow from Sara Lopez. It's humiliating.'

He was shouting now, his face flushed. My neighbour from the garret room, Howard, the water haulier, stared at us as he passed in the street.

'Hush, Simon.' I looked around, embarrassed. 'What ails you? Of course I want to help, and so will Sara.'

My heart was thrumming painfully. Simon had never spoken to me like this. He was glaring at me as though he hated me. Oh, God! Don't let me lose Simon over this.

'I will not, I cannot, humble myself to borrow from a woman.' He was hissing now, keeping his voice down, but sweat had broken out on his forehead.

'Simon, please . . . !'

I reached out my hands to him, imploring. He turned abruptly on his heel and walked, almost ran, away from me.

Stupid tears had sprung into my eyes and I brushed them away angrily as I began to trudge toward the hospital.

There had been another outbreak of measles amongst the children of Southwark and I was kept busy until late that evening, for measles is a dangerous and often fatal disease, especially amongst children of the poor who are so often weak and undernourished. I was dismayed not to find Simon at home when I reached my room, for the play would be long finished, but I supposed he had gone afterwards to the Lion with our friends. Surely he had not left me? All day I had tried to push away the memory of that bitter little scene in the morning, but I had to confront it now, faced with a cold hearth and a darkened room.

I was too tired to join the others at the Lion, and perhaps a little afraid of confronting Simon, so I cut myself some bread and cheese and had just started to eat when I heard feet in the street outside, half running, half scrambling, followed by a pounding on the outer door of the house.

I ran down the stairs and flung open the door. Two figures showed against the glow of the torch outside the whorehouse. One appeared to be supporting the other.

'Kit, help me get him inside. Quick!'

It was Will. Simon was on his feet, but only just. Between us we half carried, half dragged him upstairs and laid him on my bed. Blood was pouring from his left shoulder, where a great rip in his doublet laid bare a slash down through the flesh to his collar bone.

'He's been badly kicked in the back as well,' Will said, 'but this is the worst. How bad is it?'

'It will have to be stitched,' I said. 'Get his doublet and shirt off.'

I put water to heat over my small fire and laid out needle, thread and dressings from my satchel. After I had cleaned away the worst of the blood I could see that the wound was sharp and straight.

'This was done with a sword,' I said.

Will nodded. He was kneeling on the bed, propping Simon up so I could reach the shoulder more easily. Simon himself had fallen unconscious, for which I was grateful. I gritted my teeth and began to stitch the edges of the gaping wound together. Seeing what was needed, Will used his free hand to mop up the blood which continued to gush out. I have sewn many wounds from swords and daggers, but I had never before been forced to drive a needle back and forth through flesh which felt so precious to me. Each time

I drew the thread through and tightened it, my own flesh recoiled. Once Simon gave a sharp cry of pain and I feared he would regain consciousness, but then he lapsed back again into the dark world of the unconscious.

When I had finished, I washed the blood from my hands and the very sight of the red-tinted water made me sick, but I busied myself spreading salve over the wound and binding the whole shoulder in a bandage.

I sat back at last on the end of the bed and wiped my face with a scrap of bandage.

'What happened?'

Will laid Simon down carefully on the bed and gave me a troubled look.

'I'm not sure. We'd all been at the Lion and I left just after Simon. I heard shouting ahead of me in the street, men yelling something about paying debts. When I caught up with them, one said, "Next time it will be your pretty face, and no playhouse will want you afterwards." Simon was lying on the ground and they kicked him in the back, but ran off when they saw me. There were two of them. Big fellows. Vicious brutes.'

'Frizer,' I said. 'Frizer's men.'

'He owes money to Frizer?' Will clicked his tongue and shook his head. 'That's bad. He's a fool to fall into the hands of Frizer.'

'You know about Frizer?' I said. 'Aye, I agree. But he has nearly enough to pay back the debt, and the bond isn't due until the end of the month.'

'You've helped him?'

I shrugged. 'As much as I could. We must help our friends. You thrust yourself into danger tonight. Those men might have turned on you. Let me give you something to eat and drink.'

I busied myself laying out more bread and cheese and a tankard of poor, thin ale, for our straightened means meant our supplies were frugal. I sensed Will watching me keenly.

'I'm sorry I have nothing better,' I said, as he drew up a stool to the table.

'Who needs fine kickshaws to eat amongst friends?' He grinned at me and drank thirstily. 'I wasn't sure I would be able to reach you while he was still on his feet.'

He looked across at Simon, then turned that sharp gaze on me.

'Does he know? You share a room . . .'

'Nay. He has known me as a boy since we were both sixteen. He sees what he expects to see. I am careful.'

He pursed his lips thoughtfully. 'I wonder. Simon is no fool. Though I have heard tell of women who have gone for soldiers, disguised as men, and never been known for years, until they were wounded. There was Joan of Arc, of course, who dressed as a man, though I think she was always known for a woman. But there was the female Pope long ago – wasn't she Joan as well?'

'Yes, I think so.'

'She was revealed as a woman at last. And there was St Marina. She went into a monastery with her father, disguised as a boy, Marinus.'

'I hadn't heard of her.'

'She had a hard life. She was accused of raping some girl and forced to undergo terrible penance until the day she died, when they discovered she was a woman and innocent.'

That distant look came into his eyes. 'It's a pretty idea. We have boys playing girls in our theatres. Think of a boy playing a girl who is disguised as a boy!'

'Who pretends to be a girl?' I laughed. Then reached out my hand to him. 'You will not tell him?'

'I have promised you that I will not.'

After Will had gone home, I sat beside Simon, watching him anxiously. Although the sword cut was not ragged, it was very deep and I also feared infection. The sword was almost certainly dirty, and Simon had been near starving himself of late. In his weakened state, he might fall victim to some foul infection. His fair skin was so thin and delicate that I could watch the pulse of blood in his temple. I took one of his hands in mine, certain he would be unaware of my touch. His fingers were cold, so with my free hand I drew up the blanket from the foot of the bed until it covered him, keeping my own hand and arm under it. Gradually I could feel his hand grow warmer and when the candle went out I did not get up to light another.

Deep into the night his breathing seemed to grow easier and he rolled over towards me, curling in his sleep like a child. I should go and lie down on his palliasse, I thought, but I could not drag myself away, for he was lying now in my arms. I might never again hold him like this. I leaned forward, laying my head beside his on the pillow. Sometime before dawn, I fell asleep.

When I woke the next morning I found Simon's face not six inches from mine, his eyes just beginning to focus. I raised myself from the bed, stiff from my uncomfortable position.

'Kit?'

'How are you this morning?' I was all briskness.

'How did I come here?'

'Will brought you. He came upon you being attacked by two of Frizer's men and managed to drag you here.'

He gave a sudden yelp as he tried to sit up, and began to feel his shoulder with his other hand.

'A sword thrust,' I said. 'I've dressed it. You'll live. Leave it be.'

I kept my back to him, afraid of what my face might betray until I disciplined it into order. Was he still angry with me?

'I'm stiff as the Devil.' His voice was cracked and hesitant.

'You will be for a few days. You had a thorough kicking as well. There will be bruises. Do you have any sharp pains in your chest?'

He felt himself cautiously. 'No. I don't think so. Just stiffness. And I think my back is bruised.'

'No broken ribs, then. You must stay in bed for the present. Give your shoulder time to heal.'

'I'm needed at the theatre.'

'No, Will says there's no need for you to go in for the next three or four days. You have no rôle until then.'

'I suppose that's right.' He lay back with a groan. He was looking very pale.

'I am going to get some food to leave for you – more cheese and a pie. Then after I finish at the hospital I am going to see Sara. We will pay off Master Frizer before this happens again.'

'They said they would disfigure my face.' He sounded very subdued. I knew it was not vanity. An actor depends upon his appearance.

'That is why I am going to Sara.'

This time he did not argue.

'Of course I will help you, Kit,' Sara said. 'I know that Simon has been a good friend to you these many years. How long is it now?'

'Six years.'

'And he still does not know your secret?'

'Certainly not. How could I associate with him as I do, if he knew that I am a woman?' If I blushed at the memory of last night, she did not notice.

'But,' she said delicately, 'he shares your lodgings.'

'Sara,' I said in exasperation, feeling the colour rise further in my face, 'he does *not* know. I am very careful.'

She raised her hands, palms forward, to hush me, and laughed. 'Very well, he does not know. But you do.' Seeing my expression, she left off teasing, and gave me the precious five pounds that were to buy Simon's freedom from Frizer, and his safety from further attacks.

'We will pay you back, every farthing,' I promised.

'Do not beggar yourself to do it.

'And Ruy's affairs march well?'

'As far as he lets me know them. There is a fellow Tinoco – whom I distrust, a shifty, sneaking fellow – he is back and forth to the Continent like a rat darting in and out of a sewer. He blows in on one wind and is gone back again the next day. I never know, when I come down in the morning, whether I shall find him in my garden. And that shabby creature da Gama, who lives in Ruy's house in St Katharine Creechurch, is forever turning up here, with his greasy hair and his dirty clothes, and huddling with Ruy over some business. The man has a stink about him, of sweat and rancid garlic.'

I smiled. That was the Englishwoman in Sara talking. Despite her Marrano blood, she was as English as her birthplace. She might light candles to welcome the Sabbath, but she was more at ease with roast beef than with olive oil and garlic.

As soon as Frizer himself was reported to be back in town, I went with Simon to redeem the bond. I was determined he should have a friend and witness and, besides, I was curious to see what manner of creature could tempt intelligent young men like Simon into his traps. Simon's shoulder was still bandaged under his shirt, but I had removed the stitches and apart from some awkwardness in his left arm he was showing little effect of the attack. If Frizer was surprised to see us, he concealed it.

'So,' said Frizer, counting the twenty pounds for the second time, insulting Simon by his caution and keeping him in humiliating suspense all the while. 'So, you have repaid the debt, and before the bond runs out! I do not think I have known a common player do such a thing before.'

He laid emphasis on the word *common*.

Simon stood with his arms folded and his lips grimly pressed together, and did not respond.

'Perhaps it was the excellent influence of your learned friend here,' said Frizer, nodding at me in a dismissive way.

I had worn my best physician's gown to impress him, but he was not a man to be thus impressed. As he moved to lock the money away in his strong box, I saw that he wore a dagger at his belt. Frizer returned and laid on the table the bond that Simon had signed. He perused it slowly, as if he could somehow catch Simon out even now. At last he nodded, then tore the paper in half. He made as if to return the pieces to his strongbox, but Simon stepped swiftly forward and seized them from his hand.

'By your leave,' he said politely, 'I believe these now belong to me.'

We left at once, running down the stairs and out into the fresh air. As soon as we had returned to my room, we threw the two halves of the poisonous paper into the hearth and burned it to ashes.

'There!' said Simon, beating the burnt flakes to a powder with the poker. 'I wish I could do the same with Frizer himself.'

Although I had never shared my fears with Simon, thinking it better not to worry him unnecessarily, I thought he stood in greater danger through his association with Marlowe than through his bond to Frizer, despite the attack he had suffered.

With the paying off of his debt and the destruction of his bond, all the lines of worry which had marked Simon's face these last weeks were smoothed away.

'Come!' he cried. 'The rest of the company will have finished at the Rose by now. They will be making for the Lion for supper. If we join them and look very hungry, perhaps someone will buy us a pint of ale and a pie.'

I smiled, and dug into the purse at my belt, then held up a coin that flashed briefly in the slant of sun through the window.

'We need not beg. I have a quarter noble left.' I shook my purse to show by its silence that it was empty. 'We shall pay our way, though we go hungry tomorrow.'

'The saints be praised! How did you manage that?'

'By careful husbanding of my pennies,' I said severely. 'A skill you needs must learn.'

'You sound like my uncle's wife,' he said, pulling a face. 'I did not live with them long after my parents died, but she was always scolding my uncle for not watching his pennies carefully enough.'

'At least he found enough to put you to school at St Paul's,' I said, slapping my leg to tell Rikki to come with us.

'That he did not,' Simon contradicted as we started down the stairs. 'Do you think that miserly pair would ever have paid for my schooling? The school took me on for my voice in the choir. And I was bright enough to gain some benefit from my lessons. My ready memory was what proved my greatest weapon there. Good training for a player.'

I did not respond. Simon's childhood had not been as bitter as mine, but mine had started well, sheltered in a loving family. He had never known that. Though he had not known the terrors of the Inquisition either. But it was too lovely a day to think of such things.

We turned left along Bankside, Rikki running ahead, only stopping from time to time to raise his leg against a favourite tree. I hoped that the poor state of many of them was not entirely due to his attentions.

As we had hoped, the others were just arriving at the Lion, and were boisterous with another successful performance.

'Back with us tomorrow, are you, Simon?' Geoffrey de Claine, who specialised in old men, raised his hand to give Simon a buffet on the shoulder, but he dodged away.

'Have a care! The stitches are but taken out this morning. My physician will eat you alive if you destroy all his good work.'

'Is he that fragile, Kit?' Dick Burbage asked.

'He is fit to start work again tomorrow,' I said, 'but I'll have the guts of any man who undoes my careful stitchery.'

We crowded on to benches at a table set out between the inn and the river. In the long June daylight it would be hours before it was fully dark. Under the cover of the pot boy bringing flagons of ale and others of beer, Will murmured to me, 'Simon looks in high spirits. Is Frizer taken care of?'

'This afternoon.' I poured us both ale. 'There is still Sara Lopez to pay back, but she will not press for it in a hurry.'

'That's Dr Lopez's wife?'

'Aye.' I took a long swig of the ale, and realised how thirsty I was. The weather had turned to summer heat and I had hardly noticed, so preoccupied had I been with Simon's affairs.

'They say Lopez is a rich man.'

'Aye, he does well, as much from his trading in spices as from physicking the Queen and courtiers. He often buys some of Drake's loot from the Spanish ships. Or he used to. Perhaps he does not do so well since his losses in the Portuguese expedition.'

'He should watch his back,' Will said. 'Kit Marlowe's play has stirred up the good people of London against Jews. Especially rich ones.'

'Are you, very politely, giving me a warning as well? Not that any man could call me rich.'

'If you wish to take it that way. I think you have turned more to your Christian faith than your Jewish heritage, but that is a matter for your private thoughts. Although it is an interesting subject. I wonder whether I might make a play of it.'

'You can make a play of anything. How goes your Harry Six?'

'Second part finished. Third part well on. I wish I had never started. It is nigh impossible to make sense of all the ambition and double dealing that marked that reign.'

'Quite unlike our own times,' I said dryly.

'Quite.' He grinned. 'Let us be thankful that we are neither of us courtiers. Ah, here comes the beef pottage, and Master Burbage with it.'

Master Burbage came smiling to join us and took his place, by right, in the cushioned chair at the head of the table. We all heard the chink as he set down a fat purse on the boards before him.

'Aye, you may well smile, lads,' he said expansively. 'Philip Henslowe and I have decided to give you a bonus, audiences having been so good.' He turned to Simon. 'Even you, Master Hetherington, despite your noticeable absence recently.'

I saw Simon let out an anxiously held breath.

The beef arrived, but as soon as it was cleared away and before the serving girls brought bowls of fruit for us to finish the meal, he had begun counting out the coins and handing over each man's share. It was a happy gathering, and the prospect of an excellent summer, to make up for last winter's anxious and hungry months, raised many tankards in toasts for the season's success.

After a while I turned my attention away from the table and looked out over the river. Wherries were plying back and forth, some taking playgoers home to their supper in the City, others bringing the rougher sort to the bear baiting and cock fighting. Later the crowds would be all men, coming for the Winchester geese.

It all looked prosperous enough. Yet there niggled at the back of my mind the knowledge that London's stocks of food had run very low, and with the late spring, and the consequent late planting, food shortages could only get worse over the next few weeks, until some of the gardens along toward Lambeth, and the others north of the City beyond Shoreditch, began to yield the new season's vegetables.

There would be no new wheat for weeks yet. Already the official weight designated for the penny loaf had been lowered, and then lowered again. There had been protests on the streets at the cruelly small size of the loaf, which was the staple food of poor Londoners. The labourers' wage had not risen, so they were able to buy less and less food for their families. We were already treating cases of serious malnutrition at St Thomas's.

There was another burst of laughter from the players. Yet it seemed to me that their merriment was like the smooth flowing surface of the river before me. What dark dangers might be lurking beneath?

Chapter Four

*T*he day Simon and I paid off his debt to Ingram Frizer, and then later celebrated cheerfully with the rest of Lord Strange's Men by the river at the Lion, was Friday, the ninth day of June. All seemed set fair for the Rose and the players. With nothing but the minor companies and a few children's players available in the City, every afternoon the crowds flocked over the river by wherry or by foot over the Bridge, to attend the ever more successful performances at the Rose. Southwark had long been popular for its bear and bull baiting, its cock fights and whorehouses, and a multitude of entertainments in Paris Garden – jugglers, conjurors, puppet theatres and the like, as well as cheap alehouses and stalls where you could buy every sort of street food from honey cakes to hot pies. Such diversions (or means of separating folk from their hard earned coins) had in the past mostly appealed to labourers and their families, or footloose apprentices.

The Rose playhouse, built five years before and the first one south of the river, had drawn in – as well as the penny groundlings, who stood in the yard to watch the play – the better off who would pay extra for a seat in one of the galleries and a cushion to sit on. Moreover, both Will Shakespeare and Kit Marlowe were gaining fame by word of mouth throughout London, so their plays brought large crowds every time they were staged. No wonder the players looked forward to a richly rewarded summer to make up for the thin time they had had of it during the previous long winter.

Perhaps, caught up in their highly charged and exciting world, they were less aware of other things happening in London. Ever since the Queen's father had destroyed the monasteries, which had done much to care for the poor, those same poor had become an increasing problem throughout England, but above all in London. For now that more farm workers and cottagers were being turned off their land by their lords in order to graze sheep, the stream of penniless folk seeking work in London had become a flood. Both St Bartholomew's and St Thomas's had some accommodation for paupers, but they could provide for very few.

A few days earlier I had heard mutterings at St Thomas's about some feltmaker's apprentice who had been wrongly arrested by the Knight Marshal and his men, and hauled away to the Marshalsea. The Knight Marshal, based at the prison, was responsible for order in Southwark, but the present incumbent of the post had made himself hated for his violence, and his men had modelled themselves on him.

'They broke into the lad's home with daggers drawn,' Tom Read told me, shaking his head. 'His married sister was there, nursing a young babe, and some old folk, and all the family were terrified. The Marshal's men dragged the boy away and shut him up in the pit of the Marshalsea, though folk are saying he's innocent and they have arrested the wrong man.'

'It would not be the first time,' I said.

'It would not,' he agreed, 'but this time there's trouble brewing. Add to it the rising price of food, and the families fallen into poverty this last winter, as well as the usual accusations that foreigners are given work which rightly belong to Englishmen. It's a dangerous brew.'

I had pushed this conversation to the back of my mind when I went to the Rose the next day to see the first performance of a new play, *A Knack to Know a Knave.*

Even while he had been confined with his injured shoulder, Simon had been learning his lines for the new play as King Edgar, who it seems was a real king some six hundred years ago.

'It might sound like the best character,' Simon said, while I had been hearing his lines, 'but it isn't really. That part is Honesty, which Ned will play.'

'Honesty?' I said. 'That sounds like one of those old morality plays.'

'Aye, some of the play is a bit like a morality – wicked sinners condemned by Honesty and dragged off to Hell, but there's this other story of King Edgar falling in love with a beautiful maid – that will be played by Edward Titheridge – but being cheated of her by one of his own men. Then there's a lot of comic business too.'

'Hmm,' I said, 'a fair hodgepodge, by the sound of it.'

'Perhaps, but come anyway. It will be good entertainment.'

I was not sure I would find it so, but I was feeling in holiday mood after the paying of Simon's debt, and it was good to see him back at work, for he had been fretful while convalescing. Accordingly, on Saturday I made my way to the Rose about half an hour after Simon, and found that most of London was cramming the streets around the playhouse. A new play always drew the crowds, and if the title of this one sounded somewhat old fashioned, it did not seem to have put anyone off.

It was indeed an odd sort of play, a sort of mixed gallimaufry of a play, into which every kind of ingredient had been thrown. The morality play of the evil bailiff and his yet more evil sons, condemned to Hell by Honesty, had the usual high jinks with devils and fireworks, and a nasty streak of cruelty too. There was knockabout comedy featuring the foolish Men of Gotham, which was remarkably silly. And the story of King Edgar, in which Simon appeared, veered toward grandiloquence and tragic drama without ever quite achieving it. Throughout, the

Knack was sprinkled with allusions to recent plays staged at the Rose and to matters of common day-to-day gossip in the city – the sort of allusions which would mean nothing in a year's time.

However, the audience was full of good humour, ready to laugh and cheer and hiss as the players romped through the tangled plot, and I laughed and cheered and hissed along with them. I joined the players at the Lion afterwards, and we all went home in high good humour.

The next day being Sunday, Simon and I went with the Atkins family and Christopher to the morning service at St Mary Overy. Afterwards, because it was a fine sunny June day, we walked to Paris Garden and bought roast mutton cutlets from one stall and savoury pastries from another, which we carried down to the river's edge. Sitting on the grass and eating with greasy fingers, we made a picnic of our dinner, like many others all about us. There were clusters of ducks and swans on the river, hoping for scraps to be thrown, though I saw little of that. Despite the holiday mood, folk were still careful with food in this time of shortages and high prices.

'A good many families here today,' Simon said, as he licked the last of the grease from his fingers, and tossed the cutlet bone in the river, 'but hardly an apprentice to be seen.'

I glanced around. He was right. On a Sunday crowds of apprentices, both from the City and from Southwark, usually pushed their way through the Paris Garden throng in rowdy flocks, unmistakable in their blue tunics.

'Odd,' I said. 'There were a fair few at the play yesterday. Where can they all be?'

'Making trouble somewhere, I'll be bound,' he said.

He was to be proved disastrously right that very evening.

Our carefree time by the river was somewhat marred at the end when a ranting Puritan set himself upon a box to lecture at the crowds, condemning us all for sinners. We should be on our knees, or living on bread and water on this

Sabbath day, instead of indulging in the sinful activities of Paris Garden. The jugglers and others were evil mountebanks, henchmen of the Devil. The stall keepers had no licence to sully the Lord's Day by dealing in filthy lucre. Quite eloquent it might have been, had we not heard it all before. Eventually he was driven off by a few local youths – not apprentices but young watermen – who pelted him with mud scooped up from the foreshore, food being too precious to waste on such a fellow, apart from a few apple cores.

About eight of the clock that evening we were having a rather desultory game of chess, not paying it as much heed as it needed, when footsteps thundered up the stairs and there was a pounding on the door.

'Come!' I called.

Christopher Haigh put his head round the door. Instead of his usual rather dapper appearance, his clothes were in some disarray, and there was a fresh and bleeding cut on his cheek.

'Trouble!' he said.

We both sprang up.

'What kind of trouble?' Simon asked.

'A great crowd of apprentices. But not just apprentices. A lot of labouring men, too. And masterless men, I'll be bound. And looking ugly and ready for a fight. They aren't only armed with clubs, they are carrying steel too. And throwing rocks and broken flasks.' He touched his cheek carefully. 'One of them hit me.'

'Let me see to that,' I said. 'You do not want to be left with a scar.'

He came in eagerly. For Christopher, perhaps even more than for most players, a scarred face would be a disaster, since he specialised in playing the young romantic heroes.

'Best to clean it,' I said, swabbing the cut with a cleansing tincture of comfrey. 'It may have been dirty, whatever hit you.'

'How deep is it?' He tried to squint down at his own cheek.

'Not deep, and it has almost stopped bleeding. I think whatever it was just grazed you as it flew past. You were lucky. It missed your eye by not much more than an inch. Keep still while I smear on some salve.'

Christopher looked somewhat comical with a large clot of whitish salve ornamenting his cheek, though he thanked me profusely.

'But,' said Simon impatiently, 'why were you caught up in the trouble at all?'

'Because they gathered at the Rose.'

'What!' We both looked at him in alarm.

'I'd gone there to pick up my new part for next week. I'd left it behind and wanted to con it. All was quiet when the doorkeeper let me in. When I came out, this great crowd had gathered.'

'Do they mean harm to the playhouse?' Simon was fastening his cloak as he spoke.

'Nay, I think not. You may believe that I did not stay to discuss matters with them, but made off as quickly as I could, being one against their many. However, I heard shouts about this hat-maker's apprentice who has been wrongly imprisoned, and his family roughly handled to boot.'

'I've heard there might be trouble coming.' I was putting on my own cloak and caught up my satchel of medicines.

'They were shouting about the price of bread and the lack of work as well,' Christopher said, 'and cursing the foreigners who have come of late to settle here. What are you both about? Surely you are not going out? Have I not made it clear? It is dangerous out there, and as far as I could tell, they are coming this way.'

Simon went to the window, thrust it open and leaned out.

'Aye, I can hear them heading along Bankside.'

'What did I tell you?'

'Perhaps they are heading for the Marshalsea. They'll get little satisfaction out of the Marshal and his men.'

'If there is going to be fighting,' I said, 'there will be injuries. I shall be needed at the hospital.'

I kept my voice firm, but my stomach had turned queasy. Fights in London can become very nasty, even when only a few are involved. If there were many out there tonight, there would be serious injuries and almost certainly deaths.

'I had best reach St Thomas's ahead of them,' I said.

'Too late.' Simon leaned further out. 'They are nearly here.'

I joined him at the window. Although it was not yet truly dark, the figures beginning to pass below the window were thrown into sharp relief by the light of the torches carried by many. A wind had sprung up with the evening, so that the flames were thrown out like comets' tails as the chanting crowd increased its pace from a fast walk to a run. They did not chant in time with each other, but the shouts thrown up from below carried fragments and words to our ears – 'death to the Marshal', 'hunger', 'damnable foreigners', 'break open the Marshalsea'.

As more and more of the men passed, the crowd thickened, like a swollen river about to overflow. Some wielded clubs above their heads. Torch light glinted on steel – not daggers alone, but swords as well. By law, such men should not carry swords in the city, but it was clear these fellows cared not for the law.

'There are hundreds of them,' Simon said in a taut voice.

'What did I tell you?' Christopher said. 'Any sane man will stay within and bar his door.'

'They are like to start a fire with all those torches.' Simon waved to take in the whole mass now stretching as far as we could see, right and left along Bankside. 'I do not care for the thought that I might roast in my own bed.'

'They are not stopping here,' I pointed out. 'I think the houses here are safe. Where are they going? And why did they gather at the Rose?'

'An easy place to choose,' Christopher said. 'Everyone in London knows the Rose. If the word was passed around in whispers, the Rose would be clear to all. And as they gathered, if they were questioned, they could claim they had come for the play.'

'On a Sunday?'

There was no answer for that.

By straining as far out of the window as we dared without tumbling headlong, we could see that the crowd did not turn aside at the Bridge, but carried on. I was not clear where they were headed, unless perhaps it was the Marshalsea, but once the last of the stragglers had passed, we saw a few curious neighbours venturing out from the houses on either side of us, as well as from Bess Travis's whorehouse, trying to make out what was afoot. Even a few of the Winchester geese in their flimsy clothes took a few steps beyond the door.

'It is safe enough now,' I said, picking up my satchel again. 'I am going to the hospital. I shall be needed.'

'I am coming with you,' Simon declared. 'Christopher?'

'I am no such fool,' he said. 'And my advice to you is to stay here. A crowd like that makes no distinction of who they attack.'

I laid my hand on the latch of the door and Rikki, taking this as a sign that a walk was in prospect, jumped down from the bed.

I shook my finger at him. 'You stay here.' He knew from my tone of voice that I meant it and collapsed on the floor with a sigh.

Christopher accompanied us down the first flight of steps, then shut himself in the room which used to be Simon's, while we continued down to the street door, which Simon opened cautiously.

All of the original crowd had passed, though we could hear shouting from further down river. The curious spectators had returned to their homes, but a few local people, mostly young men, were sauntering in that direction, either to watch out of curiosity, or else to join in the trouble-making.

'We need to have a care we are not taken to be part of that crew,' Simon said. 'I will come with you as far as St Thomas's, then I think I will take Christopher's advice and shut myself up at home. You'd best stay in the hospital until morning. It should be safe there, behind those high walls.'

'I shall do that. If the Marshal turns out his men, there will be injuries done, certain sure. I wonder where they are headed.'

Even as we spoke, we heard a confused shouting and the sound of breaking glass behind us. Some of the crowd, it seemed, had not headed east with the rest but had turned aside at Winchester Palace, the London residence of the Bishop of Winchester, who owned much of the land hereabouts.

We looked at each other in alarm.

'Why should they attack the Bishop's Palace?' I said. 'He has nothing to do with this apprentice.'

Simon looked grim. 'Once the lust for violence is woken, why should they heed who they attack? They threw something at Christopher, a harmless player coming out of the Rose. Of course they will attack the richest man in Southwark from sheer envy. Best we keep moving.'

We hurried on toward St Thomas's, and as we went it became clear that although most of the crowd had headed east, there were breakaway groups tearing down the shutters of shops and houses along the way, and a large crowd bent on attacking the Marshalsea.

'That will cook their own goose,' Simon said, short breathed as we neared the hospital gates. 'Attacking the prison will rouse the Marshal if nothing else will. As well poke a hornets' nest with a large stick.'

I pounded on the hospital gate, which unsurprisingly was closed and barred.

'Who's there?' Tom Read's voice.

'Tom, it is Dr Alvarez. I've come to help, in case there is violence done.'

Even as I spoke there came the thunder of many feet as a gang of men ran toward us, almost certainly those who had been attacking the palace and the prison. The wicket in the gate opened enough for Simon and me to slip through. Tom slammed it shut behind us and dropped the bolt.

'Jesu's bones,' Tom said, mopping his face. 'What are you both doing out in the street? This is going to turn nasty.'

Beyond the gate we could hear the sound of splintering wood and a woman's scream.

'It started at the Rose,' Simon said. 'Or at least that was where they gathered. We don't think they've done any harm there.'

'Nay.' Tom shook his head. 'Why should they spoil their place of entertainment? I'll warrant you they won't touch the bear pit or the whorehouses either.'

'They are smashing shops,' I said. 'Just small men's shops, as well as places like Winchester Palace and the Marshalsea.'

'Men with nothing will envy and destroy men who have something, Tom said grimly, 'however little it may be.'

'Aye,' Simon said. 'You have the right of it. I wonder where they are heading now? They seemed to be going down river. But there is not much there, unless they attack the Beer House at Horsley Downe, but if your idea is right, Tom, they are leaving be the places of entertainment.'

'Plenty of shops and craftsmen's workplaces to loot,' Tom said.

'They wouldn't try to get as far as Deptford docks and Greenwich Palace, would they?' I said slowly. 'Is the Queen at Greenwich?'

We looked at each other in alarm, just as there came another hammering on the gate.

'Open this b'yer lady gate, Tom!' someone shouted.

He rushed to do so, clearly knowing the voice. A man burst through as Tom shoved it closed again.

'God's nails, that were a near thing.' It was a man called Job, who worked in the printing house, one of the many businesses left over from the time when St Thomas's was a monastery – more like a small town all of its own than a simple home for monks.

'What's happening?' Tom demanded.

'Smashing up shops,' Job said. 'Beating up the Watch, grabbing any women fool enough to be outside on the streets. Now they're starting fires.'

There was a note of panic in his voice, with good reason. Much of London, but for the churches and the great nobles' houses, was timber built, and even buildings of stone had roof timbers. A fire started in one corner, in one small shop, could spread in minutes along a whole street. Rikki! I thought, trapped in my room. He would not be able to get out.

'Where are they starting fires?' I cried.

'Mostly around the end of Bermondsey Street,' Job said. 'That's where the most of them have gathered now. It's not so far off that we're safe hereabouts, though the hospital wall and the space inside should keep it off.'

'I'm going up the chapel tower,' I said. 'It's not very tall, but it should be possible to see better from there what is happening.'

I could not endure any longer being shut inside the walls around the hospital grounds, able to hear the tumult outside without knowing what was happening. I began to run toward the chapel, followed by Simon and Job. Tom, perforce, must remain by the gate, but he shouted after us, 'Come back and tell me what's afoot.'

'Aye,' I called over my shoulder.

We went up the spiral steps of the chapel tower so fast that we were all gasping by the time we reached the leads of the roof. Although it was a modest tower, it was high enough to allow us to see over the houses nearby. Only Lewes Inn was of substantial size on this side of Tooley Street, and, on the river side, St Olave's church and St Augustine Inn. Away to the right, east of where we stood, was the junction of Bermondsey Street with Tooley Street, where Job said most of the men were gathering. Sure enough, there were fires burning there, more than the flames of the torches the rioters had carried.

'God help us,' I whispered, 'they will burn down the city.' Even as I spoke there was the huge sound of collapsing wood and stone, and more screams.

'Where is the Marshal?' Simon said furiously. 'It was he and his men started this. Why is he not here to stop it?'

I looked away to the left. If the Marshal did come, it would be from that direction. The minutes seemed to drag out as the fire grew more fierce, then I could hear the pounding of horses' hooves and the slap of leather shoes on cobbles as a party of men riding and on foot poured down Southwake Street and turned right into Tooley Street. It must be the Marshal and his men.

If I had expected the rioters to turn and flee, I was much mistaken. This was no casual crowd, drawn together by chance. This riot had been organised. The men did not flee, far from it. They turned to face the oncoming forces of the law and formed themselves up like a disciplined army, waiting with swords drawn and clubs raised.

Suddenly I had a sense that all this had happened before. Three years ago a band of five hundred men had marched on Bartholomew Fair, also with all the discipline of a regular army. They were some of the men who had survived the disastrous Portuguese expedition and found themselves beggared and without work on their return. They had threatened to seize their rightful reward from the Fair unless they were compensated. On that occasion the men had been turned away with false promises, only to find themselves betrayed. Were any of those who had survived that stand-off at Bartholomew Fair now out there in the streets of Southwark tonight? This group had the same discipline. And if so, they had not waited for specious words from those in authority, they had gone to work at once, taking out their anger wherever they could.

The present mob was said to be made up of apprentices, bent on avenging one of their number wrongly imprisoned, but now that I cast my mind back to the crowd we had seen passing the window of the lodging house, many of the men had not been apprentices, as Christopher himself had suggested. Too old, for one thing. For another, it was mostly these older men who had carried swords, while apprentices – who could not afford swords, nor were allowed them – normally equipped themselves with stout clubs made of some hard and heavy wood. With so many armed men, the Marshal would find that he had something more than a crowd of unruly youths to contend with.

From where we watched, we were able to see the exact moment when the two sides came together. This was not now a case of the Marshal's men breaking into a frightened citizen's house, threatening unarmed women and old people with daggers and fists. This was a battle.

Although it was growing dark, the fight was illuminated by the torches still carried by some of the rioters and by the flames of the burning houses, almost as if it were enacted upon the stage of a playhouse, but this was no play. The blood spilled here would not be dyed water, and the dead would not rise at the end to take their bows.

'If someone does not start tipping water on those fires,' Simon said, 'there is going to be serious damage done.'

'How can they?' I said. 'No one dare venture into that, for fear of being killed. Those men will cut down the Watch with their fire buckets as readily as the Marshal's men.'

Even at this distance we could hear the defiant yelling from both sides, the clash of the swords, and soon the screams of injured men.

'Look,' Job said, pointing down to the short portion of Bermondsey Street that we were able to see. 'The Marshal has sent some of his men round that way, to come at the rioters from behind. Where has he found so many men? They must equal the rioters now, or even outnumber them.'

He had the right of it. I could see them myself now, a large band of armed men closing in on the rioters at a run. Perhaps the Marshal had called in help from the City. Suddenly it seemed that the rioters were entirely encircled. A few last clashes, but there was no doubt of the outcome now, despite the desperate defiance of the mob. The rioters were down on their knees, kicked and punched by the Marshal's men. We could hear the screams of pain even from here. It needed little imagination to picture the pools of blood gathering amongst the cobbles. And amid the violent shouts on both sides the moans of the dying would be blown away on the wind.

'I have seen enough,' I said, sickened. I turned away toward the stairs. 'I hope we will be allowed to bring in the seriously injured. And the dead.'

I scrambled down the stone steps of the tower so fast I missed my footing and slithered part of the way, but apart from a few bruises I came to no harm. Simon and Job followed me more circumspectly. I ran across to the gatehouse to tell Tom what we had seen. By now the whole of St Thomas's was roused, with sisters from the hospital and craftsmen from the various workshops – those who lived here – gathering in the yard. Even some of the heartiest of the old folk from the almshouses had hobbled out and clustered together in frightened groups.

'The Marshal's men are rounding them up,' I said to anyone who asked. 'The worst of it should be over, can they but smother the fires. We'll be having the injured here soon.' I spoke with more confidence than I felt.

Superintendent Ailmer had not come into the yard, but when I knocked on the door of his house near the chapel, he opened it at once, so I suspected he had been watching through a window. I told him quickly what we had seen.

'I will send someone to the Marshal at once,' he said, 'to say that the injured should be brought here for care.'

'I hope he may agree,' I said grimly. 'From all I have heard, he is more likely to cast the severely injured into the pit of the Marshalsea along with the rest.'

'Aye.' He thought for a moment. 'I had best go myself.'

'Take a few stout men with you,' I said. 'Who knows what is yet a-doing out there?' For the sound of shouting still carried in over the walls.

'I shall, never fear. Do you see to what beds there are in the men's wards, Dr Alvarez. I fear there are no other physicians here tonight.'

'I will so. Mistress Maynard will know which of the sisters are most skilled to help with the wounded. Goodwife Appledean, my senior midwife, is as competent with wounds as with the dangers of childbirth. Between us we will manage.'

As I herded the medical staff back into the hospital, I saw that Superintendent Ailmer was gathering up a party of strong men, workers from the printing and glassworks, two of the gardeners, and some of the servants. Between them they carried a number of stretchers for the wounded as they set off in a tight pack through the gate.

'Tell me what you want me to do.' It was Simon, appearing at my side out of the patchy darkness of the yard.

'You can come and help set up more trestle beds in the men's wards,' I said. 'In the hope that the Marshal will allow the injured to be brought in.'

He followed me willingly into the hospital building, looking about him with interest. It occurred to me then that this place, which was so familiar to me, was entirely unknown to him.

'Along here,' I said, 'on the right. The men's wards are on the ground floor.'

'Where are your wards?' he asked curiously.

'Upstairs. I pray the noise has not woken the babies and the children. I will send one of the nursing sisters to calm them, if need be.'

There were two men's wards, long narrow rooms adjoining each other, each lined with rows of beds along their sides, with a clear passages down the middle. Most of the time there was ample space between the beds, but when the number of patients demanded it, we could fit in extra beds, narrow cots supported on trestles which could be folded away and stored when not in use. Mistress Maynard had already set several of the servants to fetching these from the storeroom, and Simon joined them, while some of the sisters and I shifted the existing beds to make room.

By the time the extra beds were set up and provided with sheets and blankets, Superintendent Ailmer had returned, looking somewhat grim, although he had been in some measure successful, for he was followed by others carrying a number of men.

'The Marshal was willing for you to bring away the injured, then?' I said, as the casualties were eased on to beds.

'Those who were able to walk, he has rounded up with the rest,' he said. 'I was only able to bargain for those so seriously injured they could not walk.'

'Any dead?'

'Aye, I counted half a dozen, but it was getting dark. I cannot be sure. Once we have these bestowed, I will send the men back to fetch in all the dead they can find, to lay in the chapel until we may discover who they are, and their families. I think there may have been some of the Marshal's own men killed as well. We have two of his men amongst these injured, though not as severely as some of those he has hauled off to the prison.'

'We'd best keep them separate.' I frowned. Slightly injured men belonging to the Marshal might cause trouble amongst the other casualties.

'I will show you which they are.'

We began to walk down the length of the room together.

'Once we have separated them, I will start checking the worst injured.'

He nodded. 'I am grateful you thought to come in, Dr Alvarez. None of the other physicians have done so.'

'Perhaps they live further away. We saw the mob pass by our lodgings. My fellow lodger, Simon Hetherington, is here helping as well.'

Ailmer pointed out the two Marshalsea men to me and I told Goodwife Appledean, who was sorting patients and beds, to put them in a small separate room at the end of the corridor.

As I rolled up my sleeves to wash my hands and begin the work of checking the injuries, I said, suddenly remembering, 'But what of the fire the rioters started? Did you see what was afoot with that?'

'The Watch and a line of volunteers had started passing up buckets of water from the river. And they had pulled down the houses on either side to make a gap the fire cannot leap over. I think by the time I came away that they had it contained.'

'Hard on the poor people who lived in those houses,' I said. 'What had they done to those fellows, that they should lose everything?'

'What indeed?' he said.

It was a long night. Although more men would have been brought in injured if the Marshal had not dragged off to prison the less serious cases, yet the ones we did take in had major wounds. A few were unconscious from blows to the head, but most had suffered stab or slash wounds. The majority of these had been inflicted by swords, although there were dagger wounds as well. Two cases I could tell from the start were beyond hope. One of these had his belly ripped half open and the other had been stabbed through the ear into the brain. The latter died quickly, which was a blessing. The other lingered for several hours in terrible

78

agony. All I could do for him was to dose him with poppy syrup to try to ease the pain, but I doubt it did much good.

Simon went with the party to collect the dead, a grim task. In my work I had learned to detach my mind, at least in part, from the horrors amidst which I sometimes worked, but for Simon it was a new experience and I could read the strain of it on his face when he came into the ward sometime before dawn.

'Is that all of them?' I asked, straightening from stitching up a deep slash in a youth's forearm. I feared he would never have the full use of it again.

'Aye,' he said, rubbing his eyes with grubby hands.

'Do not do that,' I said crossly, for I was tired. 'You will infect your eyes. There is water over there where you may wash.'

He gave a shaky grin. 'Aye, doctor. At any rate, I have one piece of good news. As we brought in the last of the dead and laid them in the chapel, I noticed that one of our earlier corpses was moving. Two of the hospital servants are bringing him now. Have you a bed for him?'

'Over there, next the window. Now wash. I do not want you infecting my patients.'

The men came in with the living dead, but he seemed far gone, so that I feared he might be truly lost before the night was over. He had a deep gash in the side of his neck, where it met the shoulder blade, and he had lost a great deal of blood. It was a wonder he had not bled to death. I set to, doing what I could for him. One of the sisters was at my side at once with a bowl of the cleansing tincture we had been using to sponge away the blood, and I saw that it was the young girl Alice Meadows, from the children's ward.

'How are the children?' I asked as I worked.

'Some woke with the noise earlier,' she said, 'but they are all asleep now. Goodwife Watson said she would mind them on her own, so that I could lend a hand here.' She nodded toward the man I was tending, one of the older ones, certainly not an apprentice. 'Will he live?'

'Difficult to say. He has lost a lot of blood, and was left in the street as one of the dead, but we will do what we may. I must stitch this, and it will be awkward, lying deep in the angle there between neck and shoulder. And whenever he moves his head, it will pull at the stitches. However, it has to be done.'

'I think I prefer working with the children,' she said, setting aside the bowl and fetching me needle and thread. She gave a rueful smile.

'Aye.' I returned her smile. 'I think we all do. But even children may have injuries like this.'

'Not from swords, surely?'

'Not,' I agreed, 'usually from swords. But when a town is overrun by attacking soldiers, even the children are not spared.'

When I had finished the stitching, awkward as it was, I let Alice smear on the wound salve and showed her how to apply the dressing, with a pad over the injury, held in place by a bandage. Then between us we laid him back on his pillow. Throughout he had remained unconscious, and I was uncertain whether he would ever wake again.

'His face seems somehow familiar,' I said, more to myself than to Alice, 'but I do not know where I might have seen him.'

'I've heard that there are men here from all over London,' she whispered. 'It was properly organised, not just a sudden gathering of angry apprentices calling "Clubs!" Or that is what I've heard.'

'Aye,' I said. 'That was certainly how it seemed.'

I had left the two Marshal's men to be tended by the sisters, but I went now to see that all was well with them after casting an eye over the regular patients in the ward, who had suffered a bad night of it, with all the disturbance. They were not my patients, and their own physician would come in once it was day, so I merely saw to it that they were comfortable.

At the end of the corridor I found Simon and – somewhat to my surprise – the printer Job.

'Have you come to study for a physician, Job?' I asked. 'Or have you a fancy to one of the sisters?'

He gave me a grin. 'They'd more likely give me a box on the ears than a kiss, doctor. Nay, I came to aid Master Hetherington here with keeping an eye on them two.' He jerked his head toward the door of the small side room. 'One on 'em has already been about, wanting to make trouble with the lads you've got in the ward.'

'Best fetch the superintendent, then,' I said. 'He's likely in his office. I'd as soon have him with me before I go in.'

He ran off and I smiled weakly at Simon. 'Cowardly of me, I know, but I think they will recognise the superintendent's authority more readily than mine.'

'Aye, a wise decision. You are looking tired, Kit.'

'So are you. I did not mean you to spend the night here, carrying the wounded and moving corpses.'

'I was glad to help.' He gave me a curious look, almost . . . deferential. 'I suppose I have never truly understood your work. It takes courage as well as skill. I could not do it, I know that for sure.'

I felt absurdly pleased, but tried my best not to show it. 'I was bred up to it, at my father's knee. But it can be hard, especially when you feel almost overwhelmed, and tired. And when you fight to save a life, only to see it slip away through your fingers at the last. I suppose that is why I like working on the lying-in ward best. Bringing life into the world, instead of watching Death have his way.'

'But women die in childbirth, do they not?'

'Aye, but less often here, where they are properly cared for. I know that Mayor Whittington left many bequests to the benefit of London, but surely this has been the best, meaning a safe start in life for children who had little chance at all in the past.'

'It is for unmarried mothers, is it not?'

'Mostly, aye. But if we have room we take in any pauper women and see the babies safe into the world.'

Superintendent Ailmer came along the corridor, followed closely by Job.

'Trouble?' he said.

'Hoping to forestall it,' I answered. 'Job and Simon have had some difficulty restraining these two fellows from setting about the injured rioters. Before I examine their injuries, I would be glad if you warned them that you will not tolerate violence in St Thomas's.'

He nodded briskly. 'We will go in together.' He turned to Job. 'Fetch two of our strongest and largest amongst the servants. There's a big fellow works in the kitchen.'

'Bill Warner,' Job said. 'I know him. And mebbe Jos Tinker from the stable?'

'Aye. If Dr Alvarez thinks these two fellows are fit to be sent home, we'll have them escorted to the gate.'

Job went off on his errand and Superintendent Ailmer and I went together into the small side room, usually kept for more deserving patients and not these ruffians. He could assume a formidable air when he chose, and I saw at once that my instincts had been right. The two Marshal's men recognised authority when they saw it.

'Dr Alvarez will now examine your injuries,' Ailmer said, 'and if he thinks you fit to leave, you will leave. If not, you will remain here until you are fit. However, I will not have any brawling or other violence within the purlieus of this hospital. This is a place of healing, not harming. Is that understood?'

Sulky and unwilling to meet his gaze, they both muttered something.

'I do not believe I heard you aright,' Ailmer said. 'You!' He pointed to a swarthy, black bearded man. 'Is it understood? No violence.'

'Aye, maister,' he said grudgingly, 'no violence.'

'And you?' The other man a hulking ginger haired fellow with a squint.

'Understood,' he admitted.

'Right. Now I will stay here while the doctor examines you, and then we shall see.'

The bearded man had a broken bruise on his upper arm, where someone's club had caught him a mighty clout.

'This will be all the colours of the rainbow by tomorrow,' I said, feeling the flesh around the bruise and the solid bone beneath, 'but it will soon mend. Let me see your hand.'

I unwound the bandage one of the sister had fixed around the fingers of his right hand. They were reddened, grazed, and swollen.

'That came from hitting someone,' I said neutrally.

'Aye.' He grinned, showing broken teeth. 'His jaw came off worse, and he's in the Marshalsea now.'

I replaced the bandage. 'Keep it covered for the next few days. You can go.'

I turned to the other man, who seemed to be intact.

'And what ails you?'

'Punched in the stomach,' he whined. 'I was doubled up with the pain. The bastard!'

'Lie down on the bed and lift up your shirt.'

He did as he was told and I felt his stomach area carefully. Although he made a great show of moaning, there was nothing seriously wrong but a little bruising.

'You'll live,' I said coldly, pulling down his shirt. 'Nothing damaged inside.'

By now Job had returned with two large men who watched with interest from the door.

I nodded to Ailmer. 'They are both fit to go home,' I said.

'These men will show you the way.' He nodded to the hospital servants, who each took one of the Marshal's men by an elbow and steered him away down the corridor and out of sight as we watched from the doorway.

'I know it was the rioters who were in the wrong,' I said. 'So why is it that I feel more sympathy for them than for those fellows?'

83

Ailmer laughed. 'Bullies who enjoy their work. Besides, it was their lot who began all this. Now go home yourself, doctor, and do not come back until the afternoon. I am grateful for all you have done this night. And it's past dawn already.'

I nodded. As we came out through the open door I saw that Simon was sitting on the floor asleep. I poked him with my toe.

'Time we went home to our lodgings,' I said.

He stumbled to his feet, yawning. 'Aye.'

'Rikki will think he has been deserted,' I said. 'Goodnight, Superintendent.'

He laughed. 'Good morrow.'

Chapter Five

*B*ack at our lodgings, Simon flung himself down on to his straw palliasse on the floor, barely stopping to remove his shoes, and fell asleep at once. I could not neglect Rikki, however, so I managed to stagger back down the stairs and sat on the front doorstep while he ran about and busied himself watering his favourite trees. A whole church choir of birds was singing joyfully as the first golden band of light streaked across the sky downriver. Greenwich lay that way. Would the rioters have gone that far? Attacked a royal palace? I shivered. I had nothing but loathing for the Knight Marshal and the men he commanded, but without their intervention, how far might the destruction of Southwark have gone?

As Tom was opening the gate for us to leave St Thomas's, he had told us the further news he had heard.

'Seems the Lord Mayor himself rode over to Southwark from the City,' he said. 'Mayor William Webbe. Him and one of the sheriffs. They brought the men with them that you saw along with the Marshal's men. Dunno if the Marshal could have held out against the rioters without them. It was a close run thing, it seems.'

By then the fires appeared to be mostly out, though the smell of burning hung in the air, and the acrid scent stung in the back of one's throat. I caught a whiff of it still, though it did not seem to trouble the plump male blackbird who was singing joyfully in the hazel nut tree directly opposite the Atkins' front door.

'Come, Rikki.' I gave a soft whistle, not to disturb the house behind me. He was making short darts along the road, a pointed hint that he expected a better walk than this, but after a night with the injured I wanted nothing but my bed. Reluctantly he followed me back upstairs.

Like Simon I removed my shoes, but then also my doublet, and fell into bed. Certain matters were awkward since he had started to share my lodgings in order to save money against his debt. Mostly I washed and changed when he was away at the playhouse, but I could no longer slip into the comfort of a night shift to sleep. Now that the debt was paid, I hoped that he might remove to a room of his own. Christopher had found our lodgings not quite fine enough for his taste and talked of moving out of Simon's old room, so I hoped that might serve to give him a push. I did not like to suggest it myself, for fear Simon might think me unfriendly. These thoughts wandered through my brain, accompanied by a swelling chorus of birdsong outside the window, as I fell asleep.

That afternoon I returned to the hospital at the same time as Simon set off for the Rose.

'*Harry Six* again today,' he said.

'You played that last week.'

'Aye, and the week before. London never tires of it. Master Burbage and Master Henslowe have decided we will play it every week until the takings fall away, which there's no sign of yet. Suits us fine. We could play it in our sleep. Will has written a gem. It will be good to see the other two parts when he has finished them.'

'And tomorrow?'

'*Muly Molocco.*'

'I don't know that one.'

'Barbary. Curved scimitars. Turbans. Lots of fighting. Usually does quite well, but not as well as *Harry Six*. No great English hero in it, of course, like Lord Talbot.'

'Oh, that one. Barbary and fighting. I've heard you speak of it, but I haven't seen it.'

When we reached the street, we parted company, Rikki following me happily this time, to stay as usual with Tom. The nearer I came to the hospital, the more noticeable was the smell of burning.

Before going up to my own wards, I looked in on the men, where Dr Edwards was back in charge.

'I thank you for your assistance last night, Dr Alvarez,' he said, a certain stiffness in his tone.

Assistance? I thought. Who was I assisting? However, I knew better than to point out that I was the only physician present. I simply smiled.

'Fortunately I live nearby,' I said, 'so I realised what was afoot and was able to come in quickly. Tell me, the man who was at first thought dead – how does he fare?'

He looked at me blankly and I realised he had not been told about the rescued corpse.

'Deep sword wound to the neck,' I said, 'grazing the left clavicle.'

'Oh, that one. Still unconscious, but holding on to life.'

'Good.' I gave him a slight bow – he did not merit a deep one – and withdrew.

At the foot of the stairs I encountered Mistress Maynard.

'Superintendent Ailmer would like to see you for a moment, Dr Alvarez,' she said, 'before you go to your wards.'

I tapped on the superintendent's door and was called in. He gestured me to a seat.

'That was good work you did last night, doctor,' he said. 'So far we have not lost any more.'

I thought he looked tired, as though he had not managed even my few hours of rest.

'Let us pray that augurs well for their recovery,' I said, 'though I fear it is chancy for the one we first thought dead.'

'Aye, well, he's with us still.'

He picked up a scrap of paper from his desk.

'I have received this from the Marshalsea – a request for medical help. It seems some of the prisoners taken in last night are more seriously wounded than first thought.'

'The Marshal has asked for help?' I did not try to keep the astonishment out of my voice.

'Nay, not the Marshal. One of the gaolers. It seems he knows you. Asks for you by name.'

'Oh,' I said. 'A man called Arthur. That was a long time ago. I treated a prisoner there when my father was absent. Do you want me to go?'

'I cannot compel you. The decision must be yours.'

'They should have been brought here.'

'Aye, they should.'

'In all Christian kindness,' I said, 'I must go. Does he say anything of the nature of the injuries/'

He shook his head. 'The man is barely literate. It is simply a brief, rough written request for help.'

'If the injuries are severe, it will not be easy to treat them. Not in the Marshalsea. When I was there a long while ago it was to one of the wealthy prisoners in a private room, and nothing worse than food poisoning. These will be sword slashes and the like. Difficult to treat in the dirty conditions in which these men are surely held.'

He tapped his teeth with his finger nail. 'You have the right of it. We need a strategy. I think I should come with you, and some of our stronger servants, in case those who could walk last night can no longer do so. We must insist that the worst injured should be brought in here. The less severe you can treat there, can you not?'

I nodded. 'Of course. But do you think the Marshal will allow any of them to be moved, even if they are badly injured?'

'He has had a number of unnecessary deaths amongst his prisoners of late. More than the usual. He might need reminding of that. There comes a point when even the governors of a prison cannot ignore too many deaths.'

'I heard that Mayor Webbe was here last night,' I said. 'He is known for a humane man.'

'Aye, he was. That's well thought on. I will send a runner with a message for the Mayor. Do you tend to your own wards now, and I will give you word when I hear his reply. Some might dispute his right to jurisdiction in Southwark, but by intervening last night he has already involved himself in this affair.'

I did as I was bid, finding all quiet in both the lying-in and children's wards. The waif Robert was up and about now, though still frail. We were keeping him until he gained some strength.

'You look tired,' I said to Alice Meadows, who was giving a drink of swish water to a small girl with a summer cough.

She smiled. 'I slept a little. I do well enough.'

It was nearly two hours by the bells from St Olave's before I received word from Superintendent Ailmer that we had authorisation from the Mayor to remove any seriously wounded from the prison. I was to join him, and we would go together to the prison. I had already packed extra supplies of the necessary medicines into my satchel and followed the messenger down the stairs. It was Eddi, one of the senior lads who ran errands about the hospital, who had come with the message.

'How does Matthew in his post here?' I asked him.

'Well,' he said. 'He works hard. But he does not join with the rest of us at sport or the ale house. Is he a Puritan of sorts?'

I hid my smile. The idea of the former beggar lad as a Puritan was a surprise to me.

'Nay,' I said. 'He feels responsible for the other children and saves his pennies. I am sure he has no wish to be unfriendly.'

Superintendent Ailmer was waiting for me outside his door, accompanied by four hearty servants carrying stretchers. He looked grim.

'We have the Mayor's authorisation,' he said, as we headed for the gate, 'but I fear the Marshal may not like it.'

89

It is but a short walk from St Thomas's to the Marshalsea, and when we arrived, the warder Arthur told one of the turnkeys to show me to the prisoners from the riot, while he took Ailmer to the Marshal.

Six years and more had passed since I had last crossed the threshold of the Marshalsea prison, yet the sound of it was unchanged, an inhuman cacophony of despair, which echoed from the walls of stone and tore at one's heart. I felt that same spasm of fear which besets me whenever I am near a prison, and yet I found I was not quite so afraid as once I had been.

I put out a hand to stay the warder Arthur. 'I shall need light to work by, and these men come with me.' I nodded toward the hospital servants. 'Also, I want a bucket of boiled water.'

He nodded. His manner was markedly more courteous than it had been all those years ago when I had been summoned to the bedside of Robert Poley, who believed himself poisoned. Now that I knew Poley, I thought that he had had good reason to fear poison.

Once within the building itself, the stench of the place made me gag, and I raised a hand involuntarily to cover my nose and mouth. Urine and faeces and filth and mould and damp stone and sweat. And, above all, the very stink of fear itself. I gritted my teeth, lowered my hand, and followed the turnkey.

As I had suspected, the man led us down a flight of greasy steps into an underground passage. The rioters were held in the worst part of the Marshalsea, known as the Pit, a deep cellar, windowless, dripping with damp. There was a narrow grille in the heavy oak door, which allowed the only light into the place, showing through from the wall sconce in the passage outside. At the turnkey's bidding, two of the prison servants carried in lamps, which they hung from hooks in the low ceiling, their light revealing a thin covering of stinking and rotted straw on the floor, amongst which a great crowd of men crouched, there being nowhere else to sit. Another servant arrived with a bucket of water. I hoped it was boiled. It was certainly hot.

By contrast, even in June this place was cold. The men were dirty and bruised, shivering and eying us with a mixture of emotions – fear, defiance, and here and there a faint hope.

'I am Dr Alvarez from St Thomas's,' I said. 'We treated a number of your companions last night. One of the wardens here has sent to us for help today, for the treatment of your injuries. If any are severely injured, we have the authority of Mayor Webbe to move them to the hospital. Other injuries I will treat here.'

That provoked a clamour of voices, but the turnkey raised his short club.

'Silence!'

They subsided into muttering. Already I could see three men stretched out very still on the ground, and these I turned to first. Two had head injuries, one had a deep slash to his thigh which had bled profusely, from the sticky blood-soaked straw amongst which he lay.

'These three to the hospital at once,' I said. Realising that the four servants we had brought were not enough to carry them, I said to the turnkey, 'We will need the help of some of your men.'

He agreed reluctantly, and I saw to the removal of the first three badly injured men. Shortly after they were taken away, Superintendent Ailmer appeared, looking about him with disgust.

'I know they have committed crimes, but this is no place to keep even criminals. Pigs live better.'

I nodded, but did not say that I had once spent weeks in just such a place as this. And I thought it unlikely these men would be subjected to torture, as my parents had been.

'The Marshal agreed, then?'

'Reluctantly. However, I think he does not wish to fall out with the Mayor and Common Council, who came to his aid last night. It seems the Mayor is writing to Lord Burghley for guidance on what is to be done with these men.' He looked about at the prisoners. 'Some of them are no more than boys.'

'And some are surely not apprentices.'

The struggle against the Marshal's men had left many with torn shirts and doublets, or in the case of the apprentices, torn tunics – which would earn them punishments from their masters – but at the same time it was clear that many of the men had been ill clad to begin with, some barely covered by their rags, and barefoot. These were the paupers and masterless men who had joined the riot not as a protest against the wrongful imprisonment of the feltmaker's apprentice, but in desperation at their destitute and starving state.

'There are at least four more here,' I said, 'who must be moved to the hospital. A few more who would be the better for it. And some who would benefit from hospital food and a suit of clothes, though I am not sure I can make a case for moving them.'

We were both speaking quietly, not wanting the turnkey to carry tales to the Marshal.

'Point out to me the ones who must and should be moved,' Superintendent Ailmer said. 'And I will see to it, while you set about dealing with the minor injuries. You may say to the weak and ill clad that once they are released they should come to us and we will do what we can for them.'

I set to work, cleaning and salving the lesser broken wounds, of which there were a great many. Scarcely a man there was unmarked, some muttering that their injuries had come not in the fight, but afterwards, from the rough treatment of the Marshal's men. There was also a great deal of bruising from fists and clubs, which I treated with tincture of arnica, though in truth it was too late. It should have been applied straight away. The bruises were already settled with the gathering of the blood beneath the skin, whereas an early application of the arnica would have dispersed them and speeded the healing. Any slash deep enough to need stitching I told Ailmer to take away, fearing the damage that would come if the filth of the Pit entered the wounds.

All in all, I suppose we managed to remove fewer than a quarter of the men, and I felt guilty as the rest, crowded together in the dirty straw, were shut once more into darkness and fear.

When I made mention of this to Superintendent Ailmer as we followed the last stretcher back to St Thomas's, he shrugged.

'We have done what we could.'

The injured men were transferred to the men's wards and would be no more a concern of mine, though I did ask after the man who had been taken for dead, and was told that he had woken and was no worse. It seemed that the terror engendered by the Southwark riot was over, save for the people who had lost their homes in the fire, and the men injured or lingering in the Marshalsea.

Simon was fully recovered from the wound inflicted by Frizer's men – or so we believed them to have been, though it could never be proved – and he returned to the busy times at the Rose, where a play was put on every day but Sundays, not just *Harry Six* and *A Knack* and the Barbary play, but *Hieronomo*, and something about Sir John Mandeville, and (to my regret) Marlowe's *Jew*. The more often Marlowe's play was staged, the more hatred against Jews and foreigners was engendered. I could believe that it had contributed to the causes of the riot, this antipathy to foreigners, suspected of stealing English jobs.

Simon came in laughing one evening after a performance of *A Knack to Know a Knave*.

'An excellent audience again! I do not think we have ever had a better season!'

He flung himself down on one of my chairs and kicked off his shoes.

'I shall soon be able to pay back Sara Lopez, and then you, Kit, but in the meantime I have it in mind to reclaim my old room.' He pointed down at the floor.

'Are you sure you have the coin?' I tried not to sound pleased.

'Christopher has found new lodgings and I have crowded you here for too long.'

He looked about my small room, and it was true. Even with his bedding rolled up during the day, there was scare a square foot of empty floor space, especially since Simon is not the tidiest of mortals. His clothes, costumes, and the sheets of paper containing his lines were scattered everywhere. I hope I am not too particular, but I like to keep my possessions, few as they are, in their rightful places. At the moment the row of medical books bequeathed to me by Dr Nuñez was buried under his Saracen costume and two spare (and somewhat grubby) shirts.

'Tomorrow I shall speak to Goodwife Atkins about it,' he said. 'Christopher moves out at the beginning of next week and I do not want her letting my room to someone else.'

'Which play is it tomorrow?' I asked.

'*Muly Molocco* again.' He grinned. 'Now that we have a regular cycle of plays that we know well, life has become a little easier. No new lines to learn! At least until Will finishes the two new plays of Harry Six. He is taking longer than usual about it.'

'Well, I expect you can play *Muly* with your eyes shut,' I said.

He nodded. But that performance of *Muly Molocco* was destined never to take place.

The following afternoon, when I returned early after a quiet day at the hospital, I was surprised to find Simon sitting on the front steps, his shoulders hunched and his chin in his hands. When I returned as early as this, it was generally another two hours at least before he was back from the playhouse. Longer if the players went off for a drink or a meal at the Lion. Rikki ran forward to Simon who lifted his head and gave me an odd look.

'What has happened?' I said. 'Not rioters at the playhouse again?'

He shook his head, standing up slowly. 'Worse.'

'Worse? What do you mean? Has someone damaged the playhouse? Is someone hurt?'

He gave me a bitter smile. 'Of course this fair season was too good to last. Fortune has truly spun her wheel now.'

'Stop talking in riddles!' I was beginning to get angry now, instead of alarmed. 'What has happened?'

'You will recall that the rioters the Sunday before last gathered at the Rose.'

'Of course I remember,' I said impatiently.

'They tried to claim that they came there to see a play. That was why they had gathered.'

'Pure folly. It was a Sunday. There was no play. Everyone knows that.'

'Aye, but the authorities have chosen to believe what suits them. They have decided that if the rioters gathered for a play, then the playhouses are to blame for the trouble. They have closed the playhouses.'

This was bad news indeed. To close the playhouses during a successful summer meant no income for the players. They had a hard enough time in the winter, when the cold weather put a stop to performances which were half in the open air, the playhouses being built on the same principle as a bear baiting, the whole centre being open to the sky.

'Which authorities?' I asked. 'The Common Council of London?'

'Worse. The Privy Council itself. They claim they have had word that more disturbances are planned and have ordered the Mayor to set a "strong and substantial watch" all about the city.'

'How do you know this?'

'Notice was sent to Master Henslowe in writing, just before we were to begin this afternoon's performance. He read it out to us, and I have it by heart.'

This came as no surprise to me. Simon was a quick study. He shut his eyes and began to recite the order in pompous tones. Even at a moment of such serious news, he could not forebear to act the part.

'The Mayor and Common Council are instructed they should order "that there be no plays used in any place near thereabouts as the Theatre, Curtain or other usual place where the same are commonly used, nor no other sort of unlawful or forbidden pastimes that draw together the baser sort of people." The Rose was not mentioned by name, but since a copy of the order was sent to Master Henslowe, the Rose is also meant.'

'You said "other pastimes" as well. I suppose that means bull and bear baiting, and cock fighting.'

'I suppose,.' He shrugged. 'I do not much care about them.'

'They may think an order to stop all entertainments will prevent further gatherings like the riot, but by depriving the people of the little they have apart from a life of drudgery, they may be provoking a worse uprising,' I said.

I saw that Simon was too engrossed by his own worries to care much about the common folk of London. It seemed that innocent players and commoners alike were being punished for the actions of one group of unruly men. As far as I knew, the prisoners were still held in the Marshalsea, apart from the most gravely injured, who remained in St Thomas's. Now it was others who would suffer.

'How long are the playhouses to remain closed?' I asked.

Simon groaned. 'Until the Feast of St Michael.'

'What! That is more than three months!' For the Feast of St Michael falls on the nine and twentieth day of September.

'Aye, more than three months. That is the end of our profitable summer season. If winter comes as early this year as last, we shall have scarce two months from the time

96

we are permitted to open before we close again for the winter.'

'And what do Master Henslowe and Master Burbage say to this? Odd, isn't it, that the Privy Council should close the Theatre, when it is already closed for the building repairs?'

'Lawyers talk, I expect,' he said bitterly. 'To cover every possibility, lest we sneak off and stage our plays to the sound of hammering on the roof beams, or with the rain coming in on the most expensive seats.'

He came down the rest of the steps to the street.

'Master Burbage came over the Bridge straightaway when he heard the news, and the two of them have their heads together now. But what can they do against the Privy Council? 'Tis done in pure spite. They are forever trying to destroy us, though they know very well we had naught to do with the riot.'

At that moment we both caught sight of Christopher coming toward us along Bankside, almost at a trot, if his dignity allowed such a thing.

'News!' he said, when he was barely near enough to make himself heard.

Simon looked suddenly hopeful. 'The ban has been withdrawn?'

'Don't be a fool! Would the Privy Council miss such a chance to shut us down? Or make a mockery of themselves by a public climb-down? Nay, it is quite other. We are to go on tour!'

'On tour?' A whole series of emotions chased each other across Simon's face – cautious relief, wariness, a touch of excitement. 'Who goes?'

'Nothing is decided yet, but Cuthbert has said he is willing to take on the management of it. Masters Henslowe and Burbage both say they are too old.'

'And so they are. Besides, they both have other business interests in London. But which of the players?'

'Ned Alleyn has volunteered, so if our chief tragedian is to go, it will be a fine company. I think I will say aye, though it may be something of a rough life.'

I grinned. 'Dirty inns, Christopher, with fleas in the beds, and maybe sleeping in fields from time to time.'

He looked uncertain at that, then laughed. 'You are just trying to scare me, Kit. With Cuthbert in charge, I am sure we will be well lodged.' He gave Simon an appraising look. 'What do you say, Simon? Are you for going?'

Simon hesitated only a moment.

'Aye,' he said, suddenly smiling with relief. 'I'm for going. Better than kicking our heels in London all summer, with no work and no pay. Who else has spoken?'

'Guy is debating. You know what he is, a Londoner through and through, but he did go to Wardhouse on that Muscovy voyage. I think he will come. All the young boys are wild to go, if their mothers will let them. We needs must have some of them for the women's parts, though we could always use you again.'

Simon swung a mock punch at him. 'You would be better to play the women, with your pretty face and pretty ways.'

I was beginning to feel very left out of the conversation.

'Where will you go?' I asked.

'Surrey, Kent, and Sussex are spoken of first,' Christopher said. 'After that, I do not know, but in three months we could travel a good way, visit a deal of towns.'

It was beginning to sound like a fine way to spend the summer, if this good weather held, wandering through the English countryside, visiting towns and the larger villages. Apart from a few journeys into England which I had made on the instructions of Sir Francis Walsingham, to Staffordshire and Sussex, I knew hardly anything of England outside London. That and my journey back from Plymouth after the Portuguese expedition, when I was too exhausted to take much note of my surroundings.

'Perhaps the closing of the playhouses will not be so bad for you after all,' I said encouragingly, 'if you can tour the countryside with your plays.'

'No playhouses outside London, of course,' Simon said thoughtfully, trying to conceal a growing sense of excitement I could read in his eyes. 'It will mean the yards of inns or – if we are lucky – some indoor place like a town hall or guildhall. A lot of contriving with our properties and acting space.'

'That does not matter,' Christopher said, 'it is our words and our playing that matter.'

'What of Will's new plays? Does he intend to send them on to us?'

'Will thinks he will come too.'

'Not Marlowe?'

'Nay, no one know where Marlowe is, unless he is down in Kent at Thomas Walsingham's place. Walsingham's pet household poet.' Christopher's tone was scornful. Such an idle life was clearly despised by the hard working players.

Poor Thomas Walsingham, I thought.

'Aye, Kit Marlowe would not be one to rough it,' Simon admitted. 'He is too fond of a comfortable life.'

He turned to me. 'I think I should go back to the Rose, to see for myself what's ado.'

'Aye, you'd best do so,' I said cheerfully. 'After all, if Cuthbert decides to limit the number he will take with him, you do not want to miss you chance.'

'Aye, I do not.'

The two of them turned away and began walking rapidly back along the river toward the Rose, talking eagerly. Followed by Rikki, I climbed the stairs to my room.

As usual, it was strewn about with Simon's possessions. He had not even stopped to fold away his bedding before leaving for the playhouse earlier that day, although he had taken his Saracen costume to wear in *Muly Molocco*. I could see my Arabic medical texts for the first time in days. I sat down on the end of my bed, and Rikki jumped up beside me. I put my arm around him and buried my face in his fur.

'Well, lad,' I said, my voice somewhat muffled. 'It seems we are to be left quite alone after all.'

Of course, they did not leave at once. It is no simple matter to organise a tour of a company of players to be absent from London and travelling for miles over the English countryside for two months or more. First, they must gain permission from their patron, Lord Strange, to leave London, which was arranged by Master Burbage when he was able to see His Lordship. Then horse-drawn carts must be hired, for the company only possessed hand carts, which they used for moving properties when they gave a performance at Court or at some lord's house. They must sort out just which properties and costumes would be needed, after they had conferred – and argued hotly – over which plays they would be performing. Any player who had a good part in one of the plays would be arguing that it must be included.

Apart from all these preparations, each player needed to make arrangements for his own lodgings in London and his belongings. Some were committed to longer leases than a mere weekly rent and had to negotiate with their landlords. Others needed to find storage for such possessions as they would not be taking with them. Simon was relieved that he had not agreed the lease of his old room with Goodwife Atkins after all, but that left the problem of his winter clothes and the other things he would not be taking with him. I agree to store them in my coffer, though it left little room for me.

Master Burbage had sent out touring groups before, but generally for a shorter time, and as a mere addition to the main work of the players in London. This tour was a much larger and more complex matter, effectively taking the Rose playhouse on the road, in everything but the physical building itself.

As well as all this activity in London, arrangements needed to be made for the first few weeks, so that the company would not be wandering at chance, like some of the rag-tag groups of lesser players who usually roamed the country. This was the greatest players' company in England, and it behoved them to maintain their dignity and reputation even on tour. Consequently, while the rest of the company was making final preparations at the Rose, Cuthbert Burbage rode off into Kent, to book appearances at some of the major towns, at each of which Lord Strange's Men would perform several plays.

When he returned a few days later, he had confirmed visits to Rye, Canterbury, Tenterden, Faversham, Folkestone and Maidstone.

'These are all places with somewhere suitable to perform,' Simon said, as he packed the clothes he was taking into a knapsack. His personal costumes had gone with all the others in the company's wicker hampers. 'There will be a guildhall or a courthouse. Somewhere. But the playing spaces will be different everywhere, and some of them really too small, but I daresay we shall contrive our best.'

There was a gleam in his eye as he spoke.

'You are looking forward to it,' I said, and tried not to sound accusing.

'Aye. I am. When I first heard that the playhouses were to be closed, I was near despair. To be thrown into months without work, just when I thought I was at last beginning to prosper a little, and would be able to repay you and Sara Lopez – it was enough to make any man despair. But now we will be working and earning. Not as much as in London, but something. And it will be good to see all these new places. Christopher spoke of Guy having only rarely ventured outside London, but nor have I. There was that tour we did in the Low Countries and the voyage to Wardhouse. That was an adventure, away in the far north of Norway! But I have seen little of my own country.'

He grinned. 'Aye, it will be exciting, despite the trials of travelling.'

'I could almost wish I were coming with you.'

'Aye, that would be good. You could come as physician to the company. We are bound to suffer some scrapes and bruises.'

I laughed. We both knew it was impossible, mere fantasy.

'Ah well, perhaps I will ride out and visit you, one of these days when you are performing not too far away. Hector could do with the exercise. He is spending too long shut up in the stable at Seething Lane.'

It was an idle suggestion, idly made, but it might be possible.

The day came for the company to leave.

'We shall not skulk out of London like beaten curs,' Simon told me defiantly as he rose at dawn, ready to go off to join the others at the Rose. 'We shall make a show of it.'

He handed me a purse, which clinked with coin.

'With our first prosperous weeks this summer I managed to save enough to repay Sara,' he said, 'if you would give it to her. And there is two pounds of the money I owe you. I hope I may earn enough on this tour to pay you the rest when we return. At least I shall not have to pay rent for my room here.'

'But will you not need this money while you are on tour? For lodgings?'

He shook his head. 'It is arranged that Master Burbage and Master Henslowe will pay for lodgings for the company. So we are spared that expense.'

He gave me a quick hug, patted Rikki, and walked jauntily away along Bankside, whistling.

'Well, here we are, left alone,' I said to Rikki, 'but we shall see them on their way.'

I fastened on his lead, in case he should take it into his head to follow the players, and we walked down to the south end of the Bridge to await them, joining the crowd which had already gathered there, having heard there would be something worth seeing. The players were to perform first at Rye, so would head directly south, along Southwalk Street, before taking an eastward road toward Kent. I remembered my own visit to Rye with Thomas Phelippes and Andrew Joplyn, six years ago now. It was a pretty place, but quietly sinking into decay, like a beautiful woman declining into old age, as the harbour began to silt up and the greater ships built nowadays passed it by. Still, I was sure that there were rich merchants and citizens even now who would welcome the entertainment of a famous company of London players come to their town.

Lord Strange's Men made quite a procession of it. Even the carts had been decorated with ribbons, and more ribbons fluttered from their horses' harness. Some even had bells attached, which caused them to shake their heads from time to time in irritation. Ordinary cart horses, they were unaccustomed to such frivolity.

At the head of the procession was Cuthbert, riding his own grey gelding, and just behind him two of the players blowing fanfares on trumpets, with another beating a marching rhythm on a drum. They were followed by the rest of the players, all but the boys, and all mounted.

'Cuthbert has hired horses for us until we reach Rye,' Simon had told me. 'After that, it will depend on how well we do. If the takings are good, we will hire horses from town to town. If not, we walk.'

'I hope your shoes will stand up to it.' New shoes had not been his greatest concern while he was paying off his debt.

I was glad to see them riding now, and very fine they looked, most of them sporting bright cloaks or feathered hats from the costume baskets. Examined closely, both cloaks and hats would show wear, but from a distance they were splendid. Simon wore a cloak of scarlet velvet, flung back carelessly over his shoulders to show a lining which almost looked like gold silk, and a black felt hat with a pointed brim, adorned with a sweeping peacock's feather which must have been two feet long. Catching sight of me, he swept it off in a magnificent bow, such as would have done credit to any courtier addressing the Queen herself. Somewhat embarrassed, but unable to keep myself from smiling, I returned it more circumspectly.

Cuthbert was tossing small coins with great swooping gestures right and left into the crowd of Southwark children, who were running alongside the procession, cheering and scrabbling for the pennies, ha'pennies, and farthings. I even saw one or two of their elders pick up a coin. I had never known anyone but a nobleman or a rich merchant toss coins into the crowd before, but I realised why Cuthbert had chosen to do so, and why all the players were making such a grand show. They were determined to ensure that the citizens of London did not believe they were being sent away like criminals punished with exile, but went forth instead of their own will, as ambassadors to bring the refinement and culture of London to country-bound townsmen, to their great wonder and enlightenment. There was no cloth of gold here, no nobleman's liveried servants, but the departure of the players was as fine a sight as if they were the household of some great royal duke.

After the riders came the carts, beribboned and jingling with bells, loaded with the company's scenery and hampers. Four of the boy players perched two and two on the leading carts, bearing the gold painted staffs of office used by royal officers when a play called for a scene in a king's court, staffs which I knew had been repainted just two days before, having become somewhat shabby. These were the lucky boys, those who had been permitted by indulgent mothers to join the tour, all of them so fizzing with excitement I thought they would explode, like the fireworks used in the devil scenes of a morality play.

At the very end of the procession I saw that not all the players had ridden at the front. Guy was mounted back to front on a raw boned horse and was followed by his apprentice Davy atop a small pony. Guy was playing the fool, while also juggling with balls, batons, and knives in a fashion that looked clumsy, but in fact required great skill.

Davy, wearing a doublet three sizes too large for him, and a hat pulled down almost to his ears, pretended to remonstrate with him, himself juggling in most solemn and serious a manner. Their antics raised cheers and laughter from the crowd.

Someone called out, 'Good fortune to you!'

'Aye,' another shouted, 'Don't let they mud-hoppers in Kent cheat you.'

A woman tossed a spice cake to Davy, who caught it and worked it into his juggling without losing his rhythm. Guy, it seemed, had taught him well.

As the last of the procession turned into Southwalk and headed south, several voices called, 'Come back soon!'

'Aye, I murmured to Rikki, 'but they cannot before the Feast of St Michael.'

The crowd dispersed, men and women and apprentices to their work, schoolboys to their lessons, girls to their mothers' kitchens, and the unregenerate mudlarks to their usual mischief.

Rikki and I turned away and headed toward the hospital. Here, in one of the most crowded cities in the world, it suddenly felt very lonely.

Chapter Six

*F*or months now my life had kept me almost exclusively south of the river. My principal work, of course, was at St Thomas's, and as for my friendship with the players, because they had been appearing at the Rose since the beginning of the year, I no longer crossed the Bridge and walked out through Bishopsgate to Shoreditch and the Theatre. My only occasions for visiting the City occurred when one of the private patients in Cheapside, transferred to me by Dr Nuñez, required my services. After his death the previous autumn a few more of his former patients had taken me on, including two of the benchers at Grey's Inn, and one at Lincoln's Inn, together with their families.

After Lord Strange's Men had left on tour, with the sudden resultant emptiness of my life, I realised with a pang of guilt that for too long I had been neglecting Sara Lopez, to whom I owed a considerable obligation in return for her great kindness to me ever since childhood. I had hardly seen her since we had borrowed the money to help with the debt Simon owed to Ingram Frizer. Now I had Simon's money to repay her. Therefore, a few days following the departure of the players, after I had been visiting the wife of one of the Grey's Inn lawyers, I decided on the spur of the moment to call upon Sara.

Ruy Lopez, who must somehow have repaired his fortunes, though I do not know how, had decided to move his family from Wood Street to an area further from that part of London which was often the centre of the plague. He had taken a house in countrified Holborn, called Mountjoy's Inn, in the district where the Inns of Court stand amongst their gardens. Mountjoy's Inn was more mansion than house, constructed around a courtyard like one of those same Inns of Court, a vast place built by the father-in-law of the present owner. Behind it was a large garden whose far wall was the boundary of the garden of Gray's Inn, so that, looking from the upstairs windows of the house, one could see the students and members of the Inn strolling in their garden. When the lawyers' dinners became too rowdy, they could even be heard in the house.

The man who had built Mountjoy's Inn was called Allington, a member of Gray's Inn, and his son had inherited it a few years ago, but had died soon afterwards, leaving it to his young widow, Mary Allington. She, finding the place too large for her own needs, decided to live in one small wing and rent out the rest of the mansion to a family. Ruy secured the lease and moved his family in, soon after a minor outbreak of the plague earlier in the summer of that year.

Sara greeted me happily, kissing me on both cheeks as soon as we were alone, and I apologised for neglecting her.

'Nay, there is no need. I know that you are kept very busy. Were you troubled at all by the recent riot, over there in Southwark?'

First, I gave her Simon's money, then I told her all that had happened, and about the departure of Lord Strange's Men after the closure of the playhouses. She knew, of course, about the ruling of the Privy Council, and agreed that the players were wise to take themselves off on tour.

'And since it looks as though this hot weather is nourishing the plague once more, they are well out of it,' she said.

'The Bills of Mortality are still quite small,' I said. 'I hope we may be spared anything worse this year.' In my heart I did not believe it. These were ideal conditions for the plague to work its insidious way in amongst us.

'Have you been visiting a patient here in Holborn?' she asked.

'Aye, but nothing serious,' I said. 'The wife of one of the benchers was suffering after having a bad tooth drawn. It was a little infected, so I have cleansed the hole and given her a paste containing ground cloves to rub in against the pain. She will do well enough. Now, are you going to show me this fine new home of yours? From the outside it is mighty impressive.'

We set off on our tour of Mountjoy's Inn, upstairs and down.

'The house is bigger than we need,' Sara said after she had led me through room after large and well proportioned room, 'but I am glad of the clean air here in the country, by the Inns of Court.'

'Yes,' I said, 'you are well away from the worst of the plague here, if it takes hold. And you have this large garden for the children.' I had also made note of the lavish furnishings Ruy had installed: furniture in rich foreign woods, a multitude of lamp stands furnished with best beeswax candles, imported Flemish tapestries on the walls, and court cupboards with open shelves displaying an array of silver dishes.

We had taken a tour around a well-designed garden with an orchard and walled vegetable plot, as well as clipped topiary and gravelled paths, and were now sitting at the centre of a knot garden beside an armillary sphere mounted on a stone pillar.

'Ruy has grandiose plans to turn the walled garden into a physic garden such as will be unsurpassed in England.' Sara laughed indulgently. 'Perhaps, someday, he will find time from all his other projects to plant it. It is time he retired. He is of an age to do so.'

I nodded. Ruy was twenty years older than Sara, his beard turning white, but I could not imagine him giving up his busy weaving of schemes for political advancement and financial enrichment. Sara, I well knew, would have preferred a quieter – and safer – life.

She gestured across the wide garden towards the house.

'You see how much room we have, Kit. Will you not come and live with us again?'

Great as the pleasure I took in Sara's company, I enjoyed the freedom of my small room in Southwark too much to yield to the temptation of all this luxury.

'Thank you for the offer,' I said, smiling and patting her arm, 'but Mountjoy's Inn is a long walk from St Thomas's,' I said. 'Even further than Wood Street. I should spend half my day walking to and fro.'

'But it is nearer to your private patients here in the City and Westminster,' she said persuasively. 'And these new patients you now have at the Inns of Court.'

I smiled and thanked her again, but would not be persuaded.

'They do not often call for my services,' I said in excuse. 'Most of my work by far is with the poor folk of Southwark.'

One of her maids brought us chilled golden wine and a plate of sweetmeats, then a concoction of half frozen fruit juice, which Sara, laughing at herself, called a *sherbet*.

'One of my cousins visiting from Constantinople showed my cook how to make it,' she explained. 'He says 'tis very popular amongst the Arabs. And there is an underground ice house here, so our cook is able to make it. He enjoys the challenge in a hot London summer.'

'Very pleasant in this trying weather,' I said. 'But – an ice house! I thought none but kings and emperors had such things.'

She laughed again, somewhat embarrassed, I thought.

'It was one of the things that persuaded Ruy to take the house. That, and the position in Holborn, and the possibility of making a physic garden.'

And – I thought, but did not say – the grandeur of a house which accorded with his own view of himself as one of the great men of the nation.

Afterwards, as I walked back the long hot road to Southwark, I thought how much I had enjoyed my time with Sara. Above all, it was the opportunity to relax, an opportunity all too rare, for with her I need have no fear of revealing myself for what I really was, since she had known me to be a girl ever since I had arrived in London as a motherless refugee child of twelve. Only when I let down my guard with her did I fully realise how much, for the rest of the time, I was as tight drawn with nerves as the cloth strung on the tenters' frames in Moor Fields, or an archer's bow string before he loosed his arrow.

For the moment, matters were quiet at St Thomas's. A nervous, waiting quiet. Although there had been a few cases of the plague over in the City, mostly around the docks, and also in the shipyards of Deptford, Southwark had so far been spared. It would not do, however, to be too comfortable or to relax our watchfulness. Often the plague seemed to begin near the docks and then spread outward, like the rings of ripples if you toss a stone into the still waters of a pond. It was frustrating, as a physician, to be unable to pin down precisely why the plague broke out or what caused it. And there was little we could do to treat it, apart from easing a patient's suffering.

Certainly it was an affliction of warm weather, for it scarcely ever struck in winter, save perhaps for a few unfortunates who had already become infected before the cold weather set in. It seemed to be somehow connected with the warm and sultry miasma which hung about London in the summer. Did people become infected merely by breathing in this air? Yet living and sleeping behind tightly closed shutters provided no protection. Some physicians and town authorities believed it was carried by cats and dogs, although as I have noted before, I have known whole families fall ill of the plague when there was no animal in the house.

That did not stop the slaughtering of any stray animals found wandering in the streets, when (to compound their folly) the town authorities would toss their bodies in Houndsditch, there to spread the infection (if that was its source) ever more widely. I have heard men say that when the Great Pestilence swept across all the world more than two hundred years ago and half mankind lay dead, there were towns left without a single dog or cat to be seen. For those who lived then, it must have seemed that the very world was ending and the Day of Judgement come. I have heard that whole villages were wiped out, never to rise again.

It had never proved that bad yet in London, though some years it was very bad indeed, with thousands dying. In an attempt to curb the spread of the disease, any house where the plague was found was marked with a red cross painted on the door. All windows and doors were nailed up, until every person within had either recovered or died. If they had no friends to bring them food to fill a basket lowered through a single opening, then they would simply die of starvation. It was a brutal measure, but no one knew how else to stop its spread. Sometimes, however, one of the inhabitants would manage to escape this cruel confinement, thus giving themselves some hope of avoiding infection, although in so doing they almost certainly spread the plague further.

Our tenuous hope of being spared this year soon proved false. After its retreat during the previous cold winter, the plague broke out more strongly than ever when the summer grew still warmer as the weeks passed, proving to be one of the worst visitations ever known. Thousands died. The Court fled. Parliament fled.

All the wealthy merchants – including my patients who lived on Cheapside – took themselves and their families off into the country to their own or their friends' estates well away from London, for it always seemed to be

London that was worst afflicted. The poor had no such recourse. Some indeed tried to flee. They took their belongings on their backs, and tramped off to the countryside with their families to escape the scourge that was killing thousands in London, only to find themselves driven back into the city by terrified villagers wielding clubs and pitchforks. The country people would turn on them, aye, and kill them too, rather than let them bring the curse of the plague with them. The Bills of Mortality mounted week by week.

As I went about the streets and examined the new patients brought in to St Thomas's, I wore our physicians' protective garb – a long black gown, fuller and more enveloping than my usual gown, and a full mask over the face, with a huge hooked beak like some monstrous bird of prey. Fearful though it looked, it was practical, for the beak was stuffed with raw wool soaked in efficacious potions to ward off infection. It served its turn, for neither I nor any of my fellow doctors at St Thomas's contracted the plague, but I was not surprised when small children ran from me screaming in the street. They must have thought me the Angel of Death, or the Devil himself, come to carry them off.

Toward the middle part of August, the plague seemed to slacken its hold a little. No one was fool enough to believe it had truly departed. That would not come about before the winter weather froze it out, but the weekly deaths posted in the Bills of Mortality dropped down almost to negligible, and I left off my fearsome garb. I hated that mask. I would almost have preferred to take my chance on the plague, but Superintendent Ailmer would not permit it.

'I cannot risk the loss of any of my physicians or surgeons,' he said. 'The masks will be worn, until I say otherwise.'

He did say otherwise that day in August, so I determined that now would be the time to take the waif Robert to Christ's Hospital. I had already exchanged letters with Mistress Wedderbury, the matron of Christ's, and she had confirmed that there would be a place for him there, but I had hesitated to take him outside the safe confines of St Thomas's while the plague was at its height. We had managed to keep it from the hospital, where it would have wreaked havoc with our sick and vulnerable, and there was no point in running risks with the boy. He was vastly improved since he had come to us, but was still hardly robust. I knew that he would be better served now by moving to Christ's, where he would have good meals, the company of healthy children, and the chance of some schooling.

When I told Alice Meadows of my plan to move Robert to the orphanage, she begged to come with me.

'For I have never been inside it, Dr Alvarez, though of course I have passed it many times. I have heard of the good they do. I should like to see it for myself.'

As the children's ward was quiet for once, and Goodwife Watson happy to manage by herself for half a day, I agreed. I thought Robert would be less apprehensive as well, if Alice accompanied us.

'We shall go by boat,' I said. 'Although the plague is much lessened, there is no need to risk ourselves on the streets. It is only a short walk from Puddle Wharf to Christ's.'

Privately, I thought that fairly steep climb up from the river would be quite enough for Robert. I was certain that he could never manage the walk all the way from St Thomas's, over the Bridge and through the streets of the City.

When Robert heard that we were to take a wherry up the river, his eyes shone with excitement.

'I an't iver bin in a boat,' he said. 'Nor niver thought I would.'

The idea of the boat trip seemed quite to reconcile him to leaving the sanctuary of St Thomas's, which had been his home for several months now, although as we walked out of the gate, he took hold of both my hand and Alice's, gripping them tightly.

We picked up a wherry at St Mary Overy Stairs. Jack, the wherryman, was one of those who knew me, for I had once given him a salve for his chapped hands. Ever since he had regarded me as a personal friend.

'Going to Christ's Hospital, are you?' he said, when I asked for Puddle Wharf. 'Ah, you're a lucky fellow, lad.' He winked at Robert. 'Three good meals a day. A feather bed, and naught to do but play and maybe learn a bit of reading and such. Wish I had such an easy life.'

He set to, pulling on his oars. Although the wherry had its small sail set, it could do little against the strong flow of the river. It was always hard work for the wherrymen, rowing up against the stream.

Robert looked about him in awe. I could understand his reaction, for it had been mine the very first time I was rowed across the river in a wherry. It is a curious thing, but from land the Thames does not seem so very wide. And when you cross it over the Bridge, the houses built along both sides allow only glimpses of the river through the few gaps between them. Down on the level of the water, however, the river suddenly grows much wider, and once aboard a wherry you can feel the thrust of the current like a live thing. When the tide is on the ebb, both river current and tide are a mighty force intent on sweeping you down river. If you are above the Bridge they could crush you against the stone pillars and starlings on which it is built. On the other hand, when the tide is rushing inland but the river is still flowing toward the sea, the battle between the two forces can toss a small boat about as if it were no more than a walnut shell.

Today, we were crossing on a flood tide, but because of the hot summer weather the flow of the river was no more than moderate, so there was no great contest between the two, but it still needed a mighty pull of Jack's oars to take us across the main flow in the centre of the river toward the relatively quiet water near Puddle Wharf.

As we went, I told Alice and Robert a little about some of the children who had gone from St Thomas's to Christ's Hospital.

'I am sure you will meet Mellie White,' I said. 'She did not want to part with her baby Hannah, and Mistress Wedderbury found her a place as a servant at Christ's, so that she could be with Hannah. Mellie has done well and she is now personal maid to Mistress Wedderbury, while Hannah is a well grown toddler now.'

Alice knew a little of Mellie's history, a young maidservant who at fourteen had given birth to Hannah after rape by her master, but I said nothing of this to Robert. For all I knew, he was familiar with such evil, but I had no wish to cast a gloom over the day. Both Mellie and Hannah were strong and happy now, and Mellie had even begun to learn to read.

'Then there is Jamey,' I said. 'Robert, you know Matthew, who works at the hospital. Jamey was one of those who was on the streets with Matthew and Katerina and the twins, but he was too young to stay with them, even after their life became better. He never even spoke in those days, but now he chatters like an African monkey.'

'Are they all babies there?' Robert frowned.

'Certainly not,' I assured him. 'Some of the children at Christ's Hospital are babies, certainly, but you will have little to do with them. You will be with the big boys who go to school. When they are old enough, some are apprenticed to a trade, depending on their aptitude.'

I saw him frown again. He did not understand the word.

'Depending on what they are good at doing,' I explained. 'Some might like to work with wood, so they will learn to be carpenters. Some want to carve stone, and become masons. Some will find work as drapers or shoemakers. No one leaves Christ's unless they go to learn a skill, so they will earn a good living. A few of the boys do so well at their book learning that they go on to Oxford or Cambridge, and become scholars or priests.'

I could see that he understood 'priest' well enough, but the word 'scholar' meant nothing.

'And the girls?' Alice asked.

'Apprentices also,' I said. 'To all the female trades. Those who do well at lessons may become ladies' maids to noble women and eventually rise to a good position in a great household.'

'Lessons? They are schooled?'

I nodded. 'Aye. Better schooled than some girls from a higher rank in society.'

'Remarkable.' Alice sounded a little ironic, as she had ever right to do.

'What do girls want with book learning?' Jack spared breath enough to ask as we drew in towards Puddle Wharf.

'To use the good minds God has given them, perhaps?' I said, but was spared the need to say more as the wherry bumped into the dock and we scrambled to our feet. I paid Jack and took the opportunity to check the condition of his hands quickly.

'I've no trouble with them in summer, doctor,' he said. 'And in winter that salve you told the hospital to give me mends the worst of it.'

'Good,' I said, following Alice and Robert on to the dock and giving Jack a farewell wave. I smiled to myself at what he might say if he knew his friend the physician was a girl with book learning.

We climbed the slope up to Newgate Street and crossed it to the gateway of Christ's Hospital. Robert continued to stare about him in wonder, at the wide street, today filled with the busy Newgate Market, the massive (if slightly crumbling) Newgate itself, and the impressive buildings of the orphanage, adapted from the monastery which had once stood here. I realised that as a pauper street child of Southwark he had probably never been to this part of London before.

Mistress Wedderbury received us in her private rooms and, as I had hoped, Mellie was there. She must be near seventeen now and had grown into a very pretty girl

116

indeed, tidily dressed in a blue gown and immaculate white apron, with her hair tucked neatly into an equally white cap, apart from a few curls which escaped around her face. She brought us ale and sweet biscuits, and set herself to make Robert feel at ease. Mistress Wedderbury smiled at me over their heads.

Alice began enquiring eagerly about the work of Christ's, so I asked whether I might go with Mellie and Robert to see the boys' quarters.

'Certainly, Dr Alvarez,' she said, 'although I am sure you know them very well. You will want to see Jamey. Indeed, I fancy you will hardly know him! He has started school with the petties.'

'Truly, I would like to see him.' I smiled at Mellie. 'And Hannah too.'

'She is talking so well, doctor,' Mellie said eagerly. 'I think she is going to be very clever.'

Every child is clever in the eyes of its mother, but when I saw Hannah she did seem a bright little thing, unmarked by the misfortune of her birth. I hoped she might be spared knowledge of it, should that be possible.

We peeped through the window of the classroom used by the petties, the youngest children, just beginning to learn their letters. There was Jamey, sitting at the front, grown to almost half as much again as when I had brought him here. His face was bright, and although we could not hear him, we could see him answering the master's questions.

After we had left Robert with two of the older boys – 'They are both kind,' Mellie whispered – I took the opportunity to ask after her own plans.

'I know you want to stay here with Hannah,' I said, 'but have you any thoughts for the future?'

To my surprise, she turned bright red at this mild question, and ducked her head away from me.

'I – I am not sure,' she murmured.

Ah, I thought, is there a man in the case? Or given her still quite tender years, a boy? I let the silence last, in the shrewd expectation that there would be more to come. We strolled to a bench at the side of the grassy sward in the centre of the quadrangle. In some ways Christ's was a little like one of the Inns of Court.

'I should go back to Mistress Wedderbury,' she said, but sat down anyway.

Hannah began to play with one of the resident cats, a half grown tabby kitten who was happy to chase Hannah's ball.

I sat down as well, and waited.

'There is an assistant clerk in the steward's office,' Mellie said, and blushed again.

'You like him?'

'Aye,' she whispered.

'And he?'

'He says . . . aye, I think he likes me. But Dr Alvarez, I am nothing, a shamed servant girl. I am not fit.'

'You came from a good family,' I said firmly. 'It was not to your blame that you were orphaned and left destitute. The parish was at fault, putting you in service when you were so young. You should have been placed here. You are already making a better life for yourself.' I hesitated. 'This young clerk. Does he know about Hannah?'

She nodded. 'I have told him everything. I would not deceive him in any way.'

'Good. And he does not mind?'

'He loves Hannah too. He is so good with her. But I – I am not good enough for him. He could have anyone. A merchant's daughter. He will be a full clerk one day, or a steward.' Her eyes widened. 'Even the steward of a manor. Imagine!'

I smiled. 'I do imagine. Think how wonderful that would be! I think you are quite good enough for this young man. How are you at your lessons now? The wife of a steward must read well and write a good hand. And be able to keep accounts.'

She was still blushing, but her voice was eager. 'I study whenever I can. The master of the grammar school sets me tasks to do when I am not working.'

She jumped up. 'And I should be working now! Mistress Wedderbury will wonder what has become of me.'

'I will say I have kept you.' I smiled at her as I rose. She had been so frail after the birth. Now she was nearly as tall as I. 'I think your young clerk sounds just the one for you and Hannah. Do not diminish yourself. Keep at your studies, and when you are both of you ready, I shall come to see you wed.'

Alice and I took another wherry back to St Thomas's after Mistress Wedderbury and I had concluded the arrangements for Robert's admission to Christ's Hospital, and we had eventually found him, still in the company of his two new friends, in the kitchen, being treated to slices of spiced cake hot from the oven. There would be no tears here, I could see.

'It is a fine place,' Alice said thoughtfully, as the wherryman allowed the boat to be carried down by the current, only taking a stroke or two to keep us on course and aiming for the south bank.

'It is,' I agreed. 'The men who thought to use the old monastery buildings before they could be pulled down showed great foresight. Otherwise, we should have had a few grand houses built there, and nowhere for the orphaned and destitute children of London to go.'

'And it is not just a place to feed and house them,' she said. 'I had not realised that before.'

'Aye. It is the way they are educated and set up for life that is most remarkable,' I said. 'Mistress Wedderbury said to me once that they would never turn out the children when they were grown to become no better than beggars on the streets. They must all be trained to earn a decent living for themselves.'

'Robert will do well there,' she said, a touch of regret in her voice. I could see that in these long weeks of caring for him she had grown very attached.

'He will do very well,' I said firmly, and smiled. 'And of course you may visit him whenever you please.'

In its usual insidious way, just when we thought that the plague was abating, it came back in full force. Once again the streets of London stank of burning tar, for there was a theory that the fumes would cleanse the poisonous miasma bred by the plague, killing it off. Whether it did indeed prevail, I do not know. What I do know is that everything was quickly saturated with the smell – clothes, hair, curtains, bedding – even inside the hospital, and a devilish smell it was too. Because it was always associated with a time of plague, it had fixed itself in my mind while I was still a child as the smell of the very fires of Hell.

And apart from such wild imaginings, the simple practical truth was that, although it may have combated the plague, at the same time it caused serious problems for those who suffered from weakness of the lungs, both the old and the very young, or those who were afflicted with breathing difficulties all their lives or in the aftermath of some sickness of the lungs. We had a new inflow of patients with such breathing problems once the fires had started up again. There was no avoiding them, for great braziers were set up on all the major street corners, minded by men recruited from Bridewell. The work assigned in Bridewell is hard, and some may have thought that escaping from its walls even to maintain a tar-burning brazier would be an improvement to their lives. After a day, sweating and smoked like some noxious fish, they may have thought otherwise, despite the facecloths and heavy gloves they were issued. If the rest of us suffered, these men were near pickled.

I was relieved that I need spend little time in the streets, with their reek of burned tar, which almost, but not quite, smothered the taint of unburied bodies, a stench which crept through the air like an aftertaste of the smoke. The city authorities (those who had not fled) knew very well that the plague dead must be buried quickly, yet it was almost impossible to recruit men to carry them from the plague-infested houses to the burying grounds. It was useless allocating Bridewell paupers to the work, for they would run away at once, heedless that they might be caught and punished. Better that than handling the bodies of the plague victims. All that could be done was to hire men for a fee of at least five times a normal labouring man's wage. A few, greedy enough, or desperate enough, would always come forward. But there were never sufficient men to move the bodies as soon as they should be, so the dead lay too long unburied and the plague spread.

So I hastened on my short journeys to and from the hospital, and was glad that my grand City patients had taken themselves off out of London, so I had no need to cross the river. However, I arrived one day to find a boy of about twelve hovering beside Tom Read's gatehouse, his face streaked with weeping, his hands unconsciously plucking at the neck of his worn tunic. I recognised him as one of the patients I had treated for lung problems in the first week of the latest tar burning. He and his mother had both suffered, but I had given them a tonic to clear the chest, and they had gone home again.

'What is it, Nick?' I asked. 'Has your mother the chest thickness again?'

At that he burst into fresh tears and gabbled something I could not understand. Tom took me by the elbow and drew me aside.

'Their house is marked as a plague house,' he whispered. 'Nick managed to squeeze out through a window where the shutter wasn't properly nailed shut. It's his younger sister, but his mother swears it isn't the plague. She's begging you to come and tell the men to open the house.'

It might even be true. Or it might be the despair of a mother who could not face the truth that her child was certain to die.

The normal procedure during an epidemic was this. Certain old women were appointed to examine possible cases of the plague and determine yea or nay. Like the carriers of the dead, they were either greedy for the fee or in desperate poverty, if they were prepared to undertake the work. The curious thing was that the majority of these old women survived their dangerous task, while hearty men in the prime of life would be struck down after the merest brush with the plague. It was another of the mysteries for which we had no answer.

Although these women were experienced, they could make mistakes, but if they confirmed a case of the plague, no one wished to run the risk of ignoring it. The house would be sealed by the men appointed, the cross painted on the door, and all those who lived within left to their fate.

There were also cases, of course, where money changed hands, and the women declared the house clear of the plague, when it was not, thus allowing the inhabitants not yet afflicted to escape – thereby spreading the disease further.

It was not for me to visit Nick's family and countermand the decision of the plague watchers. And if it was the plague, to enter the house would be to put myself at serious risk. Yet this child, who could have run off and saved his own skin, had come to me for help. Could I be so heartless as to refuse?

Mindful of Superintendent Ailmer's orders about wearing our plague masks, I had mine with me, though in disobedience I was not wearing it but had it hanging round my neck by its cord. I could put it on in the house, although I loathed the feel of it on my face. Wearing it, I felt myself to be suffocating, trapped inside its airless prison, for one had to fight for breath though the stuffed beak of a nose. Besides, peering through the narrow eye holes, I found it almost impossible to see, certainly well enough to see a patient. Fortunately I had only needed to wear it in the street, not in the hospital.

'Very well, Nick,' I said, 'I will come and see your sister, but you had best go back the way you came. If you are found to have climbed out, you will be punished, or else simply shut up inside again, with an extra board across the window. Tell your mother that I will come as soon as I have found one of the constables to break open the door for me.'

The boy ran off, with a gleam of hope in his eyes. I donned my plague mask, and went in search of a constable.

It was an hour or more before I could gain entry to the house. It was but around the corner from St Thomas's, but it took me that long to find one of the parish constables and to argue him into accepting that I believed a local child had been wrongly identified as a plague victim. If it were to prove that Nick's sister did have the plague, I would have more than Superintendent Ailmer to answer to. However, I prevailed at last. Perhaps my unearthly voice, booming from within the mask, convinced the constable that I knew what I was about. Then it took more time for him and his deputy to find the tools they needed, before ripping off the planks which had been nailed over the door of the house.

As soon as the door was opened, the two men backed away hastily.

'We'll be over there,' the constable said, jerking his head at an ale house across the street. 'You come and tell us what you find, doctor, nor don't waste no time about it. We'll have that door nailed up again fast as wink. Old Matilda knows what she's about. That'll be plague, right enough.'

'Aye,' said his fellow grudgingly, 'but she's been downing the beer pretty free lately. Got the money now, see? And the beer takes away the memory o' what she's seen.'

So, I thought, if the woman was a drunkard, perhaps she *had* made a mistake.

I stepped over the threshold, pulling the door to behind me. I had a moment of blind panic. What if the constable were to nail up the door with me inside? And this was a house of plague? My heart began to beat faster, but I heard no sound of hammering.

Pulling off the mask, I called, 'Nick? I am here. Dr Alvarez. Where is your Mama?'

The house was dark, with all the windows nailed up, the only illumination a sliver or two of light daring to creep in through cracks around the shutters. There was a stirring in the shadows ahead of me, and Nick materialised out of them.

'Upstairs,' he whispered. 'Mama is there with my sister.'

I knew that was all there were of this family, no other children having lived past infancy and the father killed in an accident in the Southwark tannery two years before. Nick's mother, Goodwife Ellis, kept the family on what she could earn as a washerwoman.

'I need to be able to see, Nick,' I said, resisting the temptation to whisper as well. 'Have you a candle?'

I could just make out that he shook his head.

'There's a rush dip.'

'That will do. Can you light it?'

I waited while he fumbled about in the dark, and eventually a dull smoky light showed that the rush dip was burning. He led me across to where a rickety ladder reached to the upper floor, where there must be a low roofed sleeping space.

When I reached it, I could barely stand upright, but in the light of the rush dip I could see that it was kept clean and neat. Also I became aware of the fact that the house did not smell like a house of plague. The buboes which are the unmistakable signs of the plague soon begin to burst and issue forth a stinking pus. There was no smell of that here.

The little girl was lying on a straw palliasse on the floor and shading her eyes with her hand, as though the light troubled them. Her mother was sitting on an old worn cushion at her side and looked up at me with an expression of mingled fear and hope. I knelt down beside her and laid my medicine satchel on the floor.

'Now then, Goodwife Ellis,' I said, 'tell me just what ails your daughter.'

She reached out her hands to me in a pleading gesture.

'Oh, Dr Alvarez, I could not believe you would come, but Nick said–' She gulped, a harsh, rasping sound, which betrayed that she had wept herself dry.

I turned back the thin blanket that covered the child. She was certainly feverish, her face flushed and, when I gently moved her hand, her eyes glittering.

'Her neck is swollen, below her ears, doctor, and the woman said it was the buboes of the plague coming. But that was last night, she said it, and they come much sooner than that, the buboes, don't they?'

I nodded. 'They do.' I felt the child's neck, and the glands were indeed swollen, but there were no obvious signs of the plague.

'I shall need to examine the rest of her body,' I said. 'Will you take off her shift?'

My further examination showed that there were no signs of plague buboes about her groin or armpits. I sat back on my heels and smiled at Goodwife Ellis.

'Definitely not the plague, though she is certainly ill. How long has she had this fever?'

'Three days. And she complains that her throat is very sore.'

I smiled down at the little girl. 'I don't know your name.'

'Bess,' she said, in a croaking voice.

Of course. Every third girl child was named after the Queen.

'And does your throat still hurt?'

She nodded. 'It hurts to swallow. And my head hurts.'

125

'It is the mumps,' I said. 'Not the plague. Painful, but we will soon have you well again.'

I sent Nick for a cup of small ale, such as children drink, and mixed febrifuge herbs in it, adding a small dose of poppy syrup. It would ease the pain a little and help Bess sleep.

'Now,' I said, lifting the little girl up to rest against my shoulder and holding up the cup. 'I know it is hard for you to swallow, but you must sip this down, a little at a time, and it will help you feel better. Can you do that?'

She nodded. She was a valiant little soul and drank it all, though I saw how it pained her.

Once she was tucked under her blanket again, Goodwife Ellis, Nick and I descended the rickety ladder to the main room of the house. I gave the woman a supply of the herbs, explaining how much to give Bess, and when.

'I will call and see her again this evening, when I am done at the hospital,' I said. 'And now I must tackle the Constable.'

I grinned at Nick. 'It is a good thing you have such a resourceful son, and one who is able to wriggle through small spaces.'

When I found the Constable and his man in the ale house, I gave them a tongue lashing.

'Do not let me hear, ever again, that you trust the word of a drunkard before you nail up a house. The child has the mumps. The whole family might have died, imprisoned there. I want the doors and windows unsealed and the red cross painted over. I shall be back this afternoon. If it is not done by then, I shall report you to the authorities.'

I stormed out, leaving them glowering, but chastened.

Chapter Seven

*A*fter my discovery of the true state of affairs at the home of Goodwife Ellis, I wondered whether there were more cases of people wrongly found to have the plague. I was not so naïve as to suppose there were no true cases. The Bills of Mortality alone were proof of that. But if there were drunken old women going about, asserting that some had the plague who had not, it needed to be looked into. It is not unknown for these women to threaten that they will report the plague, in the hope of receiving a bribe to keep silence, even when there is indeed a genuine occurrence of the plague. In cases like that of Bess Ellis, where swollen glands are claimed to be incipient buboes, the diagnosis (if one can use such a grand term for something so haphazard) may simply be a stupid mistake. Or it may be an attempt to extract money.

It might seem folly to try for a bribe amongst the poor of Southwark. However, Goodwife Ellis, despite her humble conditions, worked hard and kept her children and home clean and neat. To the women who pointed the finger at plague victims, themselves amongst the very poorest in London, Goodwife Ellis might even seem well-to-do. For such women, a bribe of a few pennies would buy enough cheap ale to bring temporary oblivion.

God knows, they probably needed oblivion, those women, doing the work they did, at constant risk of the plague themselves, but that did not excuse bringing down a death sentence on those imprisoned in their houses for no good reason until they starved to death.

As I made my way back to St Thomas's past the reeking braziers, I shuddered at the thought that London was turning into Hell itself – not only from its hellfire reek but from a world turned to hellish madness, where a child's mumps could bring about the death of an imprisoned family, alone and unshriven.

When I reached the hospital, I went straight to Superintendent Ailmer's office and told him quickly just what I had discovered at the home of Goodwife Ellis. He knew the woman, for she worked sometimes in the hospital laundry.

'So you see,' I said, 'if the boy had not managed to squeeze out of the ill-fitting window, they would all have been left there to starve, the woman and two children.'

'It was fortunate indeed,' he said, 'that the boy came for you. But perhaps it was no more than an honest mistake. I suppose the swollen glands might have been taken for the first sign of plague buboes.'

I shook my head.

'I do not believe so. The women who do this work day after day must know the right signs. Either it was sheer carelessness or the Constable's man was right and the woman was drunk, Or–' I paused.

'Or?'

'Or it was a trick to get money.'

'A bribe? In Southwark?' He laughed.

'A bribe is a bribe,' I said. 'Even in Southwark. Your pauper may not bribe on the grand scale, like your courtier. But in relative terms, even a penny may be a bribe for some. And if the woman – or women – are addicted to drink . . .'

He nodded, conceding the point.

'What troubles me,' I said, 'is that mumps rarely occurs as an isolated case. Why does Bess Ellis have the mumps? Where has she caught it? I am certain there must be other children with mumps in Southwark, for I doubt she ever strays far from here. Yet we have had no cases in my children's ward.'

That had certainly caught his attention.

'You think there may be other children hereabouts, who have been shut up in houses marked for the plague, when they have no more than the mumps?'

'We cannot be sure, but why should there be just this single case?'

He drummed his fingers on the desk. 'We cannot open up every plague house in Southwark to investigate. That would be madness. It would risk spreading the plague even further.'

'I have been thinking on this as I walked back to the hospital,' I said. 'There would be no need to open every house, only ones where there are children. Adults may catch the disease, but only rarely. It is commonest amongst children.'

'And how do you suggest we identify such houses?' He raised his eyebrows, giving a doubtful smile.

'Easily. Children know children. In every street the children will be known. First we need find those plague houses where there are known to be children.'

'And then?'

'Open up one window only, and question the people within. Have them describe the symptoms of whoever is afflicted. If the victim is a child, and the symptoms sound like mumps, only then need we get the parish Constable to unbar the door so that we can go inside to investigate. If it is mumps, the house may be unsealed, though the child should be kept within until the disease is gone. We do not want an epidemic of the mumps as well as the plague!'

He grunted. 'Aye, I think that plan might work. I must speak to the aldermen of the local parishes, for we shall need their authority for such an interference with the normal regulations for controlling the plague.'

'Of course.' I nodded. 'If we can gain their permission, I am prepared to examine any children we think might have the mumps.'

129

'It could be risky. There might still be plague amongst the family.'

'I suppose there might, but better me than one of the other physicians, who have wives and families dependent on them. I have no one.'

I had not meant to sound pathetic, although I am afraid my words came out that way.

'You have Rikki.' He smiled at me.

I smiled back. 'Aye. For Rikki's sake I will be very careful.'

It required a few days to organise, but Superintendent Ailmer managed to persuade the parish aldermen of the plan. One even took it upon himself to visit the Ellis family personally and give them a dignified apology. He also had the two plague women who were known to be drunkards dismissed from their work. We were never to know whether they had been trying to extract bribes or were simply incompetent, but I veered to the former conclusion when I discovered one openly admitted case of mumps in the son of a comfortably off shopkeeper, who avoided my question about bribery with shifty looks. I was convinced he had paid to avoid his boy being marked as a plague victim.

Superintendent Ailmer lent me one of his clerks and together we criss-crossed Southwark, checking the plague houses and making enquiries about local children. All this took a great deal of time, so that every day I was obliged to stay at my work in the hospital well into the evening to make up for the hours I had spent in the streets.

In the end we identified eleven cases of mumps shut up as plague victims. One boy was in the last stages of a tertiary fever, and we were too late to save him, but at least the rest of his family would no longer be imprisoned. The remaining ten children I physicked, then appointed two of the sisters from the hospital to visit them twice a day, going back myself occasionally. Afterwards, several more cases of mumps occurred, but they were reported openly and we treated them in the normal way, thus managing to control the outbreak.

I am usually as strong and hearty as anyone, but the time spent searching out the misdiagnosed mumps cases, as well as my usual work, meant long exhausting days and little sleep at night. How it was, I do not know, but one day, to my shame, I fainted as I was on the point of leaving St Thomas's in the evening. The next thing I knew, I was lying on the floor just inside the door, with Mistress Maynard bending over me and loosening the strings of my shirt at the neck. I became aware of what she was about before she could undo the buttons on my doublet, and struggled to sit up. Too close an examination would immediately reveal everything that I had been at such pains to conceal all this time.

'I thank you, mistress,' I managed to say, albeit somewhat groggily. 'I am well enough now.'

She sat back on her heels – with some difficulty, for she was a plump woman – and clicked her tongue impatiently.

'You have driven yourself past your strength this last week and more, Dr Alvarez,' she said. 'You would never allow one of your patients to behave so foolishly. And what good will you be to them, if you fall ill?'

'Nothing a good night's sleep will not cure,' I said more firmly, though in truth my head was swimming and I was curiously reluctant to get up off the floor.

'I think not,' she said, in the tone she used when disciplining one of the sisters under her orders. 'I have sent to fetch Superintendent Ailmer.'

'There is no need to worry him,' I said in alarm, trying to draw my legs under me, and not succeeding very well.

At that moment the Superintendent himself came bustling along the corridor from his office. Mistress Maynard got stiffly to her feet.

'Now what is to-do?' he said. 'Have you taken a fall, Dr Alvarez?'

'He has fainted,' Mistress Maynard said briskly, before I could answer. 'Working all hours, he's been, day and night, for I have seen it, and so have the sisters. What with these plague victims who were not plague victims at all, and the two wards, and not a decent meal these two weeks, I'll be bound. These young fellows, they think they can defy the limits the Lord sets on our bodies. They need the sense you and I have gained with our greater years . . . Sir,' she added, thinking, perhaps, that her speech was a little too familiar, given Superintendent Ailmer's position.

By this time I had managed to get to my feet, and kept there by leaning surreptitiously against the wall. I ran an exploratory hand up through the hair on the left side of my head, for I could feel that I had struck the floor there none too lightly.

'I am well enough now,' I insisted. 'It was nothing but a moment of dizziness. It is true, I believe I have not eaten much today.'

Indeed, now I recollected, I realised that I had eaten nothing, which was reinforced by Mistress Maynard's scornful sniff.

'With your good leave, I will be off home now, and eat something there. Besides, Tom Read will be waiting for me to collect Rikki.'

'Aye,' Mistress Maynard said dryly, 'Tom is usually away to his bed by now.'

'You will not come in tomorrow.' Superintendent Ailmer shook his finger at me with authority. 'In fact, it is Wednesday now. I do not want to see you again until this day week. I am not sure when you last had a break from your duties, Dr Alvarez, but I do not think it has been since you rejoined us, this autumn past.'

'My patients,' I objected. 'My wards.'

He looked at Mistress Maynard. 'What say you, mistress?'

'Aye, we can spare him for a week. Only a quarter of the beds are full in the children's ward, and no difficult cases in the lying-in ward at present. We can manage well enough for a week. Should there be an emergency, I am sure one of the other physicians can assist. Off you go, Dr Alvarez, and rest your body and your brain. Be as kind to them as if they were your patients.'

I saw Superintendent Ailmer smile at hearing the mistress of the sisters laying down the law to one of the physicians under his very nose. I bowed my head in submission. I did indeed feel somewhat weak about the legs and still dizzy in my head. The thought of a peaceful few days, without work, was suddenly very appealing.

'If you are sure?' I said to Ailmer.

'I am certain sure,' he said. 'Now, get you away to food and sleep. Are you steady enough on your feet to walk home?'

'Indeed I am,' I said, with more conviction than I felt. 'It is no distance to my lodgings. I will just collect Rikki and be away.'

Mistress Maynard seemed reluctant to let me venture forth on my own, but I bowed to them both, and made a dignified exit, though I may have stumbled a little as I crossed the yard to the gatehouse, retying the strings of my shirt as I went. It had been a very near thing there, for a moment. If I had not come to myself quickly . . . I shivered at the thought. My true sex revealed, I should have lost my position for sure, and then how could I have lived?

Once I had collected Rikki from a sleepy Tom – and felt guilty to have kept him up so late – I hurried back to my lodgings. The air along the river revived me somewhat. I few days ago the tar braziers had been taken away, deaths from the plague being well down. London air is not fresh and clean at the best of times, but at night, before winter comes with the smoke of its sea coal fires, it is better than by day.

Back on the stairs up to my room I remembered that Goodwife Atkins had promised that morning to leave me some soup, and there it was in a pot beside my door. Perhaps, like Mistress Maynard, she had seen that I had become somewhat fine drawn. Gratefully I carried the soup in and took the trouble to light a fire so that I was able to heat it on the trivet. Following it with a heel of bread and a piece of good cheese, I made a sustaining supper, even sharing a little with Rikki, although I knew he would already have been fed by Tom.

It was a luxury to peel off my clothes at last, for of late I had been too tired and so late home that I had simply lain down in all but my shoes at night. I pulled on my night shift, blew out my candle, and climbed into bed. On the thought that I need not be abroad early for work tomorrow, I fell asleep.

The next day I rose late, despite having woken at the usual time. It felt strange to lie abed and listen to the bell of St Mary Overy sound the hours. At last, however, I could no longer ignore Rikki's importunities, and my own nagging sense that I should be up and doing. Rikki and I walked as far as the butcher's shop just beyond Bess Travis's whorehouse, where I bought bacon and two mutton collops.

'I've a good bone here you may have for your dog, Dr Alvarez,' the butcher said, wrapping it together with the meat in a sheet of rough grey paper. 'I heard what you done about them children with the mumps. Disgraceful, I call it. Them women should be locked up to starve themselves. See how they fare then.'

'I thank you, Goodman Parsons,' I said. 'As for the women, poor old crones themselves. Perhaps it was no more than a mistake.'

He gave a disbelieving snort, then tossed Rikki a misshapen sausage, which Rikki caught neatly and devoured in a couple of bites.

We went round the corner to the bakery for a fresh loaf, still warm from the oven, and then to the dairy for cheese, butter, and eggs. As I strolled back to my lodgings, I felt a curious mixture of pleased leisure and guilt at being so idle, when everyone else about me was busily at work.

After we had broken our fast with buttered eggs, I leaned on my window sill and gazed out over the river, wondering what I was to do with the rest of the day. My life allowed no place for idleness, at least idle hours spent on my own. In the usual way of things, if I had time from my work, I would spend it with Simon and the rest of Lord Strange's Men. With them away on tour, that was out of the question. I could visit Sara, of course, but somehow felt disinclined to walk all the way to Holborn, merely to kill time. Or I could go and see my horse Hector, in the stables at Seething Lane.

Indeed, there was no reason why I should not take Hector for a ride out into the countryside. That was the very thing! Rikki could run alongside, and it would be good for all three of us. I would take food with me and make a day of it. On that thought, I set the remaining eggs to boil hard, and fried the mutton collops, which would be just as good eaten cold as hot. While they were cooking I fetched my knapsack out from under my bed where I kept it stored, and as I did so, caught sight of the folded paper on my table.

Simon had sent me a letter by carrier a few days before, recounting the company's adventures in Kent. He made a comical tale of it – lost costume baskets, performances in open inn yards, where hardly any of the audience paid their penny, cramped spaces in tiny guildhalls, where the players could hardly move about without falling over each other's swords. He listed the remaining places they were to visit before moving on to Hampshire.

'We have milked the good folk of Kent dry of their reluctant pennies,' he finished, 'but we have saved one good town till last. We will spend a full week in Canterbury before we shake the dust of this county from our feet.'

I pondered a moment, calculating. They would reach Canterbury today. Why should I not ride there and meet them, enjoy their company for a day or two, watch a play? Instead of riding Hector out and back again today, a day's ride would take me halfway to Canterbury. I could be there by Friday, and start back to London on Monday, to take up my work again on Wednesday.

So pleased was I with the scheme that I nearly let the collops burn, but rescued them just in time.

'Rikki,' I said, 'we are going to Canterbury, to see Lord Strange's Men!'

I almost wanted to sing, and secretly admitted to myself that it was Simon I was longing to see. Though of course I would be glad of Guy and Will and Dick and the rest.

Once my mind was made up, I hurried to make ready. I could have been on my way an hour ago, had I thought of it sooner, and I had still to fetch Hector from the other side of the river. Having doused the fire, I packed my knapsack with food and a few clothes, rolling up my cloak to fit in the top, in case the present dry weather should turn to rain. I glanced around my room to see that I had all I need, tucked Simon's letter in my doublet pocket, picked up my knapsack and satchel, and set off.

One advantage of starting out somewhat later than I might have done was that the crowds of people walking across the Bridge to their work were long gone, leaving only those strolling between the shops. Hector picked his way between them, and Rikki wove about our feet. Once back in Southwark I headed east along the Kentish road called Watling Street. It was one of those ancient roads built, so 'tis said, by the old Romans, and to this day remains a sturdy paved road laid with dressed slabs over a base of pounded layers of gravel. Although centuries of frost and rain had shifted the stones in places, it was still a very fine road, running straight and true across the high ground south of the Kent marshes which lie in a great swathe south of the Thames estuary.

Once clear of the last straggling houses of Southwark, I could fill my lungs with clean air such as we never know in London. I felt I was washing them clear of those weeks of tar smoke and the stench of the sick and dying. Hector tossed his head and snorted, as though he too felt the same. Rikki would dodge aside from time to time from the road to investigate interesting smells in the hedgerows, and on one occasion pursued a hare across a field of stubble, but was hopelessly outrun. He never wandered too far, however, and if he saw Hector drawing ahead would come loping after us, tongue hanging out.

Excellent road though it was, clear of clogging mud in wet weather or ankle deep dust in fine, Watling Street with its stone paving was hard on a horse's feet, so I mostly kept to the grass verge. According to law, whoever owns the land through which a highway passes is required to maintain a verge clear on either side, at least a bow shot in width, to keep travellers safe from ambush. It is a law more honoured in the breaking than the keeping, but this being one of the most important highways in the kingdom, the verges here were indeed kept clear, and made for easy riding. So that it would not be too difficult for Rikki to keep pace, I held Hector down to a trot or a gentle canter, only now and then allowing him a brief gallop where the going was clear and firm. I went bareheaded for once, having stuffed my cap into my saddlebag, and felt the joy of wind through my close cropped hair. I may have been exhausted enough to turn dizzy the previous day, but a good night's sleep, food, and freedom from responsibility had restored me, save for a slight soreness where the left side of my head had struck the tiled floor at St Thomas's.

Most of the fields we passed had been harvested, though in some the country people were still at work, cutting and binding wheat and barley. Overhead arched a clear azure sky, across which no more than wisps of cloud were passing, promising enough fine weather to dry the grain. The fields already harvested were now providing stubble grazing for sheep and cattle, and, near one village, geese.

Around midday I stopped at a village ale house to rest Hector and Rikki, while I bought a pint of the ale wife's fresh brew, and a mutton pasty to take with it, and with one of my boiled eggs, feeling it would be ill mannered to eat none but my own food while seated on the bench at her door. In front of me lay a village green with a somewhat weedy pond, and beyond it the doors of a barn stood wide to let the wind blow in, where men were beating the harvested grain with threshing flails, while the women were tossing the threshed grain in winnowing baskets, a swooping motion up and back, in the age old rhythm that separates the chaff from the true grain. The winnowed chaff floated away in clouds, borne on the wind, and drifted down to lie along the street and half the green, where an inquisitive duck or two investigated it, before turning away in disgust.

It was pleasant sitting there in the sun, watching other people work, with Rikki lying in the shade under the bench and Hector taking the advantage of a few mouthfuls of grass from the edge of the green. However, I must not linger too long, nor cause annoyance to the villagers if Hector made too free of their own grazing, so I returned my cup to the ale wife, bought another pasty to eat as I went, as well as one for Rikki, and set off again along my straight road.

Until now the sun had been in my face, but while I lingered it had begun to move behind me. I decided I would not overtire Hector, who had had no chance of a long ride for some while now. When it began to draw near dusk, I would look out for a likely place to spend the night. For preference a decent inn. I have often shared a stable with my horse, but today I would try for a comfortable bed. I had no wish to arrive in Canterbury dishevelled and with straw in my hair.

As it turned out, I reached the city of Rochester in good time to find an inn, the Black Swan, which lay directly on Watling Street. The innkeeper assured me I could have a room and bed to myself, and stabling for my horse, at rather less than I would have paid in London.

'How far from here to Canterbury?' I asked, as I handed over the fee for my night's lodging.

'You'll be from London, master?' he said. 'Why then, you're just halfway. Thirty mile, London to

138

Rochester. Thirty mile, Rochester to Canterbury. And a fine road all the way.'

I nodded. That was what I had hoped. If I made an earlier start tomorrow than I had today, I should reach Canterbury with time in hand to seek out the players before it grew late, probably soon after they ended their afternoon performance. As for today, it would be an hour or more before the inn served supper, so I decided to wander a little around the town. There was a deal of activity about the river, where there were docks and ship building, as well as the bridge over the Medway, the last before it spreads out and flows into the Thames. Indeed, this lowest crossing of the Medway is the very reason for Rochester's existence. However, I headed away from all this busy activity and turned my steps toward the cathedral instead. After so much vigorous riding, I felt the need of some quietness.

Like all great churches, Rochester Cathedral held within its walls a concentrated essence of centuries upon centuries of worship and prayer, as if the half heard voices down the ages still whispered here. I took a seat on a bench in a quiet corner, having left Rikki to wait outside, and found that I was quite alone. Yet it seemed as though, if I but turned my head quickly enough, I would catch a glimpse of all those who had knelt and prayed within this sacred space, as if their presence wrapped me around with kindness. I felt myself relaxing into ease, and thought how the hostility of recent months in London against foreigners had frayed away at me. Marlowe's play *The Jew of Malta* had helped to stir up an evil that was already lurking there, but by bringing hatred of the Machiavellian Jew on to the public stage, he had somehow made it concrete, given it a kind of permission to exist. Certainly the hatred had been more open after half London had been to see the play performed.

Then there had been the riot in Southwark. Although the ostensible cause was the brutal arrest of the apprentice, it had been more than that – a manifestation of this growing restlessness and anger which had begun to contaminate the citizens of London. Hunger, poverty, resentment of authority, and belief that foreigners were stealing the jobs of Englishmen – all this had fuelled the riot, and other more minor disturbances which had followed. The closing of the playhouses might have sent the players out of London – and thus led to my own presence in Rochester – but it could not change the underlying sickness of mind which was tainting London. Insidious as the plague, though concealed from view, surely it would continue to grow until it burst out once more, like an infected boil, spilling its poison and wreaking havoc.

These were uncomfortable thoughts. If I was right, serious trouble lay ahead, and I might find myself in danger, Stranger that I was.

I wondered where Marlowe was at the moment. He had not gone with the players, I was sure. Was he still courting the patronage of Sir Francis's cousin, Thomas Walsingham? He lived in Kent, I knew, but where, I had no idea. Was Marlowe busy writing yet another of his plays which dealt with the dark and evil side of man's nature? Another play which might stir up the citizens of London to worse riots, to killings such as there had been in France, which he had written about in his play, *The Massacre at Paris*? I shivered. Why had I begun to think about Marlowe? He hated me, despised me, taunted my New Christian origins, my Portuguese ancestry. Yet somehow in recent months I had had a sense of him, lingering always on the periphery of thought.

This was not why I had come to the cathedral. I had come for peace, not for such disquieting thoughts. I got up and began to walk about, taking note of my surroundings. The cathedral must be very ancient, I thought. The pillars were huge and heavy, like aged oak trees, supporting rounded arches, probably Norman. Being so old, it had none of the light, airy grace of more recent cathedrals, although there were windows of stained glass, not large, but beautiful. As I walked up the nave toward the choir, the westering sun flooded through the window behind me, casting pools of coloured light on the heavy flagstones, so that I walked through a rainbow of crimson and azure and jade and gold.

The altar was covered with a fine white cloth, heavily embroidered with swirls of gold and green and rose, which seemed to catch up and mirror the colours of the windows. At the moment, only a small altar lamp was lit, a tiny rosy glow, but huge altar candles awaited the next service, standing in exquisite silver candlesticks, twined about with delicate vine leaves. It would be time for the evening service soon, and I was reluctant to stay and find myself caught up amongst a company of strangers. I walked back down the nave, and let myself out through the massive oak door. Rikki jumped up to greet me, as relieved as if I had been gone for hours. Together we made our way back to the inn under evening gilded clouds.

I checked on Hector, who was content and seemed well cared for by the elderly stableman and his boy. It would be time for whatever evening meal the inn would serve, then I would go early to bed, for an early start on the morrow.

The next day was something of a repeat of the previous one, save that I was stiff, having been little in the saddle for weeks past. I had bought a leather jack of ale from the inn to carry with me, so that I need not find another inn or an ale house for a midday meal, for I still had the food I had carried with me. The weather continued fine and the ride along the grass verges was easy for both Hector, and for Rikki running alongside. On either side of Watling Street there were fields of stubble, and, in a few, the last of the harvest was being brought in.

A short while before the sun reached its zenith, I found a pleasant small meadow near the road, with a clear stream running about its edge in a gentle curve, so I decided that we would have our dinner here. I let Hector drink, then left him to graze while Rikki and I shared the cold mutton collops and the last of the eggs. I lay back on the grass for a time, but did not sleep, for I did not want those riding muscles to stiffen any further, and besides I was anxious to reach Canterbury and find the players.

After less than an hour, judging by the sun, we were on our way again. From London to Rochester the road had been quite busy, much of the traffic going to and from the docks on the Medway. On this stretch of the road, between Rochester and Canterbury, it was quieter, although as I neared that most holy of cities I was aware of more people on the road, many on foot, some on horseback. There were the usual farm carts carrying produce to the town markets, but I noticed a few carts which carried not barrels and bales, but people, some lying down, some leaning against the supporting arms of friends.

Pilgrimages had been banned ever since the great iconoclasm in King Henry's time, when the relics of saints were looted not only from the abbeys and monasteries as they were pulled down, but also from the great churches and cathedrals which were allowed by the king and his commissioners to survive. Even Canterbury Cathedral, where Christianity was brought to Kent by St Augustine, even Canterbury was plundered. I have heard that the shrine of St Thomas à Becket was formerly a most wondrous sight, a thing of gold and precious jewels, but all was robbed to fill the king's coffers, in order to finance his disastrous wars in France. Though, of course, one may not speak of such things.

For centuries the halt, the lame, the blind, the barren, the incurably sick had walked, limped, or been carried to beg the saint's help in their need. But no longer. Or at any rate, not legally. Yet here I could see about me the very signs of such pilgrims. When I was living in the Lopez house, after returning from Portugal only to find my father dead, my home gone, and myself penniless, I had taken advantage of Sara's collection of books to read beyond my normal fare of medical treatises. One book I had enjoyed – and read more than once – was Master Chaucer's stories of the pilgrims riding together along this very road to

Canterbury. The language of the book was somewhat old-fashioned, but that did not take away the pleasure of such a variety of tales, from the lewd and comical to the high and heroic. Such a band of pilgrims would never be seen today, yet I had a feeling that many of those I now saw heading for Canterbury would be making their way to the cathedral, and quietly sending up a prayer for help, not only to Our Lord Himself, but to St Thomas.

The crowd on the road thickened as we reached Canterbury, the cathedral soaring clearly into view above the town walls as we approached. The road led over a drawbridge, crossing what might have been either a river or a moat, though I suspected by the movement in the water that it was a river. The very town seemed like a fortified castle. Then we passed in through a massive gateway, the West Gate, protected by two vast circular towers, as imposing as the entrance to the Tower of London itself. On our right hand, just within the gate, stood a church.

'That is the Church of the Holy Cross. It was built to replace the one which once stood above the gateway.'

We had been brought to a standstill, crushed together by the crowd, and another horseman was pressed up close beside me. By his appearance, he was a prosperous merchant, not one of the surreptitious pilgrims, clad in a peasecod doublet of fine scarlet wool, with a scrolling pattern of silk threads running through it, above full breeches of dark blue. His cloak, thrown back over his shoulders on this fine sunny day, was fur lined. He must have noticed me looking about with the air of a stranger to the town.

'You are of Canterbury?' I enquired politely.

'Nay.' He beamed at me. 'I am of the Drapers Guild in London, but I come once a year to the cathedral.'

So, perhaps he was a pilgrim after all. I judged it politic not to ask. However, if he knew the town . . .

'Can you tell me where to find the Guildhall?' I asked. Simon had said in his letter that they would be performing there.

143

'The corner of High Street and Guildhall Street. You cannot mistake it. A fine building. Timber framed, with flint walls.'

'I thank you, sir.'

The pressure eased and the crowd began to move forward. Mindful that it was still too early for the players to have finished their performance, I thought to ask about an inn.

'I have heard that there is an inn here in Canterbury with a curious name. The Chequer of Hope? Have I it right?'

I knew that this was the inn where Master Chaucer's pilgrims had stayed some two hundred years ago, but I did not know whether it was real, or whether he had invented it. I hoped I would not be taken for a fool, but the merchant simply smiled and nodded.

'Aye, on the corner of the High Street and Mercery Lane. Best inn in Canterbury. I am on the way there myself. Stay with me – if you can, in this throng – and I will take you there.'

It was fortunate that my new acquaintance wore a large black velvet hat, adorned with a swan's plume, and sat high on his horse, or I might have lost him. As it was I reached the inn shortly behind him, and identified it by its sign, a barrel top painted with a board chequered in black and red. I have heard that the name Chequer of Hope is a corruption of Chequer of Hoop, referring to the practice in past times of using a painted barrel (the 'hoop') as an accounting board. Nowadays we are more sophisticated, and do our accounting in ledgers, though I believe some merchants, and indeed royal clerks, still prefer to count out their coins on chequer boards.

The inn was mightily impressive, every bit as fine as the best of the London inns. It was a full three stories, the upper floors jettied out over the elegantly arcaded ground floor. Its frontage on the High Street gave some idea of its massive size, while down the narrow lane at the side it was impossible to see how far it reached. The merchant and I rode in through an arch wide enough and high enough to accommodate the largest carriage, into a large galleried central court. Ahead of us was another party, consisting of several ladies and gentlemen who were clearly gentry, accompanied by their attendants and servants. I thought we should be kept waiting while they received all the attention of the inn's servants, but it seemed the merchant was well known here. A stableman hurried forward to take our horses as we dismounted.

'Master Durham,' he said, 'it is good to see you again.' He looked at me. 'And your companion?'

'I am afraid we have just met,' I said. 'I am Dr Christoval Alvarez, of the Royal College of Physicians.'

In circumstances such as these, I have found it is wise to establish my credentials at the outset.

'Forgive me,' the merchant said, bowing, 'we have been too much pressed by the crowds. I am Alexander Durham, of the Drapers Company, as I mentioned. At your service, doctor.'

'At yours, sir.' I returned his bow.

These niceties over, there was all the business of securing a room and stabling. Despite the large party ahead of us, and the busyness of the inn servants rushing to and fro, it appeared that the Chequer of Hope had ample space. I was able to secure a chamber to myself and a stall for Hector, seeing to his needs, as I always preferred to do, on my own account. No one demurred when I took Rikki into the inn with me, for he was not the only dog, one of the gentlemen in the large party having a greyhound with him, while a lady in the same group carried a pet squirrel with a gold collar and chain.

A maid servant showed me to my chamber, leading me first up stairs to the first floor, then along one of the galleries overlooking the inn courtyard. My chamber opened off the gallery, having one window facing on to the gallery and one window in the outer wall of the inn, giving a view into a narrow street of houses, not Mercer Lane, but on the other side of the inn.

145

I had barely shaken out the clothes from my knapsack before the girl returned with a jug of hot water and a towel, which she set down beside a bowl on a small table standing against the outside wall. When I thanked her, she smiled, curtseyed, and hurried away to attend to other guests. I had not been so well cared for at an inn since I had stayed in Amsterdam. It was a pleasure to wash in clean water after a warm day's riding.

'Well, Rikki lad,' I said, easing off my boots and wriggling my toes. 'We are well provided here. I reckon the players must be near finished their performance now. Shall we go and surprise them?'

Master Durham had pointed out the way to the Guildhall to me as we turned in through the archway of the Chequer of Hope, both inn and Guildhall lying close together, centrally on the High Street. I walked the few yards to the Guildhall quickly, and found a crowd of prosperous burgesses and their wives just emerging, so the play must be over. I stood aside to let them pass, then made way inside, following the sound of voices to what must be the central hall, where meetings would be held, and which Lord Strange's Men would have adapted temporarily for their purposes. Slipping through the door, I found a place to stand in the shadows near the wall, and watched the familiar bustle that ended a performance. As usual Guy was tenderly returning his instruments to their cases and Davy was turning handstands across the width of the room until chased back by Cuthbert to help with the packing up of the properties. From what I could see, they had been playing *A Knack to Know a Knave* and I groaned inwardly, hoping that they might be playing something better the next day, for Saturday would be the only chance I would have of seeing a play, before starting back for London on Monday.

Dick Burbage and Simon stepped down from the mayor's dais, which they had been using as a stage, the two of them deep in earnest discussion. Dick was gesturing in his usual flamboyant way as he held forth, while Simon had his head bent, looking serious and interjecting a few words from time to time. It was curious – for a moment I saw him almost as a stranger might see him. He was a man now, nearly three and twenty, yet somehow I had still been thinking of him as the wind-blown boy of sixteen who had first come to fetch me to the Marshalsea from the old cottage in Duck Lane.

Where had all those years gone? I found I was suddenly afraid. He was of an age to marry now. Will was married, with children back in Warwickshire. Ned Alleyn, joining their discussion now, was married to Master Henslowe's daughter. There was talk of a betrothal for Cuthbert. What if Simon should join this rush to the church door? I felt cold, and shivered, as though a bitter wind, carrying news of the future, had blown across my life. If only time could be made to cease. Let us grow no older, but stay just as we are now. Break the hourglasses. Stop all the clocks. Ring no more bells to mark the passing hours.

It was Guy who saw me first, and came bounded across the hall.

'Behold, a vision!' he cried. 'Kit Alvarez, by all that is remarkable! What are you doing in Canterbury?'

I had no time to answer before they were all crowding around me, shaking my hand, thumping me on the back, exclaiming their surprise with all the drama of a wondrous revelation in one of their plays.

When at last I could insert a few words of my own, I said, 'Superintendent Ailmer has instructed me to take a week's holiday. Hector was growing fat and lazy in the Seething Lane stable, and Rikki and I were growing fat and lazy in Southwark. As you were not far away, I decided to ride over to Canterbury to see you, before you are off on your further travels.'

More talk, more explanations, as we moved in a body out of the Guildhall, Rikki following, his tail sweeping the air in his pleasure at encountering so many friends.

'There's an tavern three doors along,' Dick said, leading the way. 'Very good beer, made with Kentish hops, better than anything you will taste in London.'

'You do not look fat and lazy to me,' Guy said quietly, under cover of the general talk. 'You look ill. What is the true story?'

'It has been bad in London,' I said, 'though the plague is dying away now. And we have had a minor epidemic of the mumps.'

I gave him a brief account of the children marked as plague victims.

'And you have been overworked because of it,' he said. 'What is the truth about Superintendent Ailmer? He would not lightly grant one of his physicians a week's holiday.'

'I was stupid enough to faint,' I mumbled. 'Mistress Maynard found me, then Master Ailmer.'

'I thought you looked ill.'

I shook my head. 'I was only tired. I had been missing meals and not getting enough sleep. Already I am better. Nearly two days out of the fug of London, and I am new made. They've been burning tar against the plague.'

He wrinkled his nose, making him look more like a monkey than ever.

'I am no physician,' he said, 'but in my opinion, the smoke from those braziers is more like to kill men than save them.'

'Aye.' I smiled. 'You probably have the right of it. I have never seen that it does any good.' I looked around the crowd of men and boys as we jostled into the tavern. 'Is Will not with you?'

'He was for a time, but he said that all the travelling made it difficult for him to write. He has some great poem in mind, that he wants to write now he has finished the three Harry Six plays. He's gone off to find himself a noble patron for his poetry. Thought he'd try dancing attendance on the Earl of Southampton for a start. An elegant young man, it seems, with a taste for painting and poetry.' His tone was amused, and slightly sarcastic.

I was alarmed. Will's plays were proving some of the company's most popular.

'Does he mean to write no more plays?'

'Oh, aye. Once we are back in London, when the playhouses are allowed to reopen at the end of September. He has promised us something new for then, once he has written this great epic poem of his. He longs for reputation and immortality, does Will, which he says he will never get through his plays – here this day, forgotten next year.'

'Kit!' Simon seized me by the arm. 'Why do you and Guy stand here, blocking the door and gossiping? Come and try this beer. You have never tasted its like.'

He threw an arm about my shoulders and drew me into the crowded room, where Cuthbert had commandeered three tables and was summoning the ale wife. I smiled, and went with him willingly.

Chapter Eight

The Kentish beer was excellent and flavoursome, but I drank of it sparingly. I am always careful how much I drink, even of the mildest of small ale, such as is fit for children, for I fear that my tongue may be loosened, and words which must be kept locked away inside my head and heart may spill out, to my great danger. So I sipped at my tankard of beer, and listened to the usual exuberant exchanges that always followed a successful performance, until, plied with questions myself, I gave an account of how matters stood in London.

'You are well away from it, these last months,' I said. 'What with the heat and the plague.' I paused, unsure how to frame the indistinct unease that had been troubling me for weeks, even as far back as the riot in Southwark.

'There is a bad feeling abroad,' I said at last. 'You remember the troubles back in June?'

'How could we forget, Kit?' Christopher Haigh gave me a rueful smile. 'Otherwise, I should be back in my comfortable new lodgings, not forced to move on from one flea invested inn to another, every few weeks. And I'll not forget being pelted by that rout of blaggards.'

One missile thrown at Christopher had not seemed to me at the time to constitute being pelted, but I did not correct him.

'The Chequer of Hoop is *not* flea invested,' Cuthbert said, stung. 'I have lodged us in the finest inn outside London.'

Momentarily diverted, I asked Simon, 'You are staying at the Chequer of Hoop?'

'We are.'

'So am I.'

'But what do you mean, Kit?' Ned Alleyn leaned over the table toward me. 'About a bad feeling abroad?'

'Closing down all entertainments in London did nothing to dampen down the causes of the riot,' I said. 'If anything, it has made matters worse, for the people have nothing to take their minds off their troubles, but merely brood on them – their hunger, their poverty. When the plague came and all the noble and rich fled London, the poor who tried to escape were driven back by the country folk. It was as if–' I searched my mind for an analogy. 'They were like helpless beasts herded into a pen in the shambles at Smithfield, helpless to escape death. And if the plague did not kill them, starvation probably would.'

'It has been a good harvest,' Davy suggested hesitantly. Usually he did not join in such discussions, but he was growing up.

'Aye,' I said, 'that's very true, so that if you have a penny, you may buy a penny loaf, and not starve today, but many are without work, and have not even the pennies for bread. And some are in such black despair that if they have the pennies, they will buy oblivion in a jug of ale, rather than go home to their starving children. If they have a home.'

''Tis true,' Cuthbert said. 'There are too many people in London. Too little work. Too little food. Too few houses.'

'A whole row of houses fell down the other day,' I said, 'in a lane off Eastcheap. There were several killed, and some twenty families lost their homes, if you can call a single room in a derelict hovel a home. Because most of the town authorities have departed for the country, nothing has been done about it. The rubble lies in the street, and so do the people.'

'But there has been discontent in London as long as I can remember,' Dick Burbage said. 'Most of my life. There is nothing unusual in that.'

'It grows worse by the day,' I said bluntly. 'And there is far greater outcry against foreigners. Many are convinced that they would have work and wages, were it not for the refugees who have been fleeing the Inquisition, the murderous French Catholics, and the Spanish invaders of the Low Countries. Perhaps my ear is more attuned to it than yours may be, since I am one of those disreputable refugees myself.'

I spoke with more overt bitterness than I had intended. I had not come here to quarrel with the closest friends I had. My words were greeted with an uncomfortable silence.

'No one thinks of you as a refugee, Kit,' Guy said at last. 'You are as English as the rest of us, even Christopher with his Scottish father!'

Everyone laughed at that, even Christopher.

'Forgive me,' I said. 'I did not mean to talk of such unpleasant matters, but you asked about how things are in London. All I will say is this. There is more trouble brewing, I am sure of it. I think there may be more riots than the Southwark one before we are done.'

Cuthbert called for another round of beer before we returned to the inn for supper, and the potboy was just handing out more tankards when the door of the tavern was flung open and a man stood silhouetted there for a moment on the threshold. The way he held his pose, then made his entrance, like a player on the stage, made me think he must be one of the company, but that could not be. Was it Will Shakespeare, returned from seeking a patron for his poetry? The man had his height and build. Then he moved so that the sunlight, flowing through from the door, fell upon his face.

Marlowe! I half started from my seat between Guy and Simon, then sank back again.

'What does Marlowe here?' I muttered to Guy.

'Did you not know?' he said. 'He is Canterbury born, attended the King's School here. I believe he still has family in the town.'

'I thought he was also dancing attendance on a patron,' I said. 'Sir Francis's cousin, Sir Thomas Walsingham.'

'So Marlowe has been, and will, no doubt, again, but Thomas Walsingham holds a manor here in Kent, at Scadbury, though not close. It must be fifty miles from here, but it seems Marlowe comes back here from time to time. He arrived in Canterbury soon after us, and has been talking to Cuthbert about what he will write for the Christmas Revels at Hampton Court. He has a new play, but Cuthbert says it will not do for Christmas, too dark. We shall probably perform it sometime early in the New Year.'

'You are summoned to Court for Christmas?'

'Aye, God and all his saints be praised! We will be fortunate if we come home with much gain from this tour. We have had good audiences, but our lodgings and our hired horses have gobbled up our profits.'

'That is good news about the Christmas Revels, but I am sorry the tour has not made you rich.'

Marlowe pulled out a stool and sat down, uninvited, almost opposite me, frowning. He turned to Cuthbert.

'What is the Jew boy doing here? Are you not afraid you will be tainted by his filthy company?'

I felt my anger rising, and clenched my fists together below the table's edge.

'That is enough, Marlowe,' Ned Alleyn said, mildly enough, but in a tone not to be ignored. 'Kit Alvarez is an old friend of this company, and your insults are not welcome.'

I was grateful for that. I did not know Ned – late of the Admiral's Men – nearly as well as the players of Lord Strange's Men, so I was pleased that he regarded me as a friend.

Marlowe gave a mocking little bow to Ned, but turned on me a look of sneering distaste. However, he held his tongue – for the present.

We did not linger long after that, Marlowe's arrival having cast a feeling of discomfort over the company. Besides, it was time for our supper at the Chequer of Hope. We made our way back to the inn, and when it was time to take our seats at the long table, I contrived to sit well away from Marlowe, down at one end with Simon, Guy, and Dick.

'Is Marlowe staying here as well?' I asked of them.

'Nay,' Dick said. 'He stays with his family, but contrives to eat a free meal with us whenever he can.'

He spoke with some sarcasm, and I wondered whether he too had suffered the sharp edge of Marlowe's tongue. If Marlowe had much influence over the way parts were assigned, I knew that Ned would be given all the great dramatic roles – and indeed he was a very fine actor – but Dick was shaping up to prove just as fine, once he was a little older, and he needed the experience now.

I turned to Guy. 'What do you play tomorrow? I hope to see you once while I am here. We have been quite starved of the playhouses in London.'

'We are trying out a new play of Will's. You will not have seen it, for we have not performed it in London yet.'

'One of the Harry Six plays?'

'Nay, not a history, a comedy. *The Taming of the Shrew.*'

'Is it some sort of slapstick?'

He shook his head. 'Comic, but not foolish. It all depends on the playing of it. I shall not mar it for you by telling any more.'

With that I must needs be content.

I slept well in my comfortable bed chamber, rose late, and spent the early part of the day wandering about Canterbury. As the players were preparing a new play, they spent the time in a final rehearsal, and so I did not see them until I arrived at the Guildhall with all the other citizens of the town come to see this new play.

'Not even played in London yet!' I heard one well-dressed matron exclaim in delight to another. 'So we have stolen the march on those arrogant Londoners.'

I smiled to myself as I wormed my way forward to the last empty seat in the front row. The seats not being raked, it was the best place to see the performance. The dais was small compared to the stage at the Theatre or the Rose, but Simon said they had played in much worse places. He had refused to tell me what part he would play, so I waited in amused anticipation.

One of the boys swaggered on to the stage and held up a placard, on which had been written: *The Taming of the Shrew*. He bowed and withdrew. The play was somewhat confusing at first, as it seemed to be a play within a play, but once we were within the inner play – which was the true story – we soon encountered the two sisters, Katherina and Bianca, the elder headstrong, assertive, and outspoken, the younger seemingly demure, beautiful, and biddable. Numerous suitors vied for the hand of Bianca, but she could not marry (it seemed) until her elder sister was wed, and no man in his right mind wanted Katherina.

The best jest for me appeared at once, and I realised why the players had kept me in the dark. Instead of the young boys playing the two sisters, the lovely Bianca was played by Christopher Haigh (falsetto) and bold Katherina by Simon. As neither had taken women's parts for some years now, this added to the fun. Indeed one of the boys played a suitor, a good six inches shorter than 'Bianca', falling over his sword from time to time.

When the swaggering Petruchio (Ned) swore that he could tame the shrewish Katherina, we knew we were in for some broad comedy, but when he at last succeeds, Katherina's submission scene was played by Simon with a wry subtlety, so that one could not be sure whether 'she' submitted truly or for policy. It was cleverly done. The audience stood to cheer at the end, and I heard more than one portly burgess admiring the taming as the best way to treat women, while the wives on the whole looked at each other with greater wisdom.

We all dined again that evening at the Chequer of Hope, but mercifully Marlowe did not join us, and on Sunday I decided to attend the morning service in the cathedral. I knew that the players would rise even later than usual on their one day of rest, though they would make time to attend one service, as they were required by law. For myself, I rose quietly and took Rikki down to share Hector's stable, then made my way to the great cathedral. I found I had only to walk down the side of the Chequer of Hope, along Mercery Lane, and there directly opposite was the gateway to the cathedral. Others were walking the same way, many of them pilgrims, I was sure, but despite our numbers, we went mostly in silence, passing in through the wide door held open for us by two clerics in snowy surplices.

It is not the same church built all those centuries and centuries ago by St Augustine, which was probably no more than a modest wooden building. It is not even, in truth, the church in which Thomas à Becket was murdered more than four hundred years since. Fire, earthquake, demolition and new building have changed, enlarged, and enhanced it. Yet it holds, cupped within its vast and airy spaces, some essence of holiness I had never felt before. I have known many churches, in Portugal and in England. St Paul's is a mighty church, but it is also a public space, where whores linger, pickpockets roam, and merchants do business. The cathedral I had seen at Rochester, on my way to Canterbury, was a prayer in solid stone, but nothing could compare with this. Slender columns rose far overhead to burst forth, like opening blooms, into the intertwining tracery of fan vaulting, as exquisitely logical as a geometrical solution to some complex God-given problem, yet as delicate as the symmetry of a full blown rose.

The very air vibrated with the numinous.

I made my way forward, circling past the tomb of that great hero, the Black Prince, untimely dead, to come as close to the choir as possible. Many were crowding towards the northwest transept, where once had stood the shrine of St Thomas, stripped and looted by King Henry. Six and twenty carts, it is said, were needed to carry away the spoils.

The sung service lifted my spirits, which had sunk this morning at the thought of returning to London tomorrow, and I made my communion at the altar steps here, thinking that there could be no better place. Marlowe had called me, in his usual insulting manner, 'Jew boy'. I was no boy. Was I a Jew? Returning to my place, with the metallic taste of the communion wine on my tongue, I knelt and prayed, but could not answer my own question. Was there not some compromise, that I might be both Jew and Christian? Or by shirking an honest answer, was I somehow tarnishing both?

At Dick's suggestion, we hired boats on the river in the late morning, taking food with us for a picnic on an island he had discovered when rowing here earlier in the week. It was too small to allow of habitation, or even the grazing of animals, but accommodated our party, which consisted of most of the players, but, I was glad to see, not Marlowe who, so it seemed, had returned to Scadbury. We ate cold pies and sausages, drank more of the Kentish beer, and contrived a scratch games of quoits, before lying about lazily under the half shade of willows, through whose branches the lingering summer sun danced and dazzled.

As we finished our supper that evening at the inn, tired with fresh air and rowing, I said my farewells.

'I must be away early tomorrow,' I said, 'before you idle players leave your beds, for I must ride at least thirty miles, then thirty miles again on Tuesday.'

'It has been good to see you, Kit,' Simon said. He looked as though he might say more, then closed his lips over it.

I turned to Cuthbert. 'When do you return to London?'

'We are permitted to open the playhouses at the end of September,' he said, 'so we should be back in the middle of the month, to make all ready.'

'Not so long, then.'

'Nay, not so long,' Simon echoed, giving me a hug.

Guy did the same, and soon all the players were slapping me on the back, and raising their beer tankards to me, but I would not stay drinking with them. Calling to Rikki, I took myself off to my chamber.

The next morning, I set off on my way back to London.

The matter of Mountjoy's Inn did not arise again until the late summer, when Sara had some surprising news for me.

'We are to take a tour abroad, the whole family, to visit our relatives in Antwerp, Venice, and Constantinople.'

I was astonished. A merchant on business might make such a journey. Or a young nobleman, sent with his tutor to learn a little about the peoples and cultures of other nations, in preparation for service to the Queen as an envoy or an ambassador. Never had I heard of a whole family touring distant lands. Constantinople was many weeks' journey away, and not an easy journey either, from the Low Countries over the Alps to northern Italy and Venice, then by ship across the Adriatic to Ragusa and on by either land or sea to the Ottoman Empire. Not everywhere would be friendly to travellers from England. And some of the children were still quite young.

'The whole family?' I exclaimed. 'Even young Anthony? I thought the Queen had placed him at Winchester at her expense. And can Her Majesty spare Ruy's services?'

'She has been gracious enough to give him leave to go. And, yes, Anthony is to come with us. The Queen believes it will enhance his experience of the world, in case she should wish to make use of his services when he is grown.'

'And all Ruy's other patients?'

'That is what he wishes to discuss with you. He plans to entrust some of them to you until he returns. It could be a great advantage to you, Kit. The Cecils and Essex.'

I looked at her doubtfully, even in shock, remembering Dr Nuñez's reason for not treating the Queen – he had told me more than once that he wished to retain his freedom. For a humble practitioner like myself, without a university degree and not a Fellow of the College, only a licensee, the care of these great men could be just as dangerous.

'I am not sure, Sara. The Cecils *and* Essex? I am too humble a physician for such responsibility.'

She smiled ruefully. 'You must talk to Ruy. And I wondered whether, for the time we are away, you would agree to come and live here at Mountjoy's Inn. You could keep a watch on the servants, and our possessions, and be closer to your City patients.'

'That was your argument before,' I said. 'I am still of the same mind. It is too far away from St Thomas's.'

A number of circumstances changed my mind. Reluctantly, I agreed to tend the Cecils and Essex if they should come to town, a task easier to accept because the plague had already driven them out of London. They were unlikely to return until it abated in the cold weather, and Ruy intended to be back in London by January. Also, Simon had come begging to sleep on the floor of my lodgings. Lord Strange's Men returned to London in late August, shortly before Sara and her family were to leave, in the expectation that the playhouses would reopen at Michaelmas, only to discover that the return of the plague had caused the Privy Council to extend the ban until the end of December, which meant no income for them until any performances they might have over the Christmas season. The Revels at Hampton Court were assured, but would not last beyond Twelfth Night, by which time it would be too cold for performances at the Rose or the Theatre. The players had therefore departed on another tour into the countryside, but Simon had said he would be glad to share the use of my room when they returned. The tour had been successful, but, as I had been told in Canterbury, the expense of lodgings in inns and the hire of horses had meant that the players themselves were not greatly enriched by it.

Simon's old room at the Atkins' house had been taken by a journeyman tailor and his wife, and Simon had fallen out with Kyd (with whom he had once lodged), in some argument over Marlowe. Indeed, to my mind he had somewhat come to his senses, having tired of the sort of company Kyd and Marlowe kept. A dangerous mob, he called them, of young men with sharp wits and good education but no money, who lived on the edge of respectability, sometimes slipping into the criminal world. One or two of their names were familiar to me, the men in this dubious set, as former agents of Walsingham's. Not from the higher ranks like Berden and Phelippes, but slippery, untrustworthy men who might, or might not, betray you.

'And,' said Simon, sitting on the floor of my room in suppliant pose, on the eve of the company's second departure from London, 'we are returned from our tour of the bumpkin towns of England with very little in our purses. I cannot afford to take a lodging of my own, Kit. At any rate unless and until we earn something for our performances at Court over Christmastide.'

I reminded him that without the company's tour of rural England, he would have had no work since June, but he still pleaded poverty. At least, I thought, Marlowe had not travelled with them, tempting Simon into expenses he could not afford.

'Nevertheless,' he said mournfully, 'I must live for the present on the little I have managed to put by during our tour. Even if someone does hire us after Christmas and Twelfth Night, and that is weeks away.'

In the end, I yielded to all their arguments. I said that Simon could live in my lodgings when they returned from this second stage of the tour, at least until the Lopez family returned in January. Ruy agreed to pay the Southwark rent six months in advance, to persuade me to take charge of his home, and so I moved into Mountjoy's Inn, to live like a landed aristocrat, or at any rate a wealthy London merchant. I had little time to enjoy it. To my relief, those great men I might be obliged to physic continued to stay away from London, along with the rest of the Court and the Parliament, although for the most part the poor were still forced to remain in the disease ridden city, and amongst them Death found most of his victims.

As I had pointed out to Sara, the distance from Mountjoy's Inn to St Thomas's was much too far to walk every day. I could not afford to waste so much time. In the end, I decided to bring Hector from the Seething Lane stable to Holborn. Mountjoy's Inn had a well appointed stable, with two stable lads who cared for the riding and carriage horses kept by Ruy Lopez and by the owner of the property, Mistress Allington. She made no objection to my stabling Hector there, and the lads cheerfully took on the care of another horse. Initially they were somewhat rude about Hector's less than handsome piebald appearance, but they soon learned to know him better. I might lodge free at Mountjoy's Inn, but Hector must now be provided for. It seemed there was an abundant supply of hay and oats bought in by Ruy, but when I left Hector at St Thomas's during the day, I was obliged to pay for his keep there, since the hospital never had spare funds to cover the feeding of an extra horse. However, I found I enjoyed riding about London, for these few months at least. It saved me a great deal of time. And indeed it saved on shoe leather.

From time to time, during my brief periods at Mountjoy's Inn in the early mornings and in the evening, I encountered the widow Mary Allington, and after some weeks I noticed that she was growing great with child. She was a very pretty woman – fair-haired and fair-skinned, with small plump hands and a dimple in her left cheek – generally pleasant in her manner to me, though I heard her speak somewhat sharply about Ruy Lopez. Then one day I overheard two of the kitchen maids whispering and giggling beneath my window.

'Why, to be sure, her a widow more than a year now!'

'Aye, it must be a miracle, to carry a babe a twelvemonth and more!'

Until then I had not known how long Mistress Allington had been widowed, and it gave me pause. In the past, there had sometimes been whispers about Ruy's very winning ways with women. Some said he was over familiar with certain of his female patients. Sara had never complained of him to me, but a wife will often choose to be blind to truths about her husband that she would rather not know. I began to wonder whether Ruy's journey across Europe might have some other cause than the pleasant duty of visiting family. Did he wish to avoid a confrontation here at Mountjoy's Inn? Then after I had been living there some weeks, I learned from one of Sara's servants that the midwife had been called to Mary Allington, who was delivered of a healthy boy. On the twentieth day of that month, the child was christened Richard Allington at the church of St Thomas's, Holborn.

I gave the matter no further thought – whether the child was Ruy's or some other man's was no concern of mine – until an evening a week or so later when I returned from the hospital about dusk. I stabled Hector, gave him a feed of oats, then walked out of the stableyard and round to the front door of the house. One of the servants had already hung a candle lantern beside it, for it had been overcast all this autumn day and by now it was growing dark. In the dim light I could just make out on the doorstep a large round basket, like the ones the baker's boy used. Wondering why it had been left here, instead of at the kitchen door for the cook, I peered at the bundled cloth inside, which stirred a little of itself.

'A rat!' I said to myself. 'Little wonder, if the baker leaves the bread here unattended.'

At that, the bundle moved again, and gave out a faint mew like a kitten, but I knew from long experience that the cry was not that of a kitten. Carefully, I folded back the cloth to reveal a very young baby boy, healthy and none the worse for his time outside on the doorstep of Mountjoy's Inn, although by now he must be growing cold. He was dark haired, of a slightly swarthy colouring, and his black eyes looked up at me in that unfocused way of the newborn. I picked up the basket and carried it indoors to Sara's private parlour, where the maid had a fire burning for me. In the brighter light cast by half a dozen candles – the Lopez family were extravagant with wax tapers – I saw that there was a piece of paper pinned to the child's swaddling blanket. I unpinned it and carried it to the nearest candle. The message was clearly written in a bold but feminine hand:

Señor Lopez, here I come,
Open the gate and take in thy son.
Thy Spanish creed I will not disgrace,
Behold the image of thy face.

I sat abruptly back in my chair. This was a curious course of action for Widow Allington to take, for this must certainly be her newborn son. She knew I was in charge of the household, in the absence of the family. Why was the note addressed to Señor Lopez? Did she hope thus to make a public scandal? She had already gone boldly to church for the child's christening, when everyone knew her husband had been dead for more than a year. A lusty widow indeed! I looked with pity at the child, whose attention had been caught by the sparkle of the candle flames. What would become of him, who was innocent in all this? At least the widow had money enough, and had not sent him at once as a foundling to Christ's Hospital. Or did she mean, by thus depositing him on my doorstep, to abandon him? Perhaps she thought, with my connections to Christ's Hospital, that I would take him there.

That did not square with the note, which seemed to shift responsibility for the baby on to Ruy Lopez's shoulders, even though he was now far away, perhaps even as far as Constantinople. I had no doubt that the child was Richard Allington, and from his looks, he could indeed be Ruy's son, despite the doctor's advancing years. The note was dangerous, with its reference to 'Thy Spanish creed'. The English cannot always distinguish between Spanish and Portuguese, but it was clear what was meant here – you are a Portingall, a secret Jew, and I can inform on you whenever I choose. In the hostility which had been growing all year, from the first performance of Marlowe's *The Jew of Malta* and the Southwark riot onwards, there was danger in being pointed out as a Jewish Portingall – for me, despite my secure position at St Thomas's, and for Ruy and his family, despite his elevated position as principal physician to the Queen, and his current absence abroad.

I took paper and ink and wrote the following note:
Mistress Allington, you well know that the family of Dr Roderigo Lopez is at present in Venice, while I am lodging in the house. This infant is in need of his mother's care. I found him in the cold on the doorstep, and rain threatening. I cannot believe you would wish your son to perish thus, so I return him to where he belongs.
Dr Christoval Alvarez

I folded the letter and placed it beside the baby in the basket. Then I sent for the housekeeper, the oldest and most sensible of the Lopez female servants, and instructed her to take the baby round to Mistress Allington's wing of the house. As she gathered up the child, I saw her eye fall upon the note which had been pinned to the blanket and which I had forgotten to conceal. I cursed myself for my carelessness. The contents would be known to all the servants by bedtime, and to all the neighbours before the next day was out.

Sara, Ruy, and the children were due to arrive back in England in January, which promised to be as cold and wretched as the previous year, and in my turn I was preparing to return, with considerable relief, to my lodgings in Southwark. I had lived royally at Mountjoy's Inn, waited upon by the servants, eating the finest food and sleeping between crisp linen sheets, but in the years since I had left Coimbra I had grown unaccustomed to such a life. My simple room, my cot bed with its rough blankets, my meals of bread and cheese taken at home, or a threepenny meal at an ordinary – these were more than enough for me. As winter drew in, I began to long for them, despite the ample fires and rich food of Mountjoy's Inn. I had heard nothing from Mistress Allington in response to my letter, and by now the existence of Richard Allington (or Lopez) was whispered throughout London.

Since Lord Strange's Men had been booked for the Christmas season to perform at Hampton Court Palace, I had hopes that Simon would now find fresh lodgings when they returned shortly to London, so that I could reclaim my room in Southwark as soon as the Lopez family reached London. The closure of the playhouses had been extended to the twenty-ninth of December, a cynical date, for no playhouse could open then, as both Privy Council and Common Council knew very well. It meant they would remain closed until spring. However, a profitable season performing at Court, together with whatever he had earned during this second phase of the country tour, should mean that Simon would be able to afford lodgings of his own. Much as I loved his company, sharing a room with him was fraught with difficulty, which I could imagine becoming even more difficult in winter weather.

I debated long over what I should do about the note from Mary Allington, accusing Ruy of being the baby's father. During the ensuing weeks I had seen the child from time to time in the arms of his nurse, as they came and went by the door leading to the separate wing. As far as I could tell, he was well, and not neglected. Two courses seemed open to me. I could tell Ruy about the baby left on the doorstep with a note attached, and leave it to his sense of honour, or lack of it, to inform his wife. Or I could tell Sara myself. I did not feel I could ignore the matter entirely, nor did I want to be the one to hurt her, but she was sure to hear of it soon enough from the servants or tattling neighbours. The story continued to spread round London in the family's absence, or at least amongst the Marranos and the intelligence community.

Although I now had no formal connection with the intelligence service, from time to time I met Arthur Gregory, who I had long regarded as a friend, taking dinner with him sometimes at an ordinary, and hearing the gossip of what was afoot in Phelippes's service with Essex and the Bacon brothers, an organisation where Arthur was not altogether happy. I had learned from him that Francis and Anthony Bacon were using the scandal of the Allington baby to damage Ruy's reputation, either from jealousy at his position and power, or because they hoped to elevate their intelligence network by undermining that of the Cecils, since, according to Arthur, Ruy had definitely thrown in his lot with Lord Burghley and his son. I wondered whether the journey across Europe to Constantinople was intended to serve some secret purpose for them, under the cover of family visits. This covert battle between Essex and Sir Robert Cecil, carried out in this case through their rival intelligence services, was part of a much wider struggle between the two men. Both factions were striving to win the trust of the Queen and the Privy Council. The prize would be the position of chief advisor to Her Majesty. Only time would tell which would triumph. On the basis of Walsingham's belief that knowledge is power – and my own belief that Essex was ill equipped to deploy it – my money was on Sir Robert Cecil. Despised by Essex for his small stature and weak constitution (resulting from some childhood illness), he possessed a powerful mind beyond anything Essex could match.

When Lord Strange's Men returned just before Christmas, I felt that my life was near to returning to normal and at the same time growing warmer and more colourful than it had ever been during those long months living in solitary and lonely state at Mountjoy's Inn.

'And do you find yourself quite comfortable, here in my room,' I said, looking about the familiar space, which was now full of Simon's usual clutter. I felt an ache, thinking I should have to leave it and ride through the dark streets all the way back to Holborn.

'Aye, and I thank you, Kit,' he said, sitting down on my bed and stroking Rikki, who had assumed, quite naturally, that it was his right to jump up there.

I went to the window and looked out at the familiar view. On the other side of the river the City sparkled with candlelit windows, those nearest to the Thames reflected in the dark mirror of the waters. Wherries plied back and forth, their canvas tilts lit by lanterns within, while the lanterns hung in each stern – by law – gave them the appearance of some kind of exotic insect darting about on the surface. Watching them, I longed to come home.

'I'll not be here for long,' Simon said behind me, as if he could read my thoughts. 'I have had speech with the family who are now living in my room.'

I turned around and he pointed to the floor beneath my feet.

'He has been doing better business of late, since the plague abated. The room is really too small for a family. They have found lodgings of three rooms on the ground floor of a house over beyond St Olave's. It comes free some time in January. I have already arranged with Goodwife Atkins to take the room again. And that will be when Sara returns, will it not?

'Aye, some time in January. I do not begrudge you the room, Simon,' I said, perching on a stool and poking the fire. 'It is just that I want to come home. So does Rikki.'

We both looked at the dog and laughed, for he was stretched out luxuriously, his nose on his paws and taking up most of the room on the bed.

'I must be going,' I said reluctantly. 'I cannot leave Hector tied up down there in the street for long. It is too cold.'

'You covered him with a horse blanket, I saw you do it.' He got up from the bed and went over to my hanging food cupboard. 'I was going to make some spiced wine. Stay to drink some before you go. It will keep out the cold.'

'Very well, if you can make it quickly. Are those my spices?'

'Aye.' He grinned at me. 'I'll replace them.'

He poured a small pottery flagon of red wine into my saucepan, added my spices, one of my bay leaves, and a strip of my dried orange peel, and set it to warm by the fire. The wine, at least, was his. I love the scent of spiced wine heating. It makes me think of sitting safe by the fire when snow is falling outside.

And not having to ride across London to Holborn in the dark and the cold.

When it was ready, I cupped my hands around the mug and carried it over to the window.

'It is starting to snow again,' I said.

'Stay here, then.'

'I can't. Hector needs a warm stable for the night.'

I drank my wine as soon as it was bearable, and felt it coursing through my body, bringing comfort. Setting down my cup, I donned my cloak and pulled up the hood.

'I will leave Rikki with you, though,' I said. 'No need for him to trail all that way in the snow.'

'He's welcome to stay.'

Seeing me about to leave, Rikki raised his head, but I signalled to him to remain where he was, and made my way down the dark stairs to the street. Hector was clearly relieved to see me, blowing anxiously into my ear as I stripped off his blanket, rolled it up, and strapped it behind the saddle. I buckled my medicine satchel into the saddle

168

bag and swung myself up on to his back, using the bottom step to give me some height.

Simon was at the lighted window and gave me a wave, then I set off to ride across London to Holborn in the dark and the cold, with a grand but lonely house waiting for me at the end of it.

Chapter Nine

The following week Guy and I were sitting in the tiring room at the Rose, while a great bustle went on around us. Goodwife Blakely, who sewed and cared for the company's costumes, was kneeling in front of Simon, pinning a hem, for he was to play Katherina again. Until now, *The Shrew* had made do with costumes from other plays, but for the Queen's Christmas Revels the entire play was to be dressed anew. The girl helping Goodwife Blakely was attempting to fit a bodice and skirt on Davy (maidservant), who was incapable of standing still. Tempers would be lost soon.

In answer to the proposal Guy had just made, I shook my head with a laugh.

'Nay, I am not one of you players. Just that once I appeared with you at Whitehall Palace, but it was merely cover. You know that I was there precisely on Walsingham's orders, after we had word there would be an attempt on the Queen. This is no such case now.'

Inwardly, I pondered why it was that everyone seemed bent on making of me something other than what I wanted for myself. Walsingham and Phelippes had made of me a code-breaker, forger, and spy. Guy wanted me to play the lute like one of the players who were to be performing at Hampton Court Palace. Even Sara wanted me to live in the luxury of Mountjoy's Inn, and (sometime soon) to cast off my male disguise and become a woman again. A woman, as I had pointed out to her numerous times, without fortune or employment.

While all I wanted to be was a physician.

I had been trained up to it by my father from childhood. I had studied all the modern Arab medical texts I could lay my hands on. I had worked as an assistant in St Bartholomew's from the age of fourteen. I had passed the examinations of the Royal College of Physicians, so that I was now fully licensed and in charge of two wards at St Thomas's. I had reached a position which would never have been open to me as a woman, and I was happy in it.

Very well, I would assist Phelippes if his need was urgent, as long as I could keep my distance from my lord of Essex. If I must work in the intelligence service, I would have preferred Sir Robert Cecil, had Poley not been in his employ. But there was no need, *certainly* no need, for me to play lute duets with Guy at this coming Christmastide.

'Nay, Guy, I will not,' I said firmly. 'And in any case, why should you want me? All of you can play some instrument or other. Are you not training up Davy, since he is your apprentice?'

'Aye, he does well enough,' Guy said, 'but he is not as skilled as you. Nay, do not shake your head at me, Kit. That is false modesty, and you know it. Your skill on the lute is excellent. 'Twould be even better, were you to practice.'

'And how might that be, since I no longer have a lute of my own?'

'You may borrow one of mine whenever you wish. Besides, for the Revels I want to use Davy as a singer. His voice is still very pure, but we cannot tell how soon it may deepen.'

'But what of the others? Surely one of them–'

He shook his head. 'All needed for the play. We are to perform *The Taming of the Shrew* for the Queen and Will has enlarged it, to make a greater show. Every man-jack of us is needed, some to play more than one part, with all the costume changes that will involve. We are to have

171

musical interludes, the Master of Ceremonies has requested them, and a request from Master Tilney is an order. Then a fine complex dance at the end. Also an order.'

'You are honoured,' I said. 'A play. Musical interludes. *And* a dance.'

'Let me show you the music at least,' Guy said persuasively. He drew a sheaf of papers out of his satchel and laid it on the box standing on the floor between us. I recognised it as the box which contained a ready prepared turban, which was unlikely to be needed for *The Shrew*.

I picked up the top sheet. 'Something you have written yourself?' I recognised his hand.

'Aye. At the heart of it is an old folk tune, which I hope Her Majesty will recognise, but I have sported with it, turning it this way and that, the two lutes passing the tune and its variations back and forth between them.'

He picked up his lute and began to play the part for the first instrument.

'Nay.' He stopped. 'It needs the other.' He reached behind his stool and – not entirely to my surprise – produced another lute. 'Do you favour me this once. Try the other part with me.'

I laughed, knowing full well what he was doing.

'Very well, I should like to see what you have done with it.'

I had recognised the underlying folk tune, but Guy is a clever composer. It would be entertaining to try it out. I tuned the lute to match his.

'I am but trying it, Guy. This is no promise.'

We set to. It was quite complicated, but we had played together often before, just for our own amusement, and apart from one or two stumbles we reached the end successfully.

'It is truly lovely, Guy,' I said, laying down my lute carefully. 'I am sure the Queen will be pleased.'

Some of the players had come over to listen to us, including Simon, who had surrendered his costume to Goodwife Blakely.

'I recall,' I said to him, 'when you could not wait to give up playing women. Why are you eager for Katherina?'

'Ah, he said, sitting cross legged at our feet. 'Katherina is quite another matter. No simpering maid, Katherina. A part to get your teeth into.'

'Also, I thought you had no taste for comedy,' I continued with mock astonishment, as Guy returned both lutes to their cases. Guy grinned at me. When younger, Simon had chafed at playing comedy with Guy, pining for the great dramatic roles which were now generally given to Ned Alleyn or Dick Burbage. I think he had come to realise that he could have a more satisfactory life as an actor if he was prepared to play a wide variety of parts.

'Once again, I cry you, this is not some stupid old farce like *Friar Bungay*,' he said. 'Aye, there is some knockabout, but Will always has something more subtle to say.'

'Very true,' I said, remembering when I had watched *The Shrew* in Canterbury. 'You think at first that Katherina is all bad, a shrew indeed, while Bianca is sweet and good. But in fact Bianca is somewhat of a sly minx, not a true angel at all, though she would have you think so. Katherina is clever and independent. She will not be ruled by men. When she is "tamed", she is merely playing them at their own game.'

'Exactly. And Petruchio, while making much of her untameable shrewishness, recognises her quality. She is ten times worth her sister Bianca. At least, that is how we play it, and Will seems content enough with us.'

'The Queen,' I said, 'being herself a woman of strong, independent mind, will appreciate your Katherina, I fancy.'

'We can only hope so. And are you to join us in the Christmas Revels?'

I shook my head.

Guy sighed lustily, then dropped to his knees in front of me, raised his clasped hands in suppliant fashion. 'I beg of you, Dr Alvarez, do us this honour!'

Copying him, Simon rolled over on to his knees, turned his eyes heavenwards, and said, 'We beseech you!'

'No need to play the fool,' I said, not sure whether to be exasperated or amused at their antics.

Simon dropped his prayerful pose and said, 'Have you ever been to Hampton Court, Kit?'

'I have not.'

'Ah,' he gave a cunning smile. 'Then you have not seen the astronomical clock.'

'There is an astronomical clock?'

'There is,' Guy said, getting to his feet and dusting his knees. 'A very fine clock installed in King Henry's time, after he had relieved Cardinal Wolsey of the tiresome burden of maintaining a palace better suited to a king.'

Unconsciously, I looked over my shoulder. It was always wise to curb one's tongue when speaking ill of the Tudor royal family. Except, of course, the Queen's elder sister Mary, soundly hated by most Englishmen.

'I have heard tell of astronomical clocks,' I said wistfully. 'There is a famous one, I know, in Prague. I did not realise that we had one here in England.'

Ned Alleyn had been listening to the lute duet and now joined the conversation.

'Not so decorated, I believe, as the one in Prague, but interesting and a magnificent scientific achievement all the same. You are interested in such devices, are you not, Kit?'

'Aye,' I admitted warily.

'Then why not come with us? The Great Hall, where we shall perform, is magnificent, lined with a famous series of tapestries also commissioned by King Henry. It is a privilege to be asked to perform there. You may never have another chance to see it.'

They were all aligned against me. And, truth to tell, it was tempting. I have seen many tapestries in my life, but a special royal commission might be remarkable. And the thought of the astronomical clock was the greatest temptation of all. I loved the thought that such clocks told not only hours and days, but the phases of the moon and

174

movement of the stars. It was surprising that Thomas Harriot had never mentioned the Hampton Court clock to me, but perhaps to him it was such common knowledge that he thought I already knew of it.

I glanced around at them – Guy looking hopeful, Ned expectant, and Simon, now sitting back on his heels, clearly aware of my wavering.

'Oh, very well,' I said. 'But I must sit near out of sight. The Queen never forgets a face, and she knows mine. She might well not approve of a licensed physician disporting amongst a band of vagabond players.'

Ned laughed. Simon stood up and punched me on the back. And Guy gathered up his music, smiling quietly to himself. I had been manoeuvred into this, as I very well knew.

So it was that on the Eve of Christmas I travelled to Richmond with Lord Strange's Men. I had left Rikki with Tom and Swifty, for I feared he might not be welcome in a palace. At first I had thought I would ride Hector there, but Master Burbage had hired one of the comfortable barges, designed for large parties, to convey us by river to Hampton Court, which lies on the Thames, about twelve miles or more from London. It was rowed by a dozen men, six to a side, while we were accommodated in a cabin with cushioned benches and a central table. I am certain that the royal barges, and those of the great nobles, are more luxurious, but this was very well furnished. Master Burbage had also arranged for a dinner to be provided by the cook at the Lion, and served by two of their men, so instead of a cold ride on horseback, I enjoyed a dinner kept hot on portable braziers, while relaxing amongst embroidered cushions and watching the snowy banks of the Thames gliding slowly by.

There had been some fear that ice on the river might make the journey difficult, but in the event there was little enough that it caused us no problem. When Christopher Haigh seemed nervous at the thought of ice floes on the river, I recounted my journeys in Muscovy, when the rivers froze solid. He had heard it all before, but nevertheless gaped at the wonder of travel in winter bound Muscovy, when even the frozen rivers are used as highways.

The excellent dinner helped to pass what might have been a tedious time, and after the servants had cleared away the remains, we sat back in comfort, while on Master Burbage's instructions the leftovers were given to the oarsmen, who took it in turn to row and eat. This may have slowed our progress somewhat, but in Heaven's name those men deserved it, for it was hard work rowing that great barge all that way against the flow of the river and the occasional encounter with floating islands of ice.

The arrangement was that the players would perform *The Shrew* after dinner on Christmas Day, perfect timing, for the Court should be in an excellent mood after wining and dining at one of the most sumptuous feasts of the year. Provided they had not wined too well. There would be so many courses that the dinner would continue for hours, and as it would also be held in the Great Hall, there would be a delay while the tables and dishes were removed and the seating set up. The play would then be performed on the royal dais, while the Queen would sit enthroned immediately in front of it. Too close, I thought, though I planned to sit at the side of the dais, as much hidden by Guy as possible. When playing the lute it is perfectly natural to bow over the instrument, which would partially hide my face.

Perhaps I was making too much of being recognised by the Queen, but she was famed for her memory. I could not rid myself of my own memory of the time I had been received by her at Richmond Palace, after my service in the Low Countries. I had been certain then that she had recognised me for a girl. Everyone who had to do with her spoke about her ability to judge people quickly and shrewdly at first glance, so it was not surprising that I had recognised in her eyes an awareness of who and what I really was. I had been in her company once more, that time in Whitehall Palace, when she had addressed me by name, so I knew she had not forgotten me.

Staring out as the river curved round a bend, listening with half an ear to Simon and Ned practising their lines, I decided that I was foolish to think that the Queen would even bother to notice me, or even care if she did. There were far more important things to occupy her mind – the unceasing state of war with Spain abroad, the uneasy atmosphere amongst the citizens of London, and the struggle for power between Essex and the Cecils.

Lord Burghley was her oldest and dearest advisor, who in her youth must have taken the place of her brutish father. An unnatural father who had rejected his gifted daughter, declaring her a bastard when he tired of her mother. A father who had executed her mother. What a tragic childhood, in spite of her royal blood. The Queen had leaned upon William Cecil since girlhood. I did not know what she thought of his son, but by all accounts Sir Robert Cecil had inherited his father's intellect and shrewd judgement, and she would value that.

On the other hand, Essex was her pet, handsome and richly dressed, risen to the position of favourite after the death of his stepfather Leicester four years ago. It was common knowledge that he wooed her and flattered her, under the pretence that she was still a young girl. I suppose she feared age and death, and he could help her forget, for a while, that time was passing and both were drawing near. No doubt he did not display in her presence the idiotic arrogance I had seen at first hand on the Portuguese expedition. Or perhaps he did, and she merely laughed and indulged him, like a spoiled child. Some day, however, it must come to a final confrontation between Essex and Robert Cecil, and she would be forced to choose.

I wondered whether both would be present at Hampton Court for Christmastide. Almost certainly they would. Should there be an opportunity, it would be revealing to see how they conducted themselves toward each other.

'Look,' someone called out, 'I can see the palace.'

Aye, I could see it myself now. Above the riverside bushes, ahead and to the right, the upper storeys and fantastical chimneys of the red brick palace were beginning to appear. There were crenellated towers, too, and a flash of gilding from figures mounted on the roof. The December sun was already dropping in the west, although it was but early afternoon, and it lit up the rosy glow of the warm brick, sparking fire from golden lions and other beasts. Were they gilded with real gold? It seemed an extravagance, but then King Henry had been extravagant when it came to his own pleasure and glorification. Thanks to his extravagance, our present Queen had inherited an impoverished nation and learned to be ever cautious over money – some would say miserly and penny pinching. I had some sympathy for her. I knew what it meant to lack money, even if her lack would have been my riches beyond belief.

The oarsmen turned the barge in toward the right bank of the river, and it bumped lightly against a capacious landing stage, with steps and a handrail, very different from the usual muddy stairs served by London's wherries.

'Let me help you, Guy,' I said, holding out my hand for one of the lute cases.

'I thank you. Can you manage it?' He cast a doubtful glance at the knapsack and satchel already slung over my shoulders. Even on a visit to a royal palace I would not leave my medical satchel behind, though there would surely be physicians in attendance here, quite possibly Ruy Lopez amongst them.

'Aye, easily enough. Look at those steps!'

'Fit for a queen.'

He went ahead of me up the steps, somehow managing to carry both the other lute and a portative organ. I saw that the steps had been freshly swept clean of snow. Was it for our benefit, or had some noble visitor arrived just before us?

There was a great deal to land before we could make our way to the palace. As well as our personal property – mainly a change of clothes, for we would be staying here two nights – there were all the baskets of costumes and properties, some of the latter too large to fit in a basket and needing to be unloaded and carried separately, such as the large carved chair used first by the father of Katherina and Bianca (played by Geoffrey de Claine) and later by Petruchio (Ned) when he is 'taming' Katherina, rather as a falconer tames a hunting hawk. Guy's smaller instruments – recorders, tabors, bells, and the like – had their own basket, which he watched like another hawk himself, although he allowed Davy to carry it. Davy still had some of his wild ways, but he was wise enough to know that if he dropped that basket Guy would probably throw him into the river amongst the ice floes.

At last we made our way up the avenue that led from the landing stage to the Great Gate of the palace. The sun had sunk even lower now, though there was light enough to admire the fine brick towers on either side of the gatehouse before we entered. Scattered about the building, windows shone with candle or lamp light, so that what was in reality a solid edifice seemed to float against a darkening sky, like an enchanted castle discovered at the end of some fearful journey by one of Arthur's knights. We had travelled but those few miles from London, yet this was another country.

Master Burbage led the way through the gate, showing some papers of authorisation to the guards on duty there, who waved us through.

'We have further luggage waiting at the landing stage,' I heard Burbage say, 'if you will be good enough to send servants to fetch it.'

One of the guards nodded.

Master Burbage had made it quite plain to us that we were not to arrive at the palace 'burdened like pack ponies' with the costumes and properties.

'It would demean us,' he said. 'It is essential to establish our status from the start, as the company under the patronage of the Queen's cousin, Lord Strange. Arrive looking like a lower servant and you will be treated as such.'

The same guard summoned another man from inside the gatehouse to show us our quarters. He led us across the first great courtyard directly to another gate as handsome as the first. Paths had been cleared of snow, criss-crossing the courtyard, although a scattering of flakes was beginning to fall again, as the last of the sunlight faded from the western sky. On either side of this second gateway, great torches burned, giving a good light at head height, but casting the surrounding area into greater darkness. A wind had begun to get up with nightfall, causing the flames to stream out horizontally, like earthbound comets.

'That is the astronomical clock,' Ned said in my ear, pointing upwards, but it was far too much in shadow for me to make out. If I were to see it, I needs must come back in daylight – that is, supposing we were free to roam about the palace and were not confined to our official quarters.

The man led us through this second gateway into another courtyard, then turned aside to a wing of the building opening from this yard. There were cheerfully lit windows here as well, and a lantern hung beside the door. I noticed Master Burbage scrutinising the hall into which we were taken, before we were led up a single flight of stairs.

'Not servants' quarters,' he murmured to Cuthbert. 'Lesser gentry, I would say.'

Cuthbert nodded. 'That is what we were promised.'

Three rooms had been allocated to us. One a sort of parlour, large enough for the players to rehearse, two others fitted up as bedchambers with rows of beds, some large enough for two sharing, some smaller truckle beds. While the players were examining the larger room, I took care to lay claim to a narrow cot hard up against the wall beside the door, depositing my knapsack and satchel on it, to make quite sure of it, before returning to the others.

The palace guard had left, but Master Burbage explained that we would sup with the household in the Great Hall.

'After,' he said firmly, 'we have run through *The Shrew* once more, to be sure you have learned the new speeches. You will not be making any more changes, Will?'

Will shook his head. 'More than my life would be worth in this dangerous company,' he said.

The players gave exaggerated sighs of relief.

'By your leave, Father,' Cuthbert said, 'I should like to take a look at the Hall before the servants lay for supper. I know we have been promised an hour there tomorrow morning, but, in case anything should go awry?'

'Aye,' Will said,' I should like to see it too.'

In the end we all went. It seemed the Great Hall was directly across the courtyard from our lodgings, a courtyard which I learned was called, not surprisingly, Clock Court. At the moment the Hall was deserted, but before long it would be bustling with servants. There were a few finely wrought candelabra standing along the walls, but not enough light to see the tapestries clearly. In any case, we were more interested in the dais which would serve as a stage.

'This will do very well,' Master Burbage said, stepping up on to the dais and surveying the Hall from there. 'It is as I remembered it. These two doors lead to a passage and smaller rooms behind, where we can store everything tomorrow, before the Christmas feast. Then we will be able to use them for changing before and during the performance.'

He paced the length and breadth of the dais, working out the movements of the players, while Cuthbert took notes.

'Are there to be other entertainments?' I asked Simon quietly. 'As there were at Whitehall?'

'Sure to be.' He turned to Guy. 'Have you heard what else is planned?'

181

'A new Christmas motet by Byrd,' he said, 'sung by the boys of the Chapel Royal, as well as some other Christmas music. They will be first. Solemn and beautiful to quieten the audience down. Then to liven matters up somewhat, I heard talk of some acrobats from Ireland, but the seas have been treacherous, so they may not come. Those performing dogs the Queen is fond of. And of course a Turkish sword swallower.'

I grinned. 'You mean your friend Henry Allinger from Bermondsey?'

'Aye, the same.'

'Then us?' Simon said.

'Our play to round off the entertainment. It's to be hoped that they will all be relaxed and in a good mood by then. *The Shrew* will make no great demands on them, not like this new play of Marlowe's.'

'You have seen it?' I said.

'Aye, and a queer thing it is, too. Troubling. Not fit for Christmas Revels, as Master Burbage rightly decided.'

We needed then to move out of the way of the servants setting up the tables and laying them for the Christmas Eve supper, which we attended a couple of hours later, along with all the rest of the household. The Queen and principal courtiers occupied the high table on the dais, while we were well down on the lower tables, but I was able to make out Lord Burghley on her right hand and the Earl of Essex on her left. From where I was sitting I could not see Sir Robert Cecil, but he was so small that he was no doubt hidden by all the people sitting between.

The next morning I rose early while the players were still deep asleep, and took myself off to the lavatorium where I was able to wash in private. It was a bright, sunny day, though very cold, as I found when I made my way back through the inner gatehouse to Base Court, the principal entrance courtyard. Once there, I turned about and looked up, high above the arch over the gateway, where the astronomical clock could now be clearly seen. I was too close to it, my head tilted back so far I felt a pain in my neck. I began to back away, hoping to view it at a better angle – and collided with someone.

'Your pardon, sir!' I exclaimed, finding my arm taken by a man in royal livery, steadying me so that I did not fall over into the snow.

He laughed. 'Never fear, you are not the first to be overcome by the sight of our wonderful clock.'

I smiled at him, a distinguished, grey-haired gentleman, clearly something more than a servant, but not quite a courtier.

'I had hoped to have a better view at a little distance.'

'Ah, that is the one problem,' he said. 'It is placed a little high. Forgive me, I should introduce myself. Gerard Orfrey, horologist to Her Majesty.'

He bowed, and I returned it.

'Dr Christoval Alvarez, physician at St Thomas's hospital.'

'You are here for the Revels? And, since it is the morning of Christ's birth, may I wish you the blessings of the day?'

'And a blessed day to you, Master Orfrey,' I said. 'Aye, I am here for the Revels.' I thought it best not to mention my part in them.

I pointed up to the clock. 'It was commissioned in King Henry's day, was it not?'

'It was, more than half a century ago now, in 1540, and runs as smoothly today as the day it was set there. So long, that is, as we treat it tenderly, clean and oil it, protect it from dust and the pigeons who sometimes find their way into the clock tower. It was designed by Nicholas Crazter and made by Nicholas Oursian, a fine pair of Nicholases.'

'It is difficult to judge from here just how large it is.'

'Fifteen feet in diameter,' he said proudly. 'The width of a very good sized room in any normal house. Not one here, of course.'

'I have always wanted to see an astronomical clock,' I said, 'and I know it not only tells the hour and the month, but the phases of the moon. I can see the phases of the moon displayed. And there are the signs of the zodiac.'

'Aye,' he said. 'But you may read also the age of the moon in days through its cycle. See, there?'

He pointed, and I screwed up my eyes to read the figure.

'And there,' I said. 'The figure of five and twenty. It tells what day of the month we are in?'

'It does. And there, the total days passed since the beginning of the year.'

'Remarkable.' I studied the complex dials and figures. 'I think we might be able to tease out more information.'

'We might.' He smiled, like a teacher encouraging an apt pupil.

'The sun . . .' I tilted my head. 'Is that the position where it lies on the ecliptic?'

'Bravo!'

'So that is traced out over the course of a whole year.'

'It is.'

I thought it best not to repeat the doubts Master Harriot and Dr Dee had expressed about the theory of the ecliptic. They both favoured the new theory of the structure of the universe put forward by the Polish astronomer Nicolaus Copernicus

'Have I solved it all?' I asked.

'Almost. The clock also tells us precisely when the moon crosses the meridian, therefore the exact time when high water occurs at London Bridge.'

'Now that is extraordinary. I am sure even the clock in Prague cannot do that.'

'I am quite sure it cannot,' he said firmly, protective of his precious charge. 'I am afraid I have duties now with other clocks in the palace, but if you are here for a few days I could show you the mechanism, if that would please you?'

184

'It would indeed!' I said in delight, and we parted in mutual satisfaction.

I spent some time watching the clock after he had left, my mind absorbed in thoughts of time. When God created the earth, he also a created a natural clock for mankind: the rising and setting of the sun to measure our days, the phases of the moon to measure our months, and the turning of the seasons to measure our years. That had never proved enough for restless humankind, who must be for ever inventing more and more accurate ways of measuring time – water clocks and sundials, simple clocks and these astrological marvels – as if, by so doing, we could somehow control time, as well as measure it and count it. Yet we are helpless. Minute by minute, hour by hour, day by day, year by year, time slips away from us. Even standing here these brief minutes I had watched tiny movements in the clock high above my head.

I shivered suddenly. Once again I felt a desperate desire to seize time by the throat and force it to halt. I was not sure why this feeling kept overwhelming me of late. Partly, I knew that uncertain times were coming, brewing amongst the discontented citizens of London and the endless, if covert, battles of great men. At the moment an uncertain quiet held, like the sudden stillness amongst the trees in a wood before a storm breaking. But a storm, I was sure, was coming.

There was more to my unease that this. Twelfth Night would see my twenty-third birthday. Had we remained in Portugal, by now I should probably be married, with children. It was a strangely disturbing thought. Here, living as a man, I could not marry. And only living as a man could I pursue my life as a physician. And yet, and yet, something in me yearned for more.

Standing there in the Base Court of Hampton Court Palace, I admitted to myself what I had never allowed myself to admit so clearly before. I wished that I could reveal the truth of myself to Simon. That we might marry and have children. But it was impossible. And still time slipped through my fingers and would not cease.

The rest of the day galloped past. All the costumes and properties were safely stored away in the rooms behind the dais before we sat down with the rest of the household for the Christmas feast. It was unfortunate for the players, because they did not like to eat heavily before a performance, so that they merely picked at the procession of remarkable dishes which were paraded before us, announced by trumpets and borne in by youths matched in pairs by height and colouring, all in royal livery. My mind soon refused to take in any more, although I do remember roast swans with their feathers carefully stuck back in place, and a sculpture of the lion and the unicorn in butter, packed about with ice to stop it melting in the Great Hall, which grew hotter and hotter from the flames of hundreds of candles as well as hundreds of people. The crowning glory was a creation in sugar which depicted the town of Bethlehem, complete with inn, hillside with sheep, an open stable holding the Holy Family, the shepherds, and the magi, while above them an angel appeared to hover, lit from below by a translucent star holding a candle.

'How does the angel stay in the air, Dr Alvarez?' Davy whispered across Guy, who was sitting between us. Even Davy was subdued by his surroundings.

'I think there must be some contrivance with fine threads,' I whispered back, as four strong men staggered past us carrying the whole structure, but we were not close enough to see for sure.

While the hall was finally cleared, after a dinner which must have lasted three hours at the very least, we took ourselves off to the rooms behind the dais. I had nothing to do but tune my lute, so I lent a hand fastening costumes and pinning headdresses in place. When the noise from the hall indicated that the audience had returned, I slipped behind the painted cloth which had been erected to hide the doors, so that I might listen to the choir of the

Chapel Royal, and perched on one of the stools Guy and I would use when playing.

There is something about the singing of young boys, with their pure treble voices, that sends a shiver down my spine. I gave myself over to simply listening. Guy soon joined me, and we sat there quietly, aware that the chatter of the audience had fallen away, so that the sound of those voices fell like the notes of a blackbird singing into the silence of that Great Hall.

After the motet, the boys sang about half a dozen more songs, some of them ancient tunes with a single line of melody, around which their harmonies were braided, much as Guy's lute music would be. At the end they were applauded roundly and we heard a strident trumpet call, followed by the pounding of feet running up from the back of the Hall.

'The Irish acrobats?' I whispered to Guy.

He nodded. 'Seems the sea calmed enough for them to cross over. Didn't want to miss the chance of a royal performance.'

From behind the hanging cloth we could not see the acrobats and could only judge their performance by the gasps and approving cries which accompanied it. Before it was over, another figure slipped out to join us.

'The blessings of Christ's Nativity on you, Master Allinger,' I murmured, 'if your Turkish faith permits you to accept them.'

I had spotted him earlier on the far side of the changing room, talking to Guy. I could not see his face clearly in the dim light, but I could hear the grin in his voice.

'I accept them with thanks, doctor,' Henry Allinger said, in a voice that was pure Bermondsey, then he switched voices. 'By Allah, this is magnificent, it is not? The hammer beam roof, it surpasses even the palace in–' He hesitated.

'In Constantinople?' I suggested.

'Aye, Constantinople.' He reverted to Bermondsey. 'By your leave, I think I am on.'

With that he strode on to the stage through the sound of the clapping for the acrobats. I heard Guy give a snort of amusement.

'Well timed. This way he prevents the acrobats being called to perform again.'

'And shall we do the same to him?' For we were to play before *The Shrew* began.

'Nay, let Harry have his moment of glory. Mostly he has to work the country fairs, and it's a hard life.'

I was not so nervous now as I had been that other Christmastide at Whitehall, perhaps because I was not also trying to decide who amongst the entertainers was the concealed assassin. Guy and I played his new lute composition to enthusiastic applause, the Queen herself leading it, then we withdrew to the very back of the dais to allow the play to begin.

Twice during the play we performed a musical interlude, allowing time for the costume changes, our second one including Davy's solo. His voice was as moving as those of the choir earlier, and – knowing him for the scamp he was – I wondered how many of those angelic voices in the choir belonged to equally naughty imps.

The Taming of the Shrew proved a great success, for I could easily see from my point of vantage how delighted the Queen was. After the formal dance which concluded our part of the entertainment, and indeed the entertainment itself, she sent for Simon, still in Katherina's costume, and spoke to him for several minutes.

As the audience withdrew, some to stroll about the palace before supper, others (I expected) to sleep off their earlier heavy meal, I asked him what she had said.

'Oh, she wanted to know how I had gained so much insight into how a clever woman may fool a man into thinking she has submitted to him in obedience, while all the while maintaining her independence of him.'

'Did she indeed! Then she was paying close attention. And what did you answer?'

'I said I was fortunate in having been able to observe a number of strong and intelligent women, and modelled my performance on them.'

He grinned at me. Startled, I decide to pursue this no further, and was relieved when Cuthbert called us to help with the packing up of the costumes.

It was some time later, when I had gone in search of Master Orfrey, but failed to find him, that I was passing along the screen passage at the end of the Great Hall and heard a voice I thought I recognised, but could not immediately place. I paused. Two men were speaking in low voices on the other side of the screen.

The second man spoke, and that voice I knew beyond doubt. Robert Poley.

'Aye, I am returned from Scotland these two weeks past, but I am sent off to Brussels come the new year, though I do not as yet know when.'

'That is all very well for you,' the other man said, 'with your fat purses of coin for every time you are sent abroad. But it means all the greater burden falling on Dick and me, keeping a watch on him.'

I could sense Poley shrugging his shoulders. He would care little how much trouble he caused other men, so long as he was well rewarded.

'It is no light thing,' he said, 'travelling to Scotland in winter. Foul weather. Foul roads. And cold enough in Edinburgh to freeze the Devil's arse.'

They shared a laugh.

'So you think King Jamie would welcome a warm billet in London.'

'Without a doubt. And, as for me, my travel to Brussels will be even worse than to Scotland, you may be sure, on these rough winter seas, so don't whine to me that you must keep watch in London and Kent. You have the easier task, however we look at it.'

There was a snort from the other man, and I suddenly realised who he was. I had only met him once, and on that occasion he took a patronising tone to Simon and me, whereas now he was on easy terms with Poley. It was Ingram Frizer, the purveyor of illegal and fraudulent loans.

Ingram Frizer and Robert Poley. What were they conspiring? Something unsavoury, I had no doubt.

'When do you look to be back in England?' Frizer said.

'I must see to affairs in France and Amsterdam as well. I'll not be back till the spring,' Poley said. 'April or May, most like. So in the meantime, keep up your vigilance and gather what evidence you can. His Lordship wants there to be no doubt, when he takes the matter to the Privy Council.'

'You are very knowing.' Frizer's voice had taken on a sneer. 'His Lordship draws you into his secret councils, does he?'

'I am His Lordship's secret hand in all this. But believe me, the man must be stopped. He knows too much, from previous missions he has undertaken, and of late he has become more unreliable than ever before. A loose tongue in a man with such knowledge is a danger to all. He is of no more use, so an end must be put to him.'

I heard a door open beyond the screen, and a cheerful voice called out, 'So this is where you are hiding, Poley. We are waiting to start that game of tables. Come you away. Will your friend join us?'

'Nay,' Frizer said. 'I have other business to attend to. Go your ways, and do not gamble away your shirts.'

Suddenly aware that Frizer might come round the screen and realise that I had been listening, I slipped away as quietly as I could through the nearest door and resumed my search for Master Orfrey.

What had I learned? Poley and Frizer and some other man – Dick – were following someone and collecting evidence against him. This man must be stopped, in the interests of some lord. I wondered what 'stopped' meant.

Did it mean 'killed'? And who was the lord? Poley worked for Lord Burghley, but he was so slippery he might equally well be working for the Earl of Essex. It had not sounded as though Frizer himself worked for the lord in question, but had his orders handed down through Poley. Who might their unfortunate 'mark' be? For they sounded like a pair of coney-catchers, setting up a victim before moving in for the trap.

I found Master Orfrey at last, but by then we were bidden to supper, once again in the Great Hall, which had been transformed with garlands of ivy sprigged with bunches of holly, the holly berries symbolising the blood of Christ and its sharp leaves His crown of thorns. Ivy, I think, stands for long life – even eternity – and its clinging nature represents love and fidelity. Introducing symbols of Christ's torture and death into celebrations of his birth has always seemed to me perverse, but these are ancient customs, not easily forgone.

'I will be happy to show you the mechanism of the clock tomorrow morning,' Master Orfrey said.

'Alas, I said, 'we are bidden to leave at first light. It has already grown colder and our barge master fears the freezing of the river altogether, so we must set off before the barge is quite trapped.'

'That is a pity,' he said, 'but if at any time you care to come back? I do not often have the opportunity to discuss the clock with someone who can truly understand its wonders.'

'In the summer,' I said, 'when there is no difficulty with the weather, I will ride out here and we can have all the time you can spare to examine the mechanism.'

'I shall look forward to that,' he said with a smile.

We shook hands and parted, with promises on both sides.

The Christmas supper was as lavish as the dinner had been, and the players were now free to enjoy it, but I found I could eat little more. Tomorrow I would be returning to Mountjoy's Inn, where the servants who had not gone to their families for the Twelve Days would no doubt be anxious to ply me with yet more rich food, for it meant feasts in the kitchen for them.

There was to be more music and dancing in the palace, well into the night, but I slipped away early and retired to my narrow bed beside the wall; yet even when the others returned, merry with wine and dance, I was still lying awake.

I lay awake most of the night, worrying about the words I had overheard between Robert Poley and Ingram Frizer. And wondering who the man might be that they were relentlessly pursuing.

Chapter Ten

Sara, Ruy, and the children reached London in a cold and wretched January, and for my part I prepared to return, with considerable relief, to my lodgings in Southwark. I had lived royally at Mountjoy's Inn, waited upon by the servants, eating the finest food and sleeping between crisp linen sheets, but in the years since I had left Coimbra I had grown unaccustomed to such a life. My simple room, my cot bed with its rough blankets, my meals of bread and cheese taken at home, or a threepenny meal at an ordinary – these were more than enough for me.

I packed up the few possessions I had brought with me into a saddle bag, for I would ride Hector across the City, returning him to the stable in Seething Lane, as I had already arranged with the stable lad Harry. However, before I left, I sought out Sara in her pretty little parlour to say goodbye. We sat together looking out at the snow drifting past the window as she insisted on my drinking a mug of hot brandy punch before setting out.

'We are grateful to you, Kit,' she said, 'both Ruy and I, for keeping an eye on matters here. I fear that otherwise the servants might have become somewhat slack. It has been a great comfort to come home after our long and often trying travels, to find the house warm and clean, and a meal ready for us.'

I reached across and patted her hand. 'I have been happy to do it, Sara, for I owe you so much for past kindnesses.'

It was difficult to continue, for I knew I was about to mar the pleasure of her homecoming.

In the end, I had decided it would be kinder to tell Sara myself about the Allington baby, rather than let her hear it from some malicious gossiper, which would surely be worse. I gave her the simple details as quickly as I could, not naming Ruy as the father, but merely telling her what the note had said, and warning her of the whispers which had spread abroad, and which I believed to have been sped on their way, in part, by some of Ruy's powerful enemies. She cried a little, but did not seem altogether surprised. Perhaps this was not Ruy's first bastard.

'I am sorry to be the unlucky messenger,' I said awkwardly.

She shook her head. 'You did right to tell me, Kit. If the child is indeed Ruy's, then he must provide for it. 'Tis not the fault of the little one.'

'Nay,' I smiled sadly. 'It is always the children who suffer, is it not? Although Richard Allington has received Christian baptism and – for all I have been able to see – is healthy and well cared for.'

Sara straightened her shoulders and wiped her eyes. Clearly she would refuse to be bowed by this. Married to Ruy Lopez, she no doubt often had worse matters to endure.

'And how did you enjoy your journey?' I asked, anxious to divert her from the unpleasant news.

She shrugged. 'Antwerp is suffering under the Spanish rule, so we avoided it, and all that part of the Low Countries. But you will understand that, from your own time there. Most of our people who used to live in Antwerp have moved to Amsterdam, where they feel safer. Some have gone to Denmark, others, of course, have come here.'

'Not that London is the most welcoming place for refugees at present,' I said. 'Not since the Southwark riot last year.'

'I am sure that will pass,' she said confidently.

'And Venice?' I asked. 'How did you like Venice?'

She gave a small smile. 'Well, I found Venice very strange and beautiful. Aye, very beautiful and strange. As you know, Amsterdam is threaded through with canals, but Venice! Why, Venice seems to float on the very water itself, a place of dreamy visions. Yet, in a city which is mostly tolerant, all acknowledged Jews are forced to live in either the Old or the New Ghetto, behind gates kept locked at night, where they govern themselves and worship openly in their synagogues. But such openness and independence are an illusion. The laws of Venice are strict, and from time to time prejudice breaks through the veneer of tolerance and there are severe persecutions and the burning of sacred books. The ghettos seemed like a prison to me. The Ottomans are more tolerant than the Venetians. The Jews in Constantinople live quite freely and publicly, at least as far as I could tell, but I was uneasy. The Sultan is omnipotent and ruthless. I could not live there.'

'Did you think you might?' I was surprised.

'Ruy has not confided his plans to me, but I think he wanted to visit these places in case we should have to leave England. The disturbances of last spring, the whispers, defaming Jews . . .'

She let her words trail away, but I understood. If the Cecils fell, Ruy would fall with them. And even if they did not, the increased hostility towards Marranos, which had grown again on the streets, once the plague had died back last autumn, might drive us all away. Like an animal pursued by hawk or hound, Ruy was looking for a bolt hole. Poor Sara! Born in England, and living here all her life, she would not want to move to some foreign land.

Once the Lopez family were settled again at Mountjoy's Inn that day, I returned to my lodgings in Southwark, where Simon was still occupying my room and still short of funds, as the players always were whenever the winter weather kept their audiences small or altogether absent. No man will pay his penny or twopence to listen to a play through the chattering of his own teeth. I had not the heart to turn Simon out on to the street, or back into the arms of Marlowe or Kyd. Besides, I was glad of his company during the dark winter evenings. Once again it required some contriving, however, to conceal my womanhood when we shared a room. I washed only when he was abroad, and slept at night in the same shift as I wore by day. He gave up the bed to me, and again brought in a straw palliasse for himself to sleep on. However, this continued for no more than a fortnight, when the tailor and his family moved out of Simon's old room and he moved back there, taking his scattering of belongings with him. At last Rikki and I were safely back in our own little home.

Some months had passed since I had last attended one of the meetings in Ralegh's Durham House. However, not long after I had left Mountjoy's Inn to return to my lodgings in Southwark, a message was delivered to me from my former mathematics tutor, Thomas Harriot. There was to be another meeting the following evening, and he hoped I would attend, for he would be bringing a new and much improved version of his perspective trunk and – if he found the time to complete it – a *camera obscura*. Ralegh had some thoughts on using one for optical experiments.

After long hours at the hospital, due to an influx of winter chest infections, too many of those patients weakened by poverty and hunger, the prospect of an evening of intellectual talk and new scientific toys was more than welcome. Harriot would have chided me for calling them toys, but I felt that was what they were, although toys of an adult and sophisticated nature. Therefore I left Rikki in my lodgings, warm, with the fire banked down, donned my thick fur lined cloak, winter boots, and gloves, and set off on the long walk through the February snow to the Strand.

I could have gone by wherry, but once again the edges of the river had frozen, making embarking on a wherry a treacherous business, besides which a bitter east wind would make for a cold time on the water. Walking, though it would take longer, would keep me warm, but I thought, not for the first time, that it would be good to have Hector stabled near my lodgings, instead of across the river and in the opposite direction from the north end of the Bridge to the one in which Durham House lay. I pondered collecting him from Seething Lane even so, but decided against it in the end, as taking too much time and exposing the poor horse to the cold unnecessarily. I would walk instead.

Once again this winter snow had continued unabated since November, so that roofs groaned under its weight. The Common Council set the sturdy beggars from Bridewell to clearing a way for horses and men through the main streets of London, though with every fresh fall they were blocked again. The lesser streets were only cleared if a householder or shopkeeper chose to undertake it. In one or two places, on the south facing sides of buildings, the midday sun had briefly melted some of the snow on roofs, which had dripped slowly from the eaves, freezing again into great swords of ice, hanging threateningly over the heads of the passersby. This forced us into the centre of the streets, obliged to dodge out of the way of horsemen and carts.

By the time I reached Durham House I was like one of those pies bought on a cold day in a poor pie shop – overcooked in parts, and near frozen in others. When I had climbed the stairs to the tower room where the gatherings were held, I was relieved to see a roaring fire in the fireplace, and one of Ralegh's servants crouched before it holding a griddle over the flames, on which chestnuts were roasting. Simple English fare, compared to the exotic foods Ralegh usually served, but I noticed that even the Earl of Northumberland received his handful eagerly, tossing them back and forth until they had cooled enough to peel, then dipping them into one of the small dishes of salt provided.

Another servant took my cloak and a third brought me hot spiced red wine as I found a seat on a cushioned bench beside Harriot.

'Far more people than usual,' I said, after sampling my wine and setting the silver goblet down on a side table so I could accept my handful of chestnuts.

'Aye,' Harriot said happily. 'Ralegh has spread word about the devices and invited a number who have not been here before. And I believe he has other entertainment planned for us.'

There were indeed at least half a dozen men I did not know, including one whose face seemed somewhat familiar, although I could not quite put a name to him. Once all of us had been served with mulled wine and chestnuts, and then with more conventional small pastries filled with spiced meat and sweet marchpane stamped with Ralegh's coat of arms, Harriot made himself busy about some large boxes on the big table under the window, bringing out his original perspective trunk to compare with the new one – smaller and lighter – as well as three slightly different versions of the *camera obscura*. I smiled. He had modestly claimed that he would fail to complete one, which I had not believed, but I had not expected three, even from Harriot.

Everyone clustered around the devices, passing the perspective trunks from hand to hand and trying for a view out of the window. When I had had my first view through the earliest one, it had been daylight and Lambeth Palace clear to see on the other side of the river, jumping suddenly and alarmingly into view, but in this winter dusk the prospect was quite different – the few wherries on the river with their lanterns brought suddenly into focus, and in Lambeth Palace a multitude of lighted windows shining forth across the snowy river bank. The Archbishop must be in residence. The *camerae obscurae*, though more familiar, also offered entertaining views of our fellows apparently standing on their heads.

Our happy discussion of the improved perspective trunk, and its wondrous possibilities for studying the heavens or aiding mariners (provided it could be made small enough and portable enough), was interrupted by the arrival of several more members of the group, including Marlowe, richly dressed as usual, and sporting a new ring with what looked like a large emerald. The newcomers all wanted to try the instruments, and for the next hour all the talk was of the perspective trunk and other optical devices which might developed from the principles behind the *camera obscura*.

'It gives me cause to wonder,' I said, as we settled down to enjoy more wine and refreshments brought in by Ralegh's servants, 'how we can trust the evidence of our eyes. For if a simple arrangement of lenses can so alter the way we perceive reality, how can we be sure of what *is* truly real? Plato said that we are like men in a cave, who see shadows on a wall and suppose that is reality. But reality lies elsewhere, with the objects casting the shadows. This perspective trunk, and the *camera obscura* whose principles you have explained, Thomas, seem to me to throw our perception of the world into even greater confusion.'

'That is very true, Kit,' said Ralegh. 'There is a blurring between the real and the imagined, between science and magic, which may never become clear.'

'But what you may call magic . . .' Dee began.

And they plunged into a familiar argument, which did not address the uncertainty I felt in my own mind. Perhaps I had not made myself clear, but I hesitated to say more.

Then a servant arrived with yet more small dishes of curious things to eat – Ralegh was always interested in unusual foods. Amongst tonight's dishes there were green and black olives, rare in England, but a favourite of mine since childhood. I settled back in my seat with a dish of olives, a slice of spiced Indian cornbread and my silver goblet of wine, and awaited the lecture, the usual feature of this part of the evening.

We were accustomed to lectures on scientific subjects, or philosophy, or the age of rocks and hence of the earth, or Dee's interest in mathesis – mystical mathematics. Harriot and Ralegh were both deeply curious about the peoples of the New World and their beliefs, Harriot having made a special study of the tribes he had encountered on his voyage to the Chesapeake some seven years before. They were somewhat troubled about how to reconcile what we were learning about these new races with the different account of the origins of the world in the Bible, and had given us talks about their findings. But the lecture that evening was not concerned with any of these matters.

I was not pleased when I realised that Marlowe was to read a paper, though I saw that the rest of the company looked at him with expectant relish. Even I had to concede that his plays were remarkable, if often distasteful, and I suppose what I expected was some passages from a new play he was working on. Simon had told me that Marlowe had returned briefly to London from Scadbury because he hoped to sell a new play to Master Burbage and Master Henslowe, to be performed when the playhouses reopened after the cold weather.

'Cuthbert has seen it,' Simon had said. 'And he says it is very strange, about some German scholar who sells his soul to the Devil. I think Guy saw it as well.'

I shivered. 'Another of his dark and unpleasant plays,' I said.

'The groundlings will enjoy it. They like to be frightened. And if we speak of dark and unpleasant–' He hesitated.

'What?'

'It seems Marlowe travelled from Kent in company with someone we both find dark and unpleasant. Ingram Frizer.'

'What is he doing in Marlowe's company?'

'It seems he is also a member of Sir Thomas Walsingham's household. Some manner of financial advisor.'

'May the saints preserve poor Sir Thomas!' I exclaimed. 'He is like to find all his coin, aye, and his lands too, in forfeit to Frizer.'

'I do not know whether he has tried his tricks on Sir Thomas, but I do know that from time to time Marlowe has been in debt to him.'

'Marlowe lives beyond his means,' I said. 'With his expensive clothes and jewels, more suited to a courtier.'

'And.' Simon said, 'he has recently bought a very fine horse.'

I wondered now whether the costly new ring – that Marlowe was taking care to flash about so that it caught the light from the standing brass candelabra – had been purchased with a loan from Frizer. Surely no one of sense who had once been cozened by Frizer would fall into his hands again? However, I firmly believed that Marlowe had more arrogance and pride than common sense, thinking himself cleverer than any man on earth. Certainly he was clever. But not that clever.

Along with the rest of the company, I prepared myself – with resignation – to hear whatever Marlowe intended for his lecture. Perhaps we would have a first reading of the heroic poem he had been writing under the patronage of Sir Thomas Walsingham. I noticed that the man who had seemed slightly familiar to me had settled himself in a corner, with paper, pen, and ink. A talk from Marlowe hardly seemed to merit such attention, unless he was indeed preparing to read his new play and this fellow was here to make an unlicensed copy. Having had one skirmish with the theft of plays, I did not expect it to be done so openly. Just before Marlowe took his stand before us, drawing out a roll of paper from the front of his doublet, I remembered who the man was.

Richard Baines, someone who had occasionally worked for Sir Francis. Not one of the regular agents, but a man who hung about the fringes of the service, sometimes trying to sell Phelippes small pieces of information for large prices. Now and then used for some small job, but never much liked or trusted. I wondered how he had managed to contrive an invitation for himself to one of Ralegh's gatherings.

Suppressing my irritation, I leaned back on the cushioned bench, hoping I should not be required to listen to Marlowe boasting and preening himself for too long. I had been pleased to see that Simon had not accompanied him here, as once he would have done. There had been a definite cooling off of the friendship between them. At one time Simon had been flattered by the attentions of this older, clever man, a graduate of Cambridge University and a gifted writer, but recently I think he had begun to see the other side of Marlowe, that dark side of cruelty and violence which manifested itself in his plays. I suppressed a sigh. I had enjoyed looking at Harriot's devices, but my long cold walk through the snow had not been worth the effort if I had to pay the penalty of listening to a man who loathed me. I began to wish I had suggested a meal at the Lion with Simon instead.

Marlowe did not read us a play. Nor did he read us one of his poems. The last time I had attended one of the gatherings here, we had been discussing John Proctor's treatise, *The Fall of the Late Arrian*. I had not read it and contributed little to the discussion. From what others said I understood little about it and liked less. In all the time since, I had thought about it no further. When it became clear that Marlowe intended to enlarge upon the discussion, I would gladly have left, but I was seated on the side of the room furthest from the door and my departure would have given him the opportunity to make more cutting remarks at my expense, so I hunched miserably in my seat and prepared to endure his posturing.

Northumberland and Dee looked eager, Ralegh quieter but attentive. Harriot glanced at me quizzically. I could not make him out. Glancing round, I happened to notice Baines. His expression was complicated, a mixture of excitement and a kind of terror. Alarmed, I tried to interpret it, as if that would provide some clue to what he was thinking, but he was entirely absorbed in Marlowe and I could not see his eyes. Why was he frightened?

'Item,' said Marlowe, in a smug preacherly tone, gesturing at us with his sheaf of notes, 'the first beginning of all religion is to keep men in subservience and awe. In this the Catholic religion is the most successful, with its gaudy ceremonies, incense, singing, shaven crowns of monks and so forth.' He paused. 'All *Protestants* are hypocritical asses.'

He ticked this item off on his first finger.

Someone gasped. All around me, I felt a stirring, as if men were not sure whether to laugh or grow angry.

'Item.' Marlowe paused again for effect, having successfully produced shock in his audience with his first so-called 'item'. He smirked. 'Item the second: the Old Testament is all lies. For example, let us take Moses, reared up by the Egyptians, so that it was an easy matter for him to deceive the rude and ignorant Jewish people.'

Here he directed a malicious smile at me and ticked this off on his second finger.

'Why do I say this, you ask? Where is my evidence?'

He pretended to search through his notes and shook his head sadly.

He is behaving like a player, I thought, *but he makes a very poor one. An honest shoemaker performing in a country mystery play would do better.* For some reason this put me in mind of Will, who was not only an excellent playmaker but a good player. He would never have had the conceit to parade himself like this.

My disgust must have shown on my face, for Marlowe glowered at me, and aimed his next words directly at me.

'Item: Moses forced the Jews to wander for forty years in the wilderness before they came to the Promised Land, yet as every man knows, even the slowest traveller, walking from Egypt to the Holy Land, cannot take more than a year about it. Forty years!'

He gave an incredulous laugh.

'His purpose was to persuade them with his trickeries and conjuring, so that all the old men who might have questioned him died off, and only those remained who knew no better. They were left in a state of everlasting superstition which has persisted to this day.'

He gave me a mocking bow as he ticked this off. I refused to meet his eye, but I could feel an angry flush rising in my face.

'Of course,' he added in a sneering tone, 'Moses was a poor conjuror, a mere juggler. Our own conjuror Herriot is far better than he.'

At that I saw Ralegh flush and open his mouth, clearly intending to protest at this personal insult to one of his guests. (The insults to the Jewish people had not made personal reference to my name.) However, I saw Herriot shrug and give the slightest shake of his head to Ralegh. He was right. It was better not to give Marlowe the satisfaction of rebuking him or arguing with him. He was being deliberately provocative with exactly that intention. Far better to maintain a cold silence in the face of his insults and mockery. Out of the corner of my eye, I noticed that Baines was writing furiously.

Marlowe continued.

'Item: the New Testament is filthily written, for see – the Angel Gabriel was pimp to the Holy Ghost. He procured Mary to be his whore and Christ was their bastard, no better than any gutter bastard in London.'

At this appalling profanity, there were gasps throughout the room and a low murmuring of voices. Someone behind me got to his feet, with a thump as his tilted chair fell forward. Ralegh and his friends possessed open and enquiring minds, ready to examine and discuss new discoveries, both geographical and scientific, but they were also men of devout faith, who would never have used such language of the Mother of Christ, never even allowed such a thought to enter their minds.

To call Mary a whore and Jesus a bastard was so shocking that no one seemed capable of attacking Marlowe. They were too stunned.

The rumble of voices becoming more hostile, Marlowe raised his voice to make himself heard.

'Item: Christ followed his whorish dam, for he had Mary Magdalene and the women of Samaria as his concubines.

Someone else at the back of the room stood up, scraping the legs of his chair on the floor with a squeal of wood, and walked out. I wished I had the courage to do the same, but I was trapped in the front row of seats, between the wall and Harriot. I could only leave by crossing directly in front of Marlowe, within touching distance. Not only did I lack the courage to leave, but I also possessed the determination not to give him the satisfaction of knowing he had driven me away. I was becoming not only sickened, but angry. How dare this filthy minded man speak so of Our Lord? But he was not finished. He was speaking now is so loud a voice I thought that the servants away in the kitchen, several floors below, must be able to hear him.

'Item: he took St John the Evangelist as his Sodomite.'

There was the sound, it almost seemed to me, of someone retching. I found I was clutching my hands so tight together that my nails were digging painfully into my skin. I tried to relax my grip, but my hands refused to obey my will.

Marlowe was openly laughing now, his eyes bright with excitement and malice as he threw away his next 'item' as a passing thought, relating his own notorious behaviour to his wickedly tainted version of Jesus.

'Item: by the bye, all that love not tobacco and boys are mere fools.'

Ralegh had half risen to his feet. He enjoyed a stimulating debate, but this went beyond anything that should be said or heard, but Marlowe held up his hand to stop him, as if indicating that he was nearly done.

'Item: the apostles were loutish fishermen who were taken in by Christ, being *too stupid* to see beyond the end of their noses.'

He spat out the words 'too stupid' from all the height of his intellectual arrogance.

And you are the man, I thought, *who owes the clothes on your back and your fame in London to the simple citizens who pay their pennies to flock to your plays. Without them and their pennies, you would be nothing.*

It seemed at last that this torment was coming to an end. Almost all of us, including myself, had risen to our feet, and Marlowe had rolled up his sheaf of papers. As he thrust it into the front of his gaudy doublet with one hand, he held up the other, pointing an admonitory finger at us.

'Item: if Christ was killed instead of Barabbas, well, the people at the time knew them both and chose rightly who should die, even if Barabbas was a thief and a murderer.'

I was surprised he had not chosen the usual argument of vilifying the Jews for choosing Barabas, but it suited him better on this occasion to vilify Jesus instead. As I had stood I felt a dizziness come over me, and I set my hand on the panelled wall to steady myself. Would this never be over?

Marlowe drew a great breath and swept a look about the room – at the angry, ashamed, and horrified company who had been forced to listen to this . . . this heresy. Nay, this more than heresy. It was like the black pit of Hell itself, swarming with devils and monsters, foul serpents and the slime of all that is ugly and debased in mankind. We were looking into the dark pit of Marlowe's own mind.

He came to his final argument with the sleek complacency of a lizard.

'Item: I could invent for you a better religion, more excellent and admirable in method than anything you can find in the Old and New Testaments.'

He held up his ten fingers triumphantly, as though he had achieved some remarkable victory in the debating schools of Oxford or Cambridge.

If I were all Jew, and not half-Jew and half-Christian, perhaps these blasphemies would have passed over me and make no mark, despite his vilification of Moses and his sneers at the Jewish people. But Marrano as I was, and lately inclining more towards the kindly Christianity I had met here in England, so different from the murderous church of the Inquisition, I was shocked to the depths of my soul.

As he glanced around, clearly expecting the praise of all of us, I excused myself and ran to the privy chamber, where I vomited Ralegh's fine foods until I was empty and shaking. As I began my weak kneed descent of the stairs, I saw Baines ahead of my, hastily bundling away his notes. I sent my apologies in to Ralegh by a servant and started on my way home alone. I stumbled along the Strand, still physically as well as mentally shocked. It had begun to snow again, and the confusion to my sight, blurred by the whirling flakes, seemed a manifestation of my maelstrom of thoughts. I had had the sense to grab my cloak from where a servant had hung it by the door, but I had forgotten my gloves. I tried to avoid frostbite by clasping my arms about myself and burying my hands in my armpits, but even before I reached the Bridge I was chilled to the bone.

Mercifully, as usually happened when ice made river travel difficult, the Great Stone Gate at the south end of the Bridge was kept unbarred at night. After what seemed hours, the Atkins house came in sight. There was a friendly light shining out around the edge of the shutters to the ground floor window where the Atkins family themselves lived, and another from Simon's window, still unshuttered. I climbed the stairs as quietly as I might, but as I passed his door, Simon called out.

'Is that you, Kit?'

'I am for my bed,' I said.

Once inside my room, after fending off Rikki's exuberant welcome, I stripped and washed all over, although the water was cold and the fire almost gone out. I felt dirty. Ashamed. Marlowe's words seemed to have covered me with their poisonous filth. I washed all over a second time. It was almost as if I had been raped. I was degraded. At last I pulled myself together and donned my night shift, then set to coaxing a little life back into the fire. Only then did I sit on the floor in front of it, with my arms around Rikki, as the deep shuddering gradually died away.

After that evening, I avoided Durham House for some time, chiefly because I had no wish to find myself in Marlowe's company again. I missed the excitement of the discussions with other members of the group, but my work as a doctor absorbed more and more of my time as the winter passed and the spring of 1593 crept into London, softening the grime and fogs of the cold weather with the pale leaf buds on the trees and here and there a clump of primroses or violets which had rooted themselves in a neglected corner.

Chapter Eleven

*P*lague came unusually early in the spring of 1593. Once again the Council took the opportunity to shut down all places of entertainment. After the losses incurred the previous year, the players were gloomy, and talked of going on tour again, but nothing came of it. What did follow in the wake of this Puritanical banning of means of enjoyment, was a growing restlessness amongst the citizens of London. I was reminded of the previous year and the riot in Southwark. So far, there was no overt trouble, but I sensed something in the air, like the sizzling of a fuse before a cannon is fired. Somewhere, sometime – and soon – there would be an explosion.

While the playhouses remained closed, Simon had much idle time on his hands. Despite the hasty ban, the plague had not become too severe, but the city authorities still refused to allow the playhouses to open. Apart from the plague cases, which were mostly confined to the areas around the docks north of the river, there was little illness abroad and St Thomas's was fairly quiet, so that I too was not as busy as usual. Since the increased hostility to Strangers, Simon had appointed himself some kind of watchman over my welfare and spent more time than usual in my company. We took to going for long walks across the city and sometimes out into the countryside.

Perhaps two weeks after the closure of the playhouses, we were crossing the City when we were brought up short by a crowd gathered about a large notice pinned up on a wall. There were angry mutters and much nodding of agreement from the men in the crowd, who were mostly craftsmen, to judge from their clothes. I could not see what they were reading, but Simon was tall enough to look over their heads. He gave a tug to my arm and we headed north towards Finsbury Fields.

'What was it?' I asked.

He did not answer at first, merely quickened his pace.

'Simon?'

'Nothing. A piece of folly.'

There was something in his manner that suggested it was not folly. I stopped dead.

'What was it? I will not stir another step until you tell me.'

'Wait until we are outside the city.'

We walked on in silence until we had passed out through the city wall at Bishopsgate, continued past Bedlam and the cluster of houses beyond, and we were finally seated under a tree beside a country alewife's house, with tankards of her own brew in our hands.

'You know that many craftsmen are without work, and beggars and paupers more than ever?'

'Of course,' I said impatiently. 'I treat them in the hospital.'

'There has been much angry complaint of late, that foreign refugees take Englishmen's jobs and substance, the very bread from their mouths and the mouths of their children. All the Protestants who have come flooding in from the Spanish attacks in the Low Countries, and the Huguenots escaping the persecution in France.'

'Simon,' I was more than a little annoyed. 'Do you seek to teach me to suck eggs? I saw as much of last year's troubles as you did, and when you were away in the country, I was here in London, through all the discontent. Do you not remember how I warned of this, when I came to Canterbury?'

I thought again of Marlowe's play, *The Jew of Malta*, which had served to stir up the latent discontent all the

210

more, every time it was played. It had been performed again before the playhouses were closed.

'England has changed of late,' I said. 'She always used to open her arms to the persecuted who have fled here. She welcomed my father and me.'

'Yes.' He gave a mocking smile. 'We like to believe ourselves tolerant and kindly to the destitute refugee. Until our own livelihoods are threatened. Indeed there was a vote in Parliament last month to extend the privileges of resident Strangers.'

'I did hear of that. I don't know whether I would benefit.'

'Probably. Did you know who was the one man who spoke against it?'

I shook my head.

'Ralegh.'

'Ralegh! I cannot believe it.' I was shocked, for Ralegh had always been kind to me, had always eagerly befriended scholars and explorers from other lands.

'Yes, Ralegh. He said,' and here Simon mimicked Ralegh's voice so exactly I was distracted enough to laugh, 'he said, "In the whole cause I see no matter of honour, no matter of charity, no profit in relieving them".'

'That was not kindly done, nor honestly spoken.' I was truly angry. It felt like a betrayal.

'Nay. It does seem unlike him. Strange. What was he thinking? However, the vote was passed anyway. But in speaking out as he did, Ralegh gave a kind of licence to others who had merely grumbled amongst themselves before. Men with hungry mouths to feed, and the price of food ever increasing.'

He gestured back over his shoulder, in the direction from which we had come. 'That placard makes real threats. It says that the apprentices will soon rise up and attempt some violence on the Strangers.'

I shivered, despite the warm April sun. Having lived in England nearly half my life, I tried no longer to think of myself as a Stranger, but, in the eyes of such people, that was what I was. In my heart, I knew I was. I did not have the gold to buy myself citizenship, though even then I would count merely as an endenizened Stranger, like Ruy, and not a true citizen.

'Do you think it is a serious threat?' I asked. 'This placard?'

'Who can tell? But I think you should be on your guard.'

Even more than usual, I thought.

When we passed the place on our return, the crowd had gone and the placard had vanished, as if it had never been.

The next day was Easter Sunday, and I took communion, for the first time since Christmas. I had not attended the Passover celebrations at Dunstan Añes's house; the first time in my life I had missed Passover. Was I betraying the inheritance of my own blood? Although I had been baptised a Christian in Portugal, in the eyes of my parents I was always a Jew. I no longer knew what to think of myself.

Take, eat, this is my Body, which is given for you . . .

Drink ye all of this; for this is my Blood . . .

Do this, as oft as ye shall drink it in remembrance of me . . .

I moved forward until I reached the head of the long line to the altar rail, and felt the dry wafer on my tongue and the sharp wash of the wine down my throat. In the moment of communion I wondered whether those who knelt beside me thought of me as a hostile foreigner. And did their faith come to them pure and unquestioned? Jesus was a good man. He preached love and tolerance. Surely that was a simple enough answer, a rule to live by, even for a devious Marrano, secret code-breaker, liar, deceiver, forger.

I turned to help the old man beside me to his feet, a neighbour of mine, whom I knew to be near four score years old. I remembered speaking to Sir Francis Walsingham, years before, about another aged man. Like that man, this one must have been baptised a Catholic, then forced to join Henry's new English church, divorced from Rome. Under Henry's son he would have been directed to a more severe form of Protestantism, only to turn to the Catholic faith again under Mary. At last, with Elizabeth, he was taken into the bosom of the independent English Protestant church, with its fear of secret Catholic priests and the Catholic king of Spain.

What did his faith mean to him? Perhaps his mind was as confused as mine in all this maelstrom of faiths. How did God look down at the old man, at me? Sometimes I felt a stirring in my heart of something that might be – not faith, but a sense of otherness, of the numinous. Then it would vanish, as elusive as mist.

The placard that Simon and I had seen proved to be but the first of many. That following week, libels – as they came to be called – were posted up all over London. On my way to visit one of my patients north of the river I saw one with my own eyes. There were half a dozen men clustered around it, who glanced at me from the corners of their eyes then turned their backs on me.

The notice was addressed to 'the beastly brutes, the Belgians, the faint-hearted Flemings, and the fraudulent Father Frenchmen'. Clearly the author had a fondness for alliteration, I thought, with a wry inner smile. It accused these refugees of cowardly flight from their own countries and of hypocrisy and counterfeit show of religion – I suppose that was what was meant by 'Father Frenchmen', that the French were not Huguenots but crypto-Catholics.

And what of Portingalls? Truly, we might be accused of a counterfeit show of religion, although we were not named here. The real root of the anger and spite came in the complaint that 'the Queen allows them to live here in better case and more freedom than her own people'. This was the response to Parliament's granting of greater privileges to resident Strangers, though I thought it an ill-considered accusation.

For we Strangers suffered many restrictions unknown to native Englishmen, not least in the conduct of our businesses, the employment of assistants or apprentices, and the prohibition on owning property, unless we were endenizened. The real danger of the placard in front of me lay in the threats it made. It warned that all Strangers must leave England within the *next three months*, or two thousand three hundred and thirty-six apprentices would rise up and strike down all 'Flemings and Strangers'.

There was something particularly chilling about that precise number. Was it a mere invention of the author? Or had that number of apprentices indeed sworn to destroy all the foreigners in London? Even half a dozen apprentices in ugly mood could strike fear into law-abiding citizens, and their cry of 'Clubs!' in the street caused most men to dive for shelter.

After treating my patient, which required no more than the poulticing of a twisted ankle, I hurried home, not feeling safe until I had closed the door of my lodgings. My worries were not misplaced. The mood throughout the City, Westminster, and Southwark soon grew even more ugly. In the inns and on the streets, Englishmen looked sideways at foreigners and muttered amongst themselves, whilst foreigners hurried about their business, looking neither to right nor to left, or else hid away in their houses.

A Flemish surgeon and a French physician at St Thomas's made plans to leave the country, although they were perplexed as to where they might go, for to return to their homelands would expose them to the same persecution they had fled in coming to England. I could not think what to do. Portugal was closed to me. I supposed I might make my way to Antwerp or Amsterdam. Nay, not Antwerp, not any more. Sara had said most of our people had left the tolerant town of Antwerp since the Spanish had seized the town, but word was that Amsterdam was a safe haven for Marranos. Seeing me worried and withdrawn, Simon asked what ailed me.

'I am wondering whether I should leave the country,' I said. 'It may not be safe to remain.'

He looked shocked and took both my hands in his. 'Oh, Kit, surely it will not come to that! This is but a moment of bad feeling. The men in power, the city authorities, know that the Strangers bring us nothing but good. Else why would they have granted those extra privileges last month?'

'They mean well, perhaps, but have they judged the mood of the citizens aright? And the timing of such a move? And can the authorities control the mob? Think of what happened in Paris! And in Portugal and Spain, there have been terrible massacres, thousands killed, and no attempt made to stop them.' I tried to speak rationally, but found I had begun to tremble and could not stop.

'Come,' he said, pulling me to my feet. 'What you need is a hot meal and glass of good French brandy to warm your heart and stomach.'

I smiled weakly at him. 'You always think food is the cure for all ills.'

'It often is,' he said cheerfully.

But I let him lead me off to an inn.

Afterwards, he could not walk back to our lodgings with me as he usually did, having a rehearsal with his fellow players. They hoped that a slight slackening of the plague meant that the playhouses would be permitted to reopen soon. It was an overcast evening, darker than usual for the time of year, and too early yet for the whorehouses to have set up flaming torches at their doorways. I had an uneasy sense of being followed, but scolded myself for allowing my fears to run away with me. The Lion being crowded with drinkers, we had taken ourselves off to an unfamiliar inn further down river and I had the longer walk home. Every dark alleyway to my left seemed a threatening mouth leading deeper into the maze of crazy buildings which were packed together in Southwark. To my right twisted lanes led down to the river, where I could hear the suck and slap of an ebb tide. Despite the rational half of my brain, I drew the small dagger I always wore at my waist.

They came at me suddenly out of the dark where my path crossed the opening to one of these right-hand alleys. I had barely time from the moment I first heard the pounding of their feet to wedge my shoulders into a crooked doorway. From the speed of their running steps I knew I could not outrun them, hampered by my long physician's gown.

There were three of them, burly young apprentices in their blue tunics and flat woollen caps. At least they would not carry swords, forbidden to apprentices, but one carried a hefty cudgel, the others had only their fists, but there was weight behind those fists. They were blacksmiths or stonemasons from their heavy build.

They stopped in front of me, sizing me up.

'So,' said the one with the cudgel, 'a dirty Stranger, a sneaking Frenchie, stealing our work and our food.'

'I am no Frenchman,' I said, trying to keep my voice steady, though sweat was pouring down my back and my hand was slippery on my dagger, which I kept down out of sight at my side. I knew my voice sounded as English as theirs. 'I am a physician at St Thomas's, caring for the poor of London.'

'Liar,' said one of the others.

'Even if he is,' said their leader, swinging his club menacingly in front of my face, 'St Thomas's employs Strangers to do filthy work no Englishman would touch. Look at his black hair. He's no Englishman.'

'I have done you no harm,' I said, ashamed that my voice had risen in pitch.

They laughed at that, and wasted no more time on words. In a moment they had me on the ground, kicking my stomach and spine. Instinctively I clasped my arms about my head and they caught the flash of my dagger just as the cudgel landed a heavy blow on my left elbow. I let out a yelp of pain.

Christ, help me! They were going to kill me!

'He's armed! Get his dagger!'

My left arm was numb from the blow, but my right hand tightened around my dagger. It had been my father's and I would not yield it without a fight. I lashed out blindly with it in the dark and felt the jarring of my arm as it met flesh, but I did no more than sting them into more violence. As they came at me again, I managed to twist around and kicked hard, catching one of them where it hurt most. He gave a grunt of pain and stumbled back, but the other two were kicking me again.

In a faint gleam reflected from the river, I saw a boot raised and realisation flashed through my head.

He's going to stamp on my right hand to seize hold of my dagger. My physician's right hand. Without it, I'm finished.

I rolled over just in time, but the boot caught me on the left side and I felt a sharp pain in my ribs.

Like a poker. Straight from the fire. Thrust into my side. Must curl tight, like an animal. Hide. Hide.

I knew I could not hold out much longer. I heard myself scream from far away. The world was darkening. I was lost. The man with the cudgel was standing over me now. He must be the one I had kicked.

'You bastard!' he shouted. 'Filthy foreigner! I'll smash your skull in for that.'

Time seemed to slow as he raised the cudgel, blurred somehow because my eyes were not working as they should. I closed them, dragging my weakened left arm across my face as some kind of pitiful protection. Then at the same instant I heard the swish of the club through the air and a shout: 'The Watch!' My head exploded in pain and I fell into darkness.

I do not know how long I lay there. Consciousness came back slowly, first as pain. It seemed to fill my whole body, so I wondered whether I was dying. And I was wet. Had it been raining? I wondered stupidly. I tried to move, for I was still lying curled up in that stinking doorway, with my right arm trapped under my body. I gave an involuntary yelp as I dragged myself into a sitting position and eased my right arm across my legs. Stupidly I peered down at my hand, which was clutching my dagger, but my sight was still blurred. As my brain began to focus again, I realised I was wet because I was bleeding. There was blood in my eyes and all down my right side and over my hand. Had I managed to wound one of my assailants badly enough to draw blood?

Then, as I pulled myself to my feet by clinging to the doorframe, I realised that I had rolled on to my own dagger, which had pierced my side. It was bleeding freely and a gash in my left temple was pouring blood over my face. I wiped my eyes with my sleeve and staggered a few steps. I must get myself home, in case those brutes were still nearby. My confused brain remembered the warning about the Watch, but how long ago had that been? A few minutes, so my attackers were lying low nearby? Or had it all happened hours ago?

Somehow I dragged myself back to my lodgings. I did not dare ask for help, for anyone I passed might be an enemy now and take the part of the apprentices. Back in my room I locked my door, lit a candle and began painfully to undress. Rikki, left behind when we had gone out to our meal, whined anxiously as he watched me. The gash in my side had bled a great deal but mercifully was not very deep. I must have rolled on to the side of the blade rather than the point. With some difficulty I managed to wind a bandage around my midriff and secure it. Every twist hurt my left side, where I was sure the kicking had broken some ribs.

It was more difficult to examine the damage to my head. When I had washed away the blood I could see in my scrap of cloudy mirror a mass of broken flesh above my left ear. Gingerly I pulled away the hair which had begun to stick to it, wincing as each hair sliced across the wound like a knife. Further round where I could not see, I could feel a lump swelling up, just above my hairline. This must be where the club had cracked against my head. I made a padded dressing and secured it above my ear. In the mirror

I looked like some desperate vagabond, so I found a woollen cap I wore in the winter and arranged it to hide the dressing. That was better, though I might be asked awkward questions.

My physician's instinct had carried me along until my injuries were attended to, but finally I sat down on the end of my bed and began to shake with cold and shock. Rikki jumped up beside me and began to lick my hand, as if he could somehow heal me. Even in the prison of the Inquisition I had not come so close to death. I saw clearly that if the Watch had not passed by I would be lying now a cold corpse in that alley, or rolled down to the river to be carried away on the ebbing tide.

I went to my work at the hospital as usual the next morning and if anyone noticed the woollen cap pulled down to my ears or the stiffness of my movements, they did not remark on it. No one mentioned hearing anything of an attack by apprentices, or of apprentices arrested for brawling, so I kept my own counsel. Ever since the outcry against Strangers had arisen, the mood in the hospital had become watchful. In one thing those men had been right. Many of the more unpleasant tasks both in this hospital and in St Bartholomew's were carried out by immigrants – the clearing away of bloody bandages and amputated limbs, the removal of corpses, the washing of vessels used for vomit or excrement. Such tasks fell to the hospital servants, many of whom were refugees. But there were also skilled foreign physicians and surgeons without whom St Bartholomew's and St Thomas's could not have cared for all the sick of London.

After a week, my injuries were healing. I would be left with a scar above my ear, but my hair would mostly cover it. The gash in my side had closed and when the scab fell off nothing would be left but a thin silver line. My ribs continued to give me pain, as I knew they would do for weeks yet. Especially at night, when any movement in my sleep woke me from dark dreams. The dreams, I knew, would leave a more permanent scar. I took care not to be abroad after dusk, and it was fortunate that Simon was so busy with his rehearsals that I managed to avoid him, for his sharp eyes would soon have observed what my fellows at the hospital appeared not to have noticed.

Just as my fears began to abate a little, I received an urgent summons from Thomas Phelippes and went to his office with a fast beating heart. I had not served in the intelligence service for months now. Either of the rival intelligence services. What could he want of me? Had Poley betrayed me at last? There was little reason now for him to keep silence. His hold over me because of my sex could serve no purpose any longer, now that he was employed by the Cecils, unless he decided to reveal it out of pure spite. But no, it was these recent disturbances in London that concerned Phelippes.

'The Privy Council has appointed a commission of five men to look into these libels and placards that have been appearing on the streets, Kit. I am one of those chosen as a commissioner, and also William Waad, whom you knew in Sir Francis's time. Dr Julius Caesar is to head the commission.'

In spite of my nervousness I had to repress a smile, for the name of the Master of the Court of Requests always seemed to me somewhat absurd. William Waad was another matter. A cruel man who took pleasure in the torture of his victims and who had been part of the projection against Babington to ensnare the Scottish queen. A strange choice, but perhaps the work of this 'commission' called for ruthlessness.

'I congratulate you, Thomas, on such a distinguished appointment, but what is that to me?'

'I must give all my time to the commission, for the next few weeks. We are charged with discovering, by all secret means, who are the authors of these dangerous libels which are appearing lately in London.'

At the words 'secret means', I grimaced with distaste. I knew what the term meant. It was by such 'secret means' that the Inquisition proceeded, though here in London they used the rack and manacles rather than the *strapado* and the water torture. I understood why Waad was to be one of the commissioners.

'My cipher clerk, Peter Townley, is well enough for straightforward tasks, when he is instructed what to do and kept to his work, and Arthur Gregory is very skilled, within his limited field, but I need someone to take charge here in my office. I want you.'

'But Thomas, I have my duties at the hospital.'

'That is all arranged. They will free you until the end of May. By then we should have rooted out this canker.'

I was angry, furiously angry, that he should take it upon himself to order my life without my consent, but I bit back my words. I wondered who had 'arranged' my absence from the hospital. Anthony Bacon? Essex himself? Surely not. However, the situation was too dangerous for me at present, I must not make a stand against Phelippes, though I was hurt that Superintendent Ailmer had not taken me into his confidence and forewarned me.

'Very well,' I said grimly. 'Tell me what you want me to do.'

It was simple enough. I would decipher and transcribe as I had always done in the past. If necessary I would prepare passports for agents travelling abroad. In addition I would sort the reports according to importance and urgency, despatch them by confidential messenger to Anthony Bacon, who would pass the most important to Lord Essex, and when required I would also pass on coded instructions from Master Bacon to agents afield. It meant assuming far more responsibility than I had ever held under Walsingham. It also suggested that Essex's attempt to set up an intelligence service to rival that of the Cecils was not proving very effective, if Phelippes had no senior man to whom he could delegate this responsibility.

'There is one other matter you should be informed about,' Phelippes said. 'The Council has ordered that a strict account should be taken of all the foreigners resident in London. A *Return of Strangers* will be made, ward by ward, under the direction of the aldermen. If you know of any of your countrymen, or any other Strangers, who might seek to conceal themselves from this account, warn them that there will be no danger to them in this gathering of information, but there will be reprisals if any seek to hide from it, or lie to those making the return.'

So, I was to be made responsible for managing Phelippes's network, but at the same time I was warned that as a Stranger I was under close scrutiny, while also being told to act as an informant against other refugees. Was there to be no escape, even here?

Although I was temporarily relieved of my hospital duties, I insisted to Phelippes that I would still visit St Thomas's once a day and I must be allowed to continue the care of my private patients. A day or two later I paid a call on one of the benchers at Gray's Inn, who suffered from recurring attacks of the gout. As usual I dosed him with physic to clear the crystals from his blood, gave him an ointment for the affected foot, and advised him, as usual, to modify his rich diet – advice which I knew he would ignore. Also as usual. On my way home I passed Mountjoy's Inn and called on Sara, whom I found agitatedly staring out of the window at the garden. I joined her. Ruy was pacing up and down a path between shrubberies, gesticulating with great animation, with two men of Iberian appearance who seemed familiar. One was a big, confident man, the other thin and shabby, but with the air of a gentleman fallen on hard times.

'Do I not know those men?' I said. 'But I cannot recall their names.'

'The burly fellow is Andrada, the intelligencer who was involved in Walsingham's last projection. Something Ruy is still pursuing, though I wish he would not. It is risky. With Walsingham gone, it is highly dangerous.'

'Ah,' I said.

'Aye.' She shuddered.

'And the other? I think perhaps I have seen him before. Could it have been at the safe house in St Katharine Creechurch?'

'Ferreira da Gama. A follower of Dom Antonio. Or once he was. I think, like Ruy, he has little love for the Dom now.'

'They seem very engrossed in their discussion,' I said thoughtfully.

'Aye,' she said again, with a bleak smile, turning away from the window. 'That is what I am afraid of.'

A copy of the *Return of Strangers* was delivered to Phelippes's office in the Customs House on the fourth day of May, for the aldermen and their servants had worked with remarkable speed. There were seven thousand and thirteen Strangers in London, including children and servants, but only four thousand five hundred and seventy (both adults and children) had been born abroad. Nearly half the 'Strangers' were first and second generation English-born, like Sara and her children. A handful, two hundred and thirty-seven, were denizens, and so – in a sense – citizens. In a population of near a quarter of a million, as the authorities estimated, I could not see how about two thousand foreign-born adults could be much threat to Englishmen, but when the mob seizes hold of an idea, it does not think rationally. We were foreigners, immigrants, with strange languages and dubious faiths, and some (for there were a few Ethiops and Lascars and Arabs amongst us) had skins of a different colour, which marked us out even more distinctly.

The following day, Saturday the fifth of May, something occurred near midnight that was to have terrible consequences. The first I heard of it was early the next morning, when I was summoned by Phelippes to the Customs House, although it was a Sunday.

'Read this,' he said, without preamble, thrusting a torn and dirty paper at me. It bore the mark of several fingers, but it was clear enough to read. It was a long piece of doggerel verse, of which one passage in particular caught my eye:

Your Machiavellian Merchant spoils the state,
Your usury doth leave us all for dead,
Your artifex & craftsman works our fate,
And like the Jews you eat us up as bread.

So, I thought, I had wondered how long it would be before they started attacking Jews.

'Look at the signature,' Phelippes said.

The document was signed 'Tamburlaine'.

'Surely this means nothing,' I said. 'Unless the author wishes to suggest that, like Tamburlaine, he will destroy utterly all those whom he considers his enemies. It is an attempt to make the threat more terrifying.'

'Perhaps.' He gave a small nod. 'But do you note the reference to a Machiavellian Jew? And notice this.'

He pointed to two more lines.

We'll cut your throats, in your temples praying,
Not Paris massacre so much blood did spill.

'What does that bring to mind?'

'The St Bartholomew's Day Massacre in Paris,' I said. 'When the Catholics massacred the Huguenots, even when they were praying in church.'

'Quite. *Tamburlaine.* A Machiavellian *Jew* – from *Malta*, perhaps? *The Massacre at Paris.* Not, I fancy, a coincidence.'

The name hung in the air between us, but, despite my dislike of the man, I would not speak it.

'Marlowe!' he said at last, impatiently. 'Do not pretend to me you are so dull-witted as not to see it, Kit. What game are you playing?'

'Someone is certainly trying to implicate Marlowe,' I said carefully.

I must watch my words. If Marlowe was implicated, Simon was too close. Once he had been a close friend of Marlowe, even shared lodgings with Kyd and Marlowe, though of recent months I had observed that definite cooling toward the fellow. Simon could be in danger. I

224

knew Phelippes of old. Like an English bulldog he would never release his prey once his jaws were clamped around it.

'Marlowe himself is the author,' he said flatly.

'I think not. Marlowe is no fool. Why should he write such a document, then point the finger at himself?'

'Marlowe is a dangerous hot-head,' he said angrily. 'He is forever brawling in the streets. He killed a man once, but managed to talk his way out of it, with that honeyed tongue of his. He is clever. Oh, yes, he is clever. But he is a filthy Sodomite and a damned atheist. He is behind this, you may be sure. He flaunts it in our faces!'

I had never seen Phelippes so impassioned before. A tightly controlled man, with his closed face behind those steel spectacles of his. Never had he given way to such emotion, not even long ago when he handed me the letter that was to seal the Scottish queen's fate. Now there were patches of high colour on his cheeks and a speck of foam on his lower lip. Had he been nursing a hatred of Marlowe all those years that he had employed him as an intelligencer and projector for Walsingham?

And yet I could not believe Marlowe would write something as crude as these limping rhymes. He might have hidden references to himself in a piece of political propaganda, but he would have done so with much more subtlety. And it would have pained him physically to write anything as paltry as this. Besides, I knew from Simon that Marlowe was at present again residing in Kent with Sir Thomas Walsingham at Scadbury, and working on a long lyrical poem about Hero and Leander. He was not posting up libels in the streets of London. The suspicion darted through my mind that Phelippes himself had written it, to discredit Marlowe, but he did seem genuinely disturbed by the paper.

'Where was this found?' I asked.

'Nailed up on the churchyard wall of the Dutch church in Broad Street.'

'What do you intend to do about it?'

I wondered in passing why Phelippes had taken possession of it, rather than the Cecils, but perhaps, since he had served as a commissioner, it was brought to him first.

'The Privy Council is meeting shortly,' he said. 'I want you to stay here today in case you are needed. I also want you to consider whether you know of anyone else who might be responsible. These references to three of Marlowe's plays – you know the players and playmakers – who among them might have done this, if not Marlowe?'

Suddenly I sensed further danger to Simon. I shook my head.

'I cannot think it would have been one of them. The verses are too awkward and childish. More likely someone else who wished to hurt Marlowe.'

I thought, but did not say, that this might be more of the battle between Essex and Cecil. Last year, after his arrest in Flushing, Marlowe had been interviewed and released by the Cecils, so he must be in favour with them. On the other hand, Phelippes worked for Essex. Was this an Essex plot to undermine the Cecils? Would Phelippes be a party to such a plot? Yet he had sounded genuinely angry and convinced that Marlowe was the author of the document. Then there was Marlowe's connection with Ralegh, currently out of favour with the Queen because of his secret marriage. Essex, a blundering man of inferior intellect, was known to loathe Ralegh, Northumberland, Harriot and all their learned circle. Accusations of heresy against Marlowe could be used to taint Ralegh as well, at this opportune moment. My head was spinning. It was a tangle of malice, conspiracy, and ambition.

For the next few days, the city was uneasily quiet. There were no more libels, as though the one from the Dutch church was the final throw of the dice and the perpetrators were waiting and watching to see what would happen next. Then on Thursday a proclamation from the Privy Council was read out at the Guildhall: a reward of one hundred crowns would be given to any man who revealed the author of the libel. A hundred crowns! Riches beyond belief! It was an open and lucrative invitation for the betrayal of enemies and the settling of old scores. Any man accused would be arrested and questioned under torture, regardless of whether there was any evidence against him or not. His dwelling would be searched, and all his papers seized.

The next night, the man with whom Simon had once shared lodgings was arrested, the playmaker Thomas Kyd. I remembered Simon's excitement when Kyd had written one of the first of the new kind of play, *A Spanish Tragedy*. I learned from Phelippes that Kyd was put to the torture at once. A weakly man, and never a brave one, he hastened to tell them anything they wanted to him to say. In his lodging was found some heretical document, which I learned later was merely a passage copied from a published work on theology, in which the heresy was refuted. The paper, said Kyd, belonged to Marlowe, though it was not in his handwriting.

Why? I pondered this in the days that followed. Kyd claimed that the paper had become mixed with his during the time when he and Marlowe shared lodgings – and for a time so had Simon, I thought with a shudder. But it was not in Marlowe's hand. Kyd swore it was not his own. Did he really believe it was Marlowe's? To me, it looked like a clumsy projection, planted there by Marlowe's enemies. The document had probably been inserted amongst Kyd's papers while the officers of the Privy Council were searching his rooms. It could easily be done. I wondered whether Phelippes had forged it. Nay, he must have samples of Marlowe's writing, and a forgery by Phelippes would have been undetectable from the handwriting he forged. I was thankful I had not been asked to forge it. What would happen next? Could this paper from Kyd's lodgings, on its own, be enough to convict Marlowe of heresy? And how could it link him to the anonymous libels, which were supposed to be the original justification for the arrests and torture and searches?

London felt like a pot about to boil over and scald anyone who was near. The players had abandoned their rehearsals when they heard of Kyd's arrest. Now that the census of resident Strangers had been completed, I was no longer left in charge of Phelippes's office and returned for much of each day to my work at St Thomas's, where nerves were strung tight amongst all of us, not only the Strangers. The men's ward became crowded with the victims of street brawls. Anxious to know what was happening, I continued to work at the Customs House for part of each day, until the month of May should be over, wanting to be sure I knew what was afoot and whether I was in danger as a Stranger, or Simon was in danger from his time sharing those lodgings with Kyd and Marlowe.

'Would there be anything of yours left behind there?' I asked him.

We were sitting at a table outside the Lion in the long spring twilight. No one else was near, but I kept my voice down nonetheless.

Simon shrugged. He was looking pale with worry. I had just told him all I knew about what had happened to Kyd, to try to make him understand that he could be in danger and must walk carefully.

'I don't know.' He smiled weakly. 'As you are always telling me, I am untidy in my habits. There may be rough papers of mine left there, but it was months ago. Years ago.'

'Nothing libellous or heretical?'

'Of course not. Perhaps one of my parts from a play.'

'Are you sure even a part from a play could not be misread?'

'Anything may be misread by those who choose to misread it for their own purposes,' he said bitterly. 'This paper you say they found in Kyd's lodgings – or put there themselves. You say that Phelippes has told you it is not in either Kyd's or Marlowe's writing and is merely something copied from a well known printed book. Yet they can use that as an excuse to torture Kyd. Poor Kyd!'

He covered his face with his hands and groaned.

I did not know Kyd well myself, but I knew what torture could do to a man. Even if they had broken him easily, he would never be the same again.

'All I am saying–' I reached across and laid my hand on his shoulder. 'All I am saying is that you should be very, very careful. Watch your tongue, watch your back.' I tried to lighten my tone. 'Do not walk down any dark alleys alone at night.'

He lowered his hands from his face. 'Not you either.'

In order to strengthen his resolve, I told him at last about the beating I had suffered at the hands of the apprentices.

'Jesu, Kit!' he said. 'Why have you kept that to yourself all this while? You could have been killed.'

I shrugged. 'It is over now, and nothing to show for it but two small scars.' Unconsciously I touched the place above my left ear, where the hair had grown to cover the place where the club had smashed into my head.

A week after Kyd was arrested, we had a partial answer as to why he had been picked out, from all the men known to associate with Marlowe. His ready confession and the incriminating piece of paper – flimsy evidence as it was – provided excuse enough. Someone must have known that he would be easy to break. A warrant was issued for the arrest of Christopher Marlowe, and an officer departed for Thomas Walsingham's estate in Kent to fetch him back to London, to face questioning by the Privy Council. All this I learned as I spent my time in Phelippes's office in the Customs House, longing for the month of May to end, so that I could return entirely to the safe anonymity of the hospital. On Sunday, the twentieth day of May, Marlowe was questioned and then released on bail, with the condition that he should report to the Privy Council every day. Again I wondered, *why*? Thomas Kyd, whom no one seriously suspected of anything, was imprisoned and tortured. Marlowe, whom Phelippes certainly hated, and many men disliked and distrusted, walked the streets, a free man, or near enough. Was someone protecting him? The Cecils? They had released him without charge after the affair in Flushing. So was it Essex who was out to destroy him, and through him damage both the Cecils and Ralegh? That would explain why Phelippes had secured possession of the 'Tamburlaine' libel.

A week later – I was working in the office again on a Sunday – Phelippes came in with a sheaf of papers in his hand, and a look of triumph on his face. He waved it at me.

'We have him now!'

'Who?'

'Marlowe! I have here a detailed deposition concerning all the villain's heresies, the atheistic lectures he has given to Ralegh's set, his vile sodomy, his practice of persuading men to heresy.'

The atheist lecture – I went cold at the memory. I wonder whether Phelippes, who knew so much, knew that I had been present.

'But who has written it?' I ventured. 'Someone trustworthy? Or another creeping informer?'

'Now, Kit, you know the man must be stopped. This has been written by Richard Baines, who knows him well.'

Richard Baines. That was the man who had been issuing a counterfeit coin with Marlowe in Flushing, and had accused him to the governor. Richard Baines, another former agent of Walsingham's. Was this some personal attack, or was Baines acting under instruction from someone else? Robert Poley, I remembered, had also been with them in Flushing. Poley, who now worked for the Cecils, and had clawed his way up to a senior position in their service.

Poley had been abroad again, to Brussels after Christmas, then to the Low Countries, on the eighth of May. But had he now returned?

'Is Robert Poley in England?' I asked.

Phelippes looked at me, startled by my abrupt question.

'He is this very day returned,' he said softly, 'but it is not to be spoken of. Matters of state.'

So Phelippes knew of Poley's movements, the Cecils' man.

Baines and Poley, both somewhere lurking in the shadows when Marlowe was twice entrapped. The affair in Flushing had been some simple projection, childish. The present scheme was much more complex and appeared to show bitter rivals working together. And there had been that conversation I had overheard in Hampton Court Palace at Christmas, between Robert Poley and Ingram Frizer. They had not mentioned by name the man against whom they had been gathering evidence, but I was sure now, beyond any shadow of doubt, that it was Marlowe. Poley, Frizer, and Baines, as slippery and untrustworthy a trio you could discover. I shivered. I did not like the man Marlowe, but I was glad I was not standing in his shoes this day.

Chapter Twelve

*T*here had been much talk amongst the players about Marlowe's latest play, which both Master Burbage and Master Henslowe had declared unsuitable for the Christmas Revels at Hampton Court Palace. Their intention, however, was to put it on in one of the London playhouses, either the Rose or the Theatre, once they opened again after the winter. However, the early outbreak of the plague had caused delay to their plans, and when they were finally able to open, comedy seemed to be what was most needed in the restless state of the city.

Yet, despite all the talk, I had very little idea of what the play could be about. Something to do with a German university scholar who sold his soul to the Devil, and it was supposed to be based on a true story. Marlowe was fond of true stories – *Tamburlaine*, *The Massacre at Paris*, *Edward II*, these all had their basis in factual events. *The Jew of Malta* (as far as I knew) did not, but grew from Marlowe's loathing of Jews.

I could learn very little more about this new play, *Doctor Faustus*, than the simple fact of its origin. The players were very evasive.

'Watch it and make your own judgement,' Guy advised. 'That is better than anything I can tell you.'

'It is a very curious play,' Simon said. 'I do not know myself what to make of it.'

'What part do you play?' I asked with cunning, thinking that in this way I would be able to find out more.

He shrugged. 'All of them? None of them anything of a part.'

'All of them!'

He numbered them off on his fingers.

'A friar. A Deadly Sin. A knight (nameless). A scholar of Wittenberg. A horse courser.'

'A what?'

'A clown of a horse dealer. A piece of farce. A kind of comic interlude. One of several.'

I frowned. 'Farce? Interlude? But it is not a comedy, is it? I thought the full title was *The Tragical History of the Life and Death of Doctor Faustus*. That does not sound much like a comedy to me.'

He shrugged again. 'Marlowe has thrown in a subplot of comedy, which mimics the main tragic story. Servants playing at magic, with silly results. And some such comic scenes involving Faustus himself. I suppose he thought it would give the audience ease from the tragedy. I am not sure that it succeeds.'

He sounded as though he disliked the play.

'And it is all about *magic*?' I said dubiously. 'Christopher Haigh said something about fireworks, like one of those old morality plays.'

'Oh, well, you see, if you have devils, you have to have fireworks, don't you? The groundlings expect it.'

I shook my head at this attempt (successful) to divert my questioning. And that was all the information I could extract from them. It certainly aroused my curiosity, and I planned to see this odd play, but the closure of the playhouses, almost as soon as they had opened after the winter, put a stop to any visit early in the year. Then I was caught up, first with my patients at the hospital, and then with Phelippes, taking over his work at the Customs House.

Now the playhouses were open again, and it was decided to stage *The Tragical History of the Life and Death of Doctor Faustus* at the Rose, shortly after Marlowe had been arrested and then set free. I think everyone in the players' world believed that the present case was just another of Marlowe's brushes with the law, like the time he had been involved with the killing of a man in Shoreditch, and that other time, just over a year ago, when there had been the strange case of the counterfeit coins. Marlowe was constantly in trouble and always managed to wriggle free. Why should this be any different? The play, if strange, had proved exciting and popular the few times they had been able to stage it, so it was a waste to let it moulder away, locked in a chest of playbooks. And Marlowe's present notoriety would spur people on to come and see it.

Thus, I believe, they reasoned.

I had the uneasy feeling that this time matters were different for Marlowe. From my work with Phelippes, I knew this was a far more serious case than any of his other crimes. Someone – or many people – had gone to a great deal of trouble to fan the existing flames of unrest in London, especially the hatred of foreigners, and had attached crude references to Marlowe's plays to the latest and worst of the placards, the one posted up on the Dutch Church. The one Phelippes claimed was incontrovertible proof of Marlowe's guilt, though I thought otherwise.

Then there was the paper found in Kyd's lodgings, and quite probably planted there deliberately. It was not in Marlowe's hand, and it was only on the word of the terrified Kyd that it was purported to have belonged to Marlowe. In any case, it was merely a passage copied from a printed book, easily available from any bookseller in Paul's churchyard. Neither of these documents was true evidence and seemed to me like crude and inept attempts to blacken Marlowe, but unsuccessfully.

The case of Baines's document, however, was very different. I had myself seen Baines furiously taking notes that evening at Durham House and could bear witness that what he had written was very close to what I had myself heard Marlowe say. I would not, however, bear such witness. From sheer cowardice, I did not want to admit that I had been present, however unwillingly, when Marlowe gave his 'lecture'. But, from more honourable motives, I hope, I would not try to turn words spoken in private company into evidence of heresy against a man, however much I disliked him.

Now, however, Marlowe had been questioned and released. He was required to report to the Privy Council every day, which meant he must stay in London, not return to Sir Thomas Walsingham's house in Kent, but apart from that he could live a normal, or fairly normal, life. So *The Tragical History of the Life and Death of Doctor Faustus* was to be staged, and I would finally see it the next day.

'Marlowe is coming to see it himself,' Simon said, when I told him of my plans. We were sitting outside in the tiny garden behind the Atkins house, with a tankard of ale and a cold beef pasty each. The garden held a vegetable bed and a herb plot, a few chickens, and a small, not very productive, bee skep. It was too warm for comfort in our rooms, so we had brought stools out here to share the fresh air with the hens, who were eying our pasties hopefully.

'He has never yet had the chance to see *Doctor Faustus* staged,' he said, 'for when we performed it before, he was down at Scadbury.'

'I shall look out for him in the audience,' I said politely, thinking to myself that I would take care to stay well away from him. I doubted whether his latest brush with the law would have made him any less insulting to me.

Since the weather had turned so warm as we approached the end of May, I thought it kinder not to shut Rikki up in my room while I was at the playhouse.

'Thank you for keeping him this extra time,' I said to Tom Read.

'We're always happy to have him, Swifty and me,' he said. 'Going to the playhouse, are you? Which play?'

'*The Tragical History of the Life and Death of Doctor Faustus*,' I said, rolling out the mouthful with a touch of sarcasm. Many of these titles the playmakers devised always seemed somewhat overblown to me.

'Ah,' Tom said.

'Have you seen it?'

'I have.'

'I gather, from the look on your face, that you did not like it.'

He looked uncomfortable. 'I don't think it is a play you can exactly *like*, doctor. It's . . . well, it's troubling, if you take my meaning.'

'I am not sure I do,' I said. 'Everyone speaks of it in such a strange way. I suppose by this evening I shall understand what you all mean.'

I reached the Rose early, so that I might have a good choice of seats, and was waved in without paying by the doorkeeper, who knew me well. The best place, I always feel, is directly opposite the centre of the stage and one story up from ground level, in one of the balconies. These hold tiers of seats, divided into blocks by narrow aisles, for the easier movement of the audience in and out of the seats. Because I was early, I found one of the choicest seats, in the front row of this balcony, next to an aisle. Higher up it is more difficult to hear; lower down you can be distracted by the groundlings standing only slightly below you; seated around to the right or left you view the stage aslant, which does not matter much when the actors are forward on the apron stage, but can hamper your view if they are using the room as the back, which they call the 'inner' stage. A seat next to the aisle allows you more room.

Pleased with my seat, I settled down to wait while the rest of the audience arrived, drifting in slowly after the flag was raised in the tower above the upper stage, then hurriedly pushing their way in after the trumpet had sounded the last call before the play started. Several people tried to make me give up my seat and move along the row, but I am wise to that trick. I twisted to one side and let them sidle past me to the inner seats. All came in parties of two or more, so they ignored the single empty seat across the aisle from me, in the front row of the next block.

At the very last moment, when Christopher Haigh (as Chorus) was striding on to the stage, there was a slight disturbance behind me, and a man ran down the stepped aisle to that empty seat. I looked across to see who had left it so late, and felt a sudden shock. It was Marlowe himself, come to watch a performance of his *Doctor Faustus* for the first time. He leaned forward, resting his loosely clasped hands on the railing in front of him as Christopher began to speak.

> *Not marching now in fields of Thrasimene,*
> *Where Mars did mate the Carthaginians;*
> *Nor sporting in the dalliance of love,*
> *In courts of kings where state is overturn'd;*
> *Nor in the pomp of proud audacious deeds,*
> *Intends our Muse to vaunt his heavenly verse:*
> *Only this, gentlemen, — we must perform*
> *The form of Faustus' fortunes, good or bad.*

I turned away from Marlowe and began to concentrate on the play. Hmm, 'heavenly verse', indeed. Marlowe did not grow in modesty as he grew in years.

Soon we were shown Faustus in his study at the University of Wittenberg, where he poured contempt on all the academic studies he had mastered – philosophy, medicine, the law, and, above all, divinity. He was, by his own estimate, the greatest master in the world of all these subjects, and they could not satisfy either his greed for learning or his lust for power. There was only one study left which could give him the power he craved, over man and beast, living and dead, over the physical world and the very heavens.

> *'Tis magic, magic, that hath ravish'd me.*

As the play proceeded, I thought that Marlowe had made precisely the correct choice of word in 'ravish'd', for the effect of necromancy on Faustus was like the rape of his soul.

I glanced across at Marlowe. He was watching intently, and it came into my mind to wonder whether the figure of Faustus was in some way a kind of self portrait. Did Marlowe recognise in himself the overweening intellectual arrogance he had given to Faustus? And was Faustus's greed for power, through whatever illicit means, a parallel to the dangerous games his creator had been playing in recent years? I knew what everyone knew about his publicly discussed crimes, but being a part of the same intelligence world as he was, which was hidden from the public, I also knew what dark and treacherous byways might be travelled there.

But I must stop thinking about the creator and think about his creation. Ned Alleyn was powerfully convincing as Faustus, a man with a brilliant mind, admired by his students, but restless, dissatisfied, unfulfilled. He is instructed by two colleagues who have dabbled in the fringes of necromancy, which reminded me somewhat uneasily of Dr Dee and the wizard Earl. But Faustus longs to go beyond these petty experiments, and calls up a major devil, Mephistophilis, played with sinister cunning, hidden under a bland and servile exterior, by Dick Burbage.

Faustus, who believes himself to be in control, is unaware that he is being manipulated by Mephistophilis. Even when Mephistophilis tells him the truth, that he is always in Hell, that Hell is here, Faustus is too self-absorbed to understand the message. Told that Mephistophilis can only act under orders from the fallen angel Lucifer, who rules in Hell, Faustus readily agrees to write out a deed of gift, granting his soul to Lucifer in return for four and twenty years of magical power, with Mephistophilis to carry out his every command during the agreed period of the bargain. The deed must be signed in his own blood. When the blood congeals, preventing him from signing, Faustus has a moment of doubt, but Mephistophilis soon has the blood running again.

Intermittently a good angel and a bad angel try in turn to persuade Faustus to abandon his devilish pact – repentance would save him – or to enjoy the pleasures of the Devil's bargain – repentance would be useless. As stage figures, these angels reminded me of the old fashioned plays I had seen performed on holy days when I had first come to London. They were long gone now, but Marlowe was using these traditional characters to embody the conflict in Faustus's (or his own?) mind.

As Simon had predicted, the demons from Hell were accompanied by fireworks, another survival from those old, crude plays.

Marlowe, I noticed, was craning forward now, his hands gripped tightly together. What was he thinking? More than ever it seemed to me that in Faustus he was working out some problem with himself. I did not think he had ever experimented with necromancy, though for all I knew he might have done, but in Faustus's heretical denunciation of divinity and the Bible there were clear echoes of Marlowe's denunciation of the Bible and the traditional teachings of the Church in his lecture at Durham House. Not quite the same words, but close enough to make me shudder.

It was clever of him not to make Faustus pure evil. This was a man of great abilities and initially his intentions were to use his magical powers for the general good.

> *I'll have them wall all Germany with brass,*
> *And make swift Rhine circle fair Wittenberg;*
> *I'll have them fill the public schools with silk,*
> *Wherewith the students shall be bravely clad;*
> *I'll levy soldiers with the coin they bring,*
> *And chase the Prince of Parma from our land,*
> *And reign sole king of all the provinces;*
> *Yea, stranger engines for the brunt of war*
> *Than was the fiery keel at Antwerp's bridge,*
> *I'll make my servile spirits to invent.*

Protection for Wittenberg and Germany, silk gowns for the students, defeat for the Prince of Parma, King Philip's general of the Spanish army in the Low Countries – all of these are public spirited intentions, even if Faustus's plans to become king, and to deploy engines of war better than those of Spain, are not.

As the play continued, it became clear that none of these noble goals would be achieved, as Mephistophilis subtly subverted them.

In all honesty, I found the scenes of low comedy irritating while I was trying to concentrate on the main story of Faustus's apparent rise to power and fortune, followed by his tragic fall. Although, not surprisingly, these comic scenes drew loud bursts of laughter and applause from the groundlings standing in the pit below me. Laughter which was, perhaps, all the louder for being a release from the tension in the audience at what was happening in the rest of the play.

Troubling, as Tom had said.

I had begun to notice something very peculiar in the way Faustus spoke. Almost invariably he referred to himself in the third person, saying that 'Faustus' does this, or 'Faustus' will do that, as though by speaking of this person as separate from himself, he could somehow divorce himself from his own blasphemy and dealings with the Devil. When I realised this, I shivered, and stole another glance at Marlowe. I could detect beads of sweat on his temple, and his hands were now so tightly gripped that the bones shone white beneath the skin.

When Mephistophilis expressed his agony and horror at being shut out for ever from the blessings of Heaven, Faustus urged him to emulate his own 'manly fortitude'. *Bluster*, I thought. When he had Mephistophilis fetch grapes in winter, preening himself, I thought: *Empty party trick*. When the two of them, scholar and devil, tormented the Pope and his fellows, I thought: *Childish foolery*. All of which I was sure I was meant to think. All through the four and twenty years of his bargain, Faustus achieves nothing but these empty tricks. And for this he has sold his soul into eternal damnation.

What I found most compelling was the fact that almost from the start, Faustus begins to be frightened, to regret his dangerous bargain, but can never quite bring himself to repent. As time begins to run out, an old man makes one final attempt to persuade him to seek God's mercy, even when he is himself threatened with physical torments by Mephistophilis. He is not afraid, for he knows his immortal soul is safe in God's hands. Faustus, however, is terrified:

Where art thou, Faustus? Wretch, what hast thou done?

Damn'd art thou, Faustus, damn'd; despair and die!
Hell calls for right, and with a roaring voice
Says "Faustus! come! thine hour is almost come!"
And Faustus now will come to do thee right.

There is no escape, he thinks. The bargain must be kept. The good angel and the old man urge him to repentance, for even now, after his evil bargain, repentance will bring him God's mercy and the saving of his soul from eternal damnation. In the end, he recognises this truth, but cannot speak the words.

There is danger in words.

Words spoken to make an evil pact. Words spoken for salvation.

The audience had fallen silent, even down in the pit, where there is usually some movement and whispering and the sound of nuts being cracked. Danger in words. The tension was palpable. My own heart was beating faster and the palms of my hands were damp. I could not like Marlowe – I mean Faustus – but I did not want to see him damned to eternal torment through the rest of time. Why did he not repent? Why *could* he not repent?

Accursed Faustus, where is mercy now?
I do repent; and yet I do despair;
Hell strives with grace for conquest in my breast:
What shall I do to shun the snares of death?

I turned to look across the narrow aisle to Marlowe. He was bowed forward, his knees drawn up as if in some pain. His face was buried in his hands.

Threatened by Mephistophilis if he does not keep his bargain, Faustus, twisting this way and that, begs Lucifer's forgiveness – forgiveness from the Devil, who will never forgive, who does not possess the quality of mercy.

Sweet Mephistophilis, entreat thy lord
To pardon my unjust presumption,

And with my blood again I will confirm
My former vow I made to Lucifer.

In so doing, Faustus fails to show the courage of the old man, who endures present physical torment to secure ultimate divine grace.

As a final boon from Mephistophilis, Faustus begs to have Helen of Troy as his paramour. By now all his vaunted intelligence and scholarship are for nothing. He is blind to elementary reason. Helen has been dead for centuries. Even if her ghostly image could be summoned up, it is nothing but illusion. She can never be mortal woman again. Faustus deliberately ignores this, instead willingly choosing to participate in the illusion:

Sweet Helen, make me immortal with a kiss.
Her lips suck forth my soul; see where it flies!

And in this he finally speaks the truth, for this is not Helen, it is a demonic *succuba*. By kissing it, Faustus does indeed at last abandon any claim on his soul.

Three scholars enter and try to reason with Faustus, but he is beyond reason, muttering like a madman, they can do nothing but leave him while they go to offer up prayers for him.

On the stage, the clock strikes eleven times. At midnight Lucifer would demand Faustus's soul.

Ah, Faustus, Now hast thou but one bare hour to live,
And then thou must be damn'd perpetually!
Stand still, you ever-moving spheres of Heaven,
That time may cease, and midnight never come;
Fair Nature's eye, rise, rise again and make
Perpetual day; or let this hour be but
A year, a month, a week, a natural day,
That Faustus may repent and save his soul!
O lente, lente, currite noctis equi!
The stars move still, time runs, the clock will strike,
The Devil will come, and Faustus must be damn'd.
O, I'll leap up to my God! Who pulls me down?
See, see where Christ's blood streams in the firmament!

242

One drop would save my soul — Half a drop: ah, my
Christ!
    Ah, rend not my heart for naming of my Christ!
Yet will I call on him: O spare me, Lucifer! —
Where is it now? 'Tis gone; and see where God
Stretcheth out his arm, and bends his ireful brows!
Mountain and hills come, come and fall on me,
And hide me from the heavy wrath of God!
No! no!

Faustus's voice had risen to a desperate shriek, but despite it, I heard a groan from the man across the aisle. I wanted to reach out to him, but sat frozen in my seat, my breath stopped, my heart swelling in my chest.

    Then will I headlong run into the earth;
Earth gape! O no, it will not harbour me!
You stars that reign'd at my nativity,
Whose influence hath allotted death and hell,
Now draw up Faustus like a foggy mist
Into the entrails of yon labouring clouds,
That when they vomit forth into the air,
My limbs may issue from their smoky mouths,
So that my soul may but ascend to Heaven.

The clock on stage tolled the half hour. A gasp from the audience.

    Ah, half the hour is past! 'Twill all be past anon!
O God!
If thou wilt not have mercy on my soul,
Yet for Christ's sake whose blood hath ransom'd me,
Impose some end to my incessant pain;
Let Faustus live in hell a thousand years —
A hundred thousand, and at last be sav'd!
O, no end is limited to damned souls!
Why wert thou not a creature wanting soul?
Or why is this immortal that thou hast?
Ah, Pythagoras' metempsychosis! were that true,
This soul should fly from me, and I be chang'd

243

Unto some brutish beast! All beasts are happy,
For, when they die,
Their souls are soon dissolv'd in elements;
But mine must live, still to be plagu'd in hell.
Curst be the parents that engend'red me!
No, Faustus: curse thyself: curse Lucifer
That hath depriv'd thee of the joys of Heaven.

And midnight struck. A groan from the audience. I had covered my own face now, for I could not bear to watch.

O, it strikes, it strikes! Now, body, turn to air,
Or Lucifer will bear thee quick to hell.

There was a roaring like true thunder, and even through my closed eyes I was aware of lightning flashes.

O soul, be chang'd into little water-drops,
And fall into the ocean — ne'er be found.
My God! my God! look not so fierce on me!

Through the noise of thunder and lightning, and the explosion of fireworks, I knew that all the devils of Hell had come to seize this man, once so fine and promising, and drag him down to eternal torment. His final cries rang in my ears:
Adders and serpents, let me breathe awhile!
Ugly hell, gape not! come not, Lucifer!
I'll burn my books! — Ah Mephistophilis!
Gradually the noise died away. I found that I was gasping for breath, as though I had myself been fighting those very devils. Chorus, who had opened the play, returned to speak the epilogue:
Cut is the branch that might have grown full straight,
And burned is Apollo's laurel bough,
That sometimes grew within this learned man.
Faustus is gone; regard his hellish fall,

Whose fiendful fortune may exhort the wise
Only to wonder at unlawful things,
Whose deepness doth entice such forward wits
To practise more than heavenly power permits.

There was a hush in the audience, then hesitant applause, that grew louder, as much, I expect, from relief that it was over as from enjoyment.

I knew with absolute certainty, then, that Faustus was Marlowe. That his desperate struggles of mind were in some sense Marlowe's struggles. And had I not known that the play had been written long before his arrest, I would have believed that the final speech by the chorus was an attempt by Marlowe to make his peace with . . . whom? The authorities, who accused him of heresy? Or with his own tormented soul?

I knew suddenly that I must myself make my peace with Marlowe, however he might despise and reject me. I had hated the man. Now I felt for him an overwhelming sense of pity. Which no doubt he would not thank me for. But I needed to unburden myself. I suffered my own inner turmoils and torments, but they were nothing to what Marlowe – Faustus – suffered.

I got to my feet, somewhat dazed, and looked across the aisle.

Marlowe was gone.

Twisting around, I saw that he had reached the top of the sloping tiers of seats and was heading for the staircase that would lead down to the street. Elbowing my way rudely through the dispersing audience, I went in pursuit of him.

When I reached the crowds outside the theatre, some talking excitedly, some looking stunned and walking off alone, I saw Marlowe not far ahead. I must catch up with him now, before my courage failed me and I could not speak. As I came almost within reach of him, I heard a familiar voice say, 'Ah, there you are, Kit.'

My heart froze. My hand, which had been reaching out to pluck Marlowe's sleeve fell to my side. I turned my head. What did Robert Poley want with me?

But Poley wanted nothing of me. He was not even looking at me. It was the other Kit to whom he spoke. Kit Marlowe. Friendliwise, he threw his arm across Marlowe's shoulders. I had seen him make just such a gesture years before, throwing his arm around Anthony Babington's shoulders. Anthony Babington, who had been betrayed to his death a few short months later.

'A fine play, Kit,' Poley said. 'Your best, I'd say. The crowning achievement of your career in the playhouse, perhaps. For are you not Sir Thomas Walsingham's tame household poet now?'

'Indeed he is.'

Another man had joined them, on Marlowe's further side. Ingram Frizer.

'Sir Thomas thinks highly of his poet,' he said, smooth as a diplomat, 'and I have some proposals to put to you, Marlowe, which I bring from him. Proposals which you may take advantage of when this unpleasant business with the Privy Council is finished.'

I could see none of their faces, for I was behind them, but I was close enough to catch the sweet persuasiveness in Frizer's tone, which reminded me of Mephistophilis. I was also close enough to observe the stiffness of Marlowe's back. I thought he did not care to have Poley's arm so close about his neck, nor to be led away from the playhouse as if he was between two of the Privy Council's officers.

'Aye,' Poley said. 'Frizer has some interesting proposals.' With his free hand he tapped the side of his nose. 'But this is not the place to discuss them. We need time and quiet, so I have bespoken a room in Mistress Bull's house in Deptford for the whole day tomorrow. She makes provision for private parties in her home. We will have dinner and the garden to stroll in, and a board to play a game of tables, should we take the fancy, while we discuss these proposals and where they might lead.'

'Aye, proposals to your advantage, Marlowe,' Frizer said. 'We have the place until supper, and she serves an excellent meal, does Mistress Bull.'

''Twill make a change from kicking your heels in London,' Poley said, 'while you await the pleasure of the Privy Council.'

'Nick Skeres will join us,' Frizer said. 'To make up the numbers for any games we play to pass the time.'

'I will fetch you after you have reported to the Council tomorrow morning.' Poley gave Marlowe's shoulders a squeeze. 'Then we can take a boat down to Deptford and be there with the whole day to disport ourselves. That's settled then.'

In all this I had not heard Marlowe utter a word, but now he said, 'Aye, as you will,' in a distracted voice.

I thought he was still brooding over what he had revealed of himself in the play and wished to be rid of them, at any price. He broke away from Poley's arm, gave them the merest of bows, then strode away.

The other two men turned aside, so that I could now see their faces. Lest they notice me, I began to back into the crowd, but not before I saw the look they exchanged. I could not but recall the conversation I had overheard at Hampton Court Palace. I was certain now that they had been speaking of Marlowe, and he was the man who must be stopped.

Leaving the playhouse I felt restless, yet I did not want company. The play had given me much to think about, especially my certainty that Faustus was, in some sense, Marlowe. I felt uncomfortable with my need to speak to him, to somehow make peace. I had misjudged him. Certainly he was arrogant. He hated Jews. He was invariably rude to me. Yet I felt I was beginning to see beneath that swaggering exterior he always affected.

From the evidence of his other plays, it was clear that he was achingly sensitive to the dark side of human existence, as all the violence and bloodletting in

247

Tamburlaine, *Massacre at Paris*, *Edward II*, and *Jew of Malta* made clear. He must live with these dark demons in his head all the time. He was also intellectually very clever, there was no doubt of that, but what had it gained him? Neither distinction in the scholarly world nor at Court. Little wonder that he was restless and unsatisfied. Little wonder that his temper was short. Little wonder that it sometimes exploded into violence against those around him.

And that very cleverness led him into questioning the teachings of the Church. How much had he actually believed of that blasphemous lecture he had delivered at Ralegh's gathering? Was it intended purely to shock his listeners? Or was it the outburst of a deeply troubled mind? Could a man with no belief in God and the fate of his immortal soul have written that terrible heart-wrenching final speech of Faustus's?

I wanted to speak to him, to . . . to apologise for misjudging him, for taking him for a crude, bigoted fellow, when I now admitted to myself that he was a man tormented by his own inner demons, as he had shown Faustus to be by their physical manifestation in Mephistophilis and Lucifer.

However, I had no idea where he was lodging in London while under restriction by the Privy Council. In backing away to avoid notice by Poley and Frizer, I had lost sight of him in the crowd, and now he was nowhere to be seen.

Simon or Will might know where he was living. Master Burbage surely would, but I was reluctant to return to the playhouse to ask them. They would want to know why I, so often the butt of Marlowe's barbed remarks about Jews, should go seeking him out now. I would not ask them. I began to make my way back toward the Bridge and St Thomas's, for I must collect Rikki from Tom. Much of the crowd from the playhouse drifted in the same direction. Some were silent and thoughtful, others arguing loudly about whether it was possible to conjure the dead.

That, I thought, was not the point of the play.

'So what did you think of *Doctor Faustus*?' Tom asked.

'As you said, Tom. It is a troubling play. I need to think about it more.'

I buckled on Rikki's lead and headed back up river. I did not stop at my lodgings, and when I passed the Lion – where some of the players were just sitting down at one of the outside tables – I skirted round it, avoiding them. Instead, Rikki and I walked on, up the river, past the last scattered houses of Southwark, where I let him off the lead to roam about the Lambeth marshes at will.

There was a family of mallard ducks on the river, a slow swimming mother followed by seven ducklings in a row, bobbing about like a row of corks. Then a pair of swans passed, gliding slowly with the current. One grey cygnet was perched on a parent's back, a dark shadow, dull against the adult's white plumage, while two more cygnets followed behind. Over on my left, Rikki had flushed out a whole colony of marsh birds which exploded suddenly upwards, startling him, so that he came rushing back to me for reassurance.

We must have walked for an hour before I turned back. By then the brightness of the day was dimming, and even Rikki seemed tired, walking quietly at my heels and paying no heed to any birds or other creatures which rustled amongst the reeds. We had walked as far as Lambeth Palace, and it now seemed a long way back. I thought of taking a wherry, but there were none moored along this isolated stretch of river bank. The ducks and swans were no longer to be seen, having withdrawn to their nests, and the birds of the marsh, having taken note of Rikki, were keeping silence. Only, now and then, a frog croaked.

I no longer felt the same urgent compulsion to seek Marlowe out. I would make discreet enquires as to where he might be found, and call on him there. It could not be the next day, for I had heard Poley arranging to collect him the next morning, and take him to spend the day in

Deptford. The following day, then. I would call on Marlowe and speak to him about *Doctor Faustus*. I would not say outright that I was convinced that Faustus was Marlowe, but I would try to probe a little into what had prompted him to write about a man who had sold his soul to the devil.

The day after tomorrow, then. When he was back from Deptford.

Chapter Thirteen

The next day at St Thomas's was suddenly very busy. Two women already well into their birth contractions were brought in, one with the baby presenting wrongly, one with twins. The first was a hard birth, hard on the mother, the midwives, and me, but the babe was brought safely into the world. It was a boy and looked healthy enough. I reckoned he would survive, but the mother was much weakened and would need great care. She had lost a considerable amount of blood, more than was normal, so I put her on a diet of the best beef broth every two hours, and gave her tincture of willow bark to ease her considerable pain.

The other woman had borne twins before. I had examined her the previous week when she had a false start to the birth pains, and I was certain I could detect twins again.

'As God wills, doctor,' she said wearily, 'but the last lot are but a twelve month old. I don't know as how I am to feed them all.'

'Are you still working at Bess Travis's whorehouse?' I said severely. If these women would not take care, what could they expect?

''Tis the only home I has.' She was somewhat inclined to self pity.

'Well,' I said firmly, 'you cannot go on in that life. Not with four babies or little more than babies. We must find you something else to do. We will speak of it later. For now, we will set our minds to bringing these little ones into the world.'

Because she had already given birth to twins, matters went much more easily for her than for the other woman. The first baby came quickly, a healthy girl. Once I had ascertained that all was well with her, I handed her over to Goodwife Appledean to be washed and wrapped in a soft blanket, then laid in one of the simple wicker cradles we keep in the lying-in ward.

The second baby lingered a while, then came with a rush. Another girl, smaller, but seemingly sound. Leaving the mother and both baby girls to the midwives, I crossed the ward to see how the other new mother was faring. I was worried by her flushed face and feared she was developing a fever. I persuaded her to take more of the willow bark infusion, which is sovereign against fevers as well as pain, but it is bitter and she was reluctant.

'Doctor Alvarez!' Goodwife Appledean called across to me, not shouting – she never shouted – but with a sharp urgency to her voice that made it clear I was needed. I handed the cup to one of the sisters.

'Make sure she drinks it all,' I said.

The mother of the twins was writhing in her bed, complaining that she still had pains.

'Just as bad as at the start, doctor! What's wrong? Am I going to die?'

She rolled panic stricken eyes at me, reaching out to clutch at my sleeve. It is little wonder she was frightened, for every woman giving birth has cause to be frightened, childbirth being the greatest killer of women next the plague.

I took the clutching hand in both of mine and tried to calm her.

'It is only the afterbirth,' I said. 'You have given birth before. It is good that your body is ready to yield it up.'

'Doctor,' Goodwife Appledean said meaningfully, nodding toward the bed.

252

I let go of the woman's hand and looked where the midwife indicated. Jesu! It was not the afterbirth. It was another baby!

This one was very small, another girl, who must have been concealed by the bulk of her two sisters. She came forth easily, but I was not sure whether she was alive. Thin and bluish, she seemed already to have left the world before she was truly here amongst us. I held out my hand, and one of the midwives put a linen cloth in it, with which I wiped the baby's nose and mouth clear of blood while Goodwife Appledean dealt with the umbilical cord.

The child was not breathing.

I picked her up by her feet, holding her upside-down, and slapped her smartly on the back.

Nothing.

The midwives are used to every kind of birth, and know that some babies will be stillborn, if it is God's will, but I saw that one of the younger ones was crying.

I swung the baby gently, then slapped her back again. It looks cruel, but sometimes in this way you can give the lungs a shock, so that they begin to function. It is remarkable, after all, that most babies know how to start breathing as soon as they are out in the air. A natural inborn instinct.

The baby twitched slightly in my hands. She was not quite dead. I was about to try one last time when the tiny mouth opened and emitted a thin wail.

She was breathing!

I sat down on the end of the bed, laid the child face down on my lap and began to knead her back, rather as if I were working a delicate piece of pastry. Her cries grew stronger, and I could feel the small lungs under my fingers fighting to draw in more air.

'Give me a blanket,' I said, without looking up. 'I do not want her to become chilled.'

Luckily it was warm in the ward, but it would seem cold after the confines of a womb shared with her two bigger sisters. I wrapped her loosely in the small blanket

Goodwife Appledean handed me, then laid her against my shoulder and continued to rub her back. In this more comfortable position, she stopped fretting and began to breathe steadily.

'I think she will do now,' I said, handing her to Goodwife Appledean. 'Put her in with her sisters. They will feel safer, all of them together.'

The mother was slumped back against the pillow, with her arm across her eyes, as I stood up and looked down at her.

'She will live,' I said.

I was not sure whether or not she was pleased.

'Five babes,' she whispered. 'What am I to do?'

'For now, rest, once the sisters have changed your bedding. You need think about nothing more for the moment.'

Goodwife Appledean turned away from the cradle and clicked her tongue, looking at me.

'You are covered with blood, doctor. It's my fault. I should have wiped her clean before you took her on your lap.'

'There was no time,' I said, smiling at her. 'What are stained clothes compared with a life saved?'

Nevertheless, I would ask Mistress Maynard for a temporary change of clothes, and tell the hospital laundry to wash mine as quickly as possible. Fortunately I had removed my doublet, so only my shirt and breeches were marked.

What had started as a difficult day, continued along the same path. Once I had changed, I was called to the children's ward, where a boy had been brought in with a terrible slash across two fingers. He had found a dagger lying in a ditch and begun playing knights and dragons with it. Fortunately the dragon (a neighbour's dog) had escaped without injury, but in pursuing it the boy, whose name was Nol, had fallen on the dagger, nearly severing the fingers.

'Not again, Nol!' I said, pretending to make light of the blood soaked cloth his mother had wound around the hand. 'Is there never to be a month when we do not see you in here?'

Nol was a wild and fearless child, for his mother Eva was somewhat simple-minded and had no control over him. There was no known father. This time I feared the consequences of his rough play might be severe.

I unwound the cloth and viewed the injury, which was unpleasant, but it might be possible to save the fingers.

'Eva,' I said, 'do you go down to the kitchen and wait there. Tell them I say you are to have some soup and bread.'

She nodded, and trotted off obediently. It would be a relief not to have her present. The young sister Alice had already brought me boiled water with antiseptic herbs to cleanse the wound, and a salve of woundwort and comfrey.

'Good,' I said. 'I also need a suturing needle and thread.'

'You are going to stitch it?' She looked dubiously at Nol's small fingers, which were bleeding profusely.

'I shall try,' I said, over Nol's howls, which had grown louder when he heard the mention of needle and thread. I had been obliged to stitch an earlier injury, and he had not cared for it.

'I shall need both you and Goodwife Walker to hold him still while I work,' I said.

It was a grim business. Luckily, the dagger had not damaged the bone, but the flesh of the two fingers was deeply severed. Nol fought us all the way, and I came near to sewing my own hand to his at one point. By the end, all four of us were sweating and exhausted, but I had managed to bring the edges of both wounds together cleanly, then salved and bandaged the two fingers.

'Now, Nol,' I said, 'you are going to stay here in St Thomas's where I can keep an eye on you. Three good meals a day, I promise you.'

He gave me a shaky smile through his tears. A minor terror he might be, but he had suffered a great deal of pain. Three good meals a day was reward enough for the child of a mother who barely knew how to boil water. I was surprised she had known to wrap a rag about his hand, but Nol told me a neighbour had done it. The owner of the dragon dog, it seemed. Rare charity.

'And,' I said, 'I am going to ask the hospital cook for some sweetmeats. Do you like marchpane? Sugar paste? I think they will help the healing.'

He grinned, showing a mixture of baby and adult teeth, interspersed with gaps. 'B'yer lady, I do, doctor!'

I did not chide him for his language – he probably knew much worse – but sent Alice down to the kitchen for the treats.

'And tell Eva to go home to her other children,' I said. 'Nol will be safe with us for this while.'

The rest of the day, what little was left of it, never allowed me a moment to draw breath, so when I arrived home, weary, with Rikki, I banged on the door of Simon's room.

'Aye?' he called.

I stepped inside. 'Have you any food?'

'I thought we were going to the Lion for supper, so you can tell me what you made of *Dr Faustus* yesterday?'

'I am too tired to walk another step. Could you fetch us some pies from the pie shop? I'll go squares with you.'

'I'll do so. Why are you wearing those odd clothes?'

'Borrowed from the hospital. Mine were covered in blood. I'll fetch mine back tomorrow.'

I flung myself down on the bed with a groan.

'A hard day?' he said, at the door.

'Nobody died. Which was a good thing. A hopeless whore gave birth to triplets. *Triplets!* And she already has year-old twins. The triplets are like to survive, so I must find her other work than whoring. It might four next time.'

He gave a snort of laughter. 'Does that ever happen?'

256

'I don't know. I've never had triplets before. Then there was the seven-year-old imp who did his best to slice off his fingers with a filthy dagger he found. I may have saved them, or may not, but his mother is the simpleton Eva, so he's like to do it again.'

'Life is ever full of excitement at St Thomas's.'

'And I fear one of the other mothers may have contracted puerperal fever. I've left word I'm to be sent for if it grows worse.'

'In that case, I'd best make haste for the pies before you are called away,' he said, going out.

By the time he returned, I was sliding into sleep, and sat up dizzily at the savoury smell he brought with him.

'I've brought one for Rikki, too.'

'You spoil that dog,' I said. 'He will grow fat. Tom has already fed him.'

'I spoil him no more than you do, and I cannot refuse him now. He heard tell one was for him.'

I laughed, and reached out for the pie he handed me. Our local pie maker was famed throughout Southwark. If you were very poor, you could still buy a tasty pie if you did not enquire too closely what meat it contained. On the other hand, if you were prepared to pay more – as Simon had done – your pie would be made with the best quality beef, with some onion and mustard, encased in a fine flaky pastry. Simon passed me a pewter plate, which I held to catch the crumbs, while I ate the pie with my fingers. And licked them clean afterwards.

'Some new brewed ale to wash it down,' Simon said, 'and apple tarts for afterwards.'

Rikki, having swallowed his pie in two gulps, watched him hopefully, his tail swishing across the floor like a broom, but Simon shook his head.

'No apple tart for you, my lad.'

I had just accepted a second cup of ale when we both heard a knocking at the street door. I groaned.

'Not so soon!' I stood up resignedly. 'I might as well have stayed at the hospital.'

Then Goodwife Atkins called up the stairs, 'Visitor for you, Master Hetherington.'

Simon threw open his door and shouted down, 'Send him up, and welcome.'

I was sitting back down again in relief that it was not a summons to the hospital, when there was a rush of feet on the stairs and Will burst in, his hair pushed awry and his doublet ill buttoned.

'Will!' Simon cried in alarm. 'What's to-do? Is it the playhouse?'

Like all the players, he always feared damage or fire to the playhouse.

Will shook his head and sank down on the bed beside me, fighting for breath.

'It's Marlowe,' he gasped.

'Marlowe?' Simon said sharply. 'What of Marlowe? What fool trouble has he got himself into now?'

'Trouble of the worst sort.' Will's mouth twisted into a grimace. 'Aye, I think you could say that.'

He took a deep breath.

'He's dead.'

At first his words made no sense to me. How could Marlowe be dead? I had been sitting not three yards from him only yesterday. I simply stared at Will. Simon, after one sharp cry, began to question him.

'Where? How did it happen? Has he been in a fight again?'

Will shook his head.

'I know very little. We were eating at the Lion. Why were you not there? We expected you. Then some friend of the innkeeper came running in, a vintner, and whispered to him. It seems the news travels fast, for it cannot have happened more than two hours ago, at most. This fellow had been in Deptford, to see to the unloading of some firkins of Kent beer, come up by water, and then had himself rowed straight back here.'

'Deptford?' I said sharply. 'Did you say Deptford?'

'Aye,' Will said. 'It seems Marlowe has been there all day, eating and gaming at the house of some respectable widow – not his usual rough tavern. With a group of fellows–'

'Robert Poley.' I said. 'Ingram Frizer. Nicholas Skeres.'

'What?' they spoke both together, and gaped at me.

'Oh, Jesu!' I said, burying my head in my hands. I had begun to shake. 'I could have prevented. I should have warned him.'

Simon took me by the shoulder and shook me, none too gently.

'What are you babbling about, Kit? What do you mean, you could have prevented?'

'At Christmas,' I said. 'At Hampton Court. I overheard Poley and Frizer discussing someone who must be "stopped". I did not know who they meant, but they are villains, both of them. It spelled ill for someone. They are villains for hire, who will do anything for gain.'

'But why should that mean Marlowe?' Simon said.

He released my shoulder and I looked up as he turned to Will.

'Who was with Marlowe in Deptford?'

'Robert Poley,' he said. 'Ingram Frizer. And Nicholas Skeres.'

Simon gasped, and turned back to me.

'How did you know that those three would be with him today?'

'After the play yesterday, I wanted to speak to Marlowe, and I followed him down the stairs to the street.'

'Why? You both dislike each other.'

'I wanted–' I broke off. 'It doesn't matter now,' I said dully.

It would never matter now. I could never make my peace with Marlowe.

'Before I could catch him,' I said, 'Poley and Frizer came up to him.'

I paused, thinking about it. The scene was still clear in my mind.

'I think they must have been waiting for him. They closed in on him like a pair of sheriff's men, though they were sugary with pretended friendship. Poley said he had hired a room in the house of a Mistress Bull in Deptford, where they could spend a pleasant day, eating, strolling in the garden, and playing at tables.'

Will was nodding, his eyes wide with shock. 'That accords with what the vintner said.'

'Poley said he would meet Marlowe after he reported to the Privy Council in the morning. This morning. And they would take a boat down to Deptford. Frizer said he would bring Nicholas Skeres. To make up the number for any games they might play.'

'It all seems to have been as you say, Kit.' Will spoke slowly. 'But then they quarrelled over paying the reckoning to Mistress Bull. And we all know that Marlowe likes to slip out of paying his share. There was a fight, and he was killed. So why do you think you could have prevented?'

'Because it was a trap. Can you not see? Three men, all of them scoundrels, lure Marlowe away from London to some quiet house in Deptford. All goes well. Even if Marlowe had any suspicion of them – and why should he? – by early evening he must have been lulled into trust.'

'But it was an accident,' Will insisted.

I looked at him steadily. 'Do you really believe that, after all that has happened of late? Someone has been building a case against Marlowe as a dangerous troublemaker and heretic. God knows, he's helped them to it! This was no accident. Had he come to trial, the evidence would have been shown up as a flimsy tissue of lies, and with the talk of heresy there would have been trouble. And Marlowe, once he was cornered like a dangerous animal, would not have kept silent about secrets he knows, which certain men in power would do anything to suppress.'

'But–' said Will.

I glared at him, impatiently. 'Like me, Marlowe worked for Walsingham. I believe he has continued to work either for Burghley or for Essex. Perhaps for both. Where does he get the money he spends so lavishly? Not from the sale of his plays, unless he is paid ten times as much as you.'

I ran my fingers through my hair. 'As for Poley, Frizer, and Skeres, they are all, every one of them, former agents of the intelligence service. Poley still works for Burghley. I do not know about the other two, though I know Frizer has been in Sir Thomas Walsingham's household. Was he there to keep a watch on Marlowe? To report if his tongue began to wag? At any rate, they would be available – and willing – for any dirty work someone with a deep purse might want carried out.'

'But you are saying they would deliberately *kill*, Marlowe,' Simon said, disbelieving. 'Why?'

'I think he had become unreliable. Dangerous. When I saw him at the playhouse yesterday, he was in great distress of mind. And while Poley and Frizer were talking to him, he hardly seemed to be listening. "What you will," he said, as if he were indifferent, and walked off.'

'But who would go so far as to want him killed?'

'Men who would arrange the killing of an anointed queen,' I said.

By the following day, all of London knew that Marlowe was dead. The whole affair of the placards, the award offered, the seizure of Thomas Kyd, the threat of dangerous foreigners in the city, as well as even more dangerous heresy, native bred, had been talked of on every street corner and in every ale house. When Marlowe had been arrested and charged, the citizens' attention had focused on him. And now he was dead in a brawl (so it was reported by Lady Rumour on the streets). The citizens of London, wise after the event, forgot how they had flocked to his plays, and instead spoke of God's vengeance against a wicked heretic.

Well, perhaps he was a heretic. Thinking back to that evening at Durham House, I tried to remember whether Marlowe had really seemed to believe in his terrible arguments, but my memory was confused, overlaid by the more recent memory of watching *Dr Faustus*, and at the same time watching Marlowe. Perhaps, like Faustus, he had begun to play with the Devil's fire, but had not totally given himself up to it. I wished bitterly that I had pursued him after he left Poley. If I had been able to speak to him, perhaps I might have seen his mind more clearly. Now I would never know.

The inquest was to be held in Deptford the following day, and I gained Superintendent Ailmer's permission to attend, as one of the last to see Marlowe alive before he had gone to Deptford. My various patients were on the way to recovery. Even the mother whose fever had concerned me was much better. So, having recovered my clothes from the hospital laundry, I joined Simon, Will, Guy, and Ned in one of the two-man wherries, to be rowed down the river very early in the morning of Friday, the first day of June. More of the players were heading the same way, and I saw Master Burbage, looking wan and ill.

'As the Queen is in residence at Greenwich,' Ned said, 'that means Deptford is within the verge, as it's less than a mile away. The inquest has to be held by the Coroner to the Royal Household, William Danby. Nothing but the best for Kit Marlowe.'

His drawn face belied his grim jest. Where would his great tragic roles come from now that Marlowe was dead?

It seemed that Ned knew his way about Deptford, leading us from the landing stage to Mistress Bull's home, a substantial merchant's house overlooking Deptford Green. Wherever possible, an inquest is held, by law, at the scene of sudden death, so that the inquest on Marlowe would be held at the widow's house. The public are permitted to attend, provided there is room, and we had taken care to come early.

It was not the first inquest I had attended and I knew whenever possible it should take place *super visum corporis*, in sight of the body. To my relief, Marlowe's body remained in the small upstairs room where he had been killed, while the formal part of the inquest would take place in the large hall downstairs, at the centre of the house. Early as we were, the coroner and the sixteen jurors had arrived earlier. They had already viewed the body and the coroner's officers had taken measurements of the wounds, and noted the arrangement of the room and the position of the body. I was thankful not to be confronted with Marlowe's murdered body, but the summer weather was hot and the coroner had wisely chosen to take the evidence of the witnesses well away from it.

As we were making our way into the hall, I drew aside from the others and accosted one of the coroner's men.

'I do not know whether you wish to have my testimony,' I said. I was not eager to give it, but thought I should speak out. 'I saw Master Marlowe the evening of the day before his death, and I saw him in company with two of the men who were with him here the following day.'

He looked down his nose at me, as though he thought I was some fool seeking attention, and answered abruptly. 'I will mention it to Master Danby, but I'm certain sure he'll have no need of you. You did not witness the accident, did you? The three witnesses are all here to give evidence.'

'Very good,' I said, and made my way after Simon and the others.

So it was already being spoken of as an 'accident', was it?

The inquest was remarkably brief. I suppose the jurors had already been sworn in before we arrived, and there were only the three witnesses to be sworn in now: Poley, Frizer, and Skeres. I wondered why Mistress Bull was not called. She had not, presumably, witnessed the 'accident', but she could have given testimony as to the rest of the day. And she could also have given her impression of how the men had seemed together. Curious that she was not called.

One by one the three men gave their evidence. Poley, Frizer, and Skeres had been sitting in a row on a bench at a table, with Frizer in the middle. Marlowe had been lying on a bed. There had been a quarrel about how they should share out the paying of the reckoning to Mistress Bull for the day's food and accommodation. Marlowe had seized Frizer's dagger.

How? No one said.

Then Frizer had seized it back and stabbed Marlowe through the eye in self defence.

He had died almost instantly.

Their stories were very neat, matching almost word for word.

If Frizer had been seated with his back to Marlowe, pinioned between Poley and Skeres, how had he been able to seize the dagger and stab Marlowe with such force through the eye that it penetrated his brain? It was physically impossible.

And if initially Marlowe had really attacked Frizer, surely the other three strong men could have restrained him, without the need for killing him.

It all sounded too neat. And too implausible. Yet with great solemnity and dignity the coroner questioned them no further, pointed out to the jurors that Poley, Frizer, and Skeres had immediately surrendered themselves to the local authorities, in the right and proper manner. The jurors, a group of sober and decent looking local men, conferred only briefly before returning their verdict. The coroner's clerk read it aloud as recorded:

And so it befell, in that affray, that the said Ingram, in defence of his life, with the dagger aforesaid of the value of twelve pence, gave the said Christopher a mortal wound above his right eye, of the depth of two inches and of the width of one inch. Of this wound the said Christopher then and there died.

264

It was over. Frizer was not held guilty. It was all an accident, in the course of an affray begun by the dead man, the unspoken conclusion being that he had brought it upon himself.

Along with the rest of the public, we began to drift toward the door. I had never known an inquest so quickly and decisively concluded. Christopher Marlowe could now be disposed of and we would all leave, but not until I had caught the merest look exchanged between Poley and Frizer, which spoke more eloquently than their brief, smooth-spoken testimonies. It was a look of complacent satisfaction.

'The funeral is to be held this afternoon,' Ned said, after speaking to a clergyman who had been standing at the back of the hall. 'Here in Deptford, at the church of St Nicholas. That was the vicar, Thomas Macander. I shall stay for it. What of the rest of you?'

'Aye, let us stay,' Cuthbert said. 'We owe that at least to the poor fellow, even if he did bring it upon himself with his brawling.'

I opened my mouth to express my doubts, then closed it again. Here was not the place or time, at the edge of the green, with all the crowd about us.

'There is no point in returning to London,' Cuthbert said. 'Let us find some quiet inn where we can take a little food to sustain us, then go back after the funeral.'

There was general agreement to this suggestion. As Ned was familiar with Deptford, he led the way once again and brought us to a pleasant small inn standing in one of the streets leading off the green. Most of the players joined us there, but we were a subdued party. I sat at a table with Simon, Guy, Ned and Will, but had no inclination to eat, though I made a pretence of it, toying with some bread and cheese, though I drank thirstily of small ale, for the day continued hot.

'It is curious,' Guy said, 'that Frizer made so much of how he was attacked by Marlowe, but did you see signs of great injuries?'

265

'Nay,' Will said. 'I did not.'

'I took a chance to sidle near him,' Guy said. 'He has a couple of small scrapes on the back of his head. Not slashes with a dagger blade, I'd swear. It looks to me as though Marlowe pummelled him with the hilt. Unpleasant, but nothing serious.'

'And *how*,' I said aloud at last, 'was Frizer able to grab the dagger back and stab Marlowe to death, while sitting on a bench with his back to him?'

They all looked at me.

'I know a little of dagger wounds,' I said, 'in my work. I have not examined the body, but from the description of the thrust that killed Marlowe, I would say it was inflicted by a man standing in front of him. And also, why had he grabbed Frizer's dagger? Why not use his own? He always wore one. Had they agreed to lay their weapons aside for the day? But Frizer had not? If Marlowe had no dagger, he could not defend himself when Frizer went for him. Yet there was no mention of wounds to his hands or arms. An unarmed man, when attacked, will instinctively put up his arms to protect his face. Why did he not do so? Were his arms perhaps being held by the other two "witnesses" to this affray? Was he gripped so that he could not defend himself, while Frizer inflicted the blow that killed him?'

There was a hiss of in-taken breath, and they stared at me, aghast.

'I believe he was lured to Deptford with the intent to kill him. He was then provoked over something, anything. Marlowe was quick tempered. It would be easily done. That gave them the excuse to jump up, grab him. To kill him. For all we know, Marlowe may not even have caused those small injuries to the back of Frizer's head. They may simply have been inflicted by one of his fellows, to give colour to their story.'

'Kit,' Ned said cautiously, 'these are dangerous suggestions. The coroner and jurors have conducted a careful inquest. Are you saying that there was some plot involving them?'

'Not the jurors, of course not. The coroner? For all I know he is a most upright and honest man. But he did not probe the story very deeply, did he?, and those three men are all trained in deception. Even an upright and honest man could be deceived. What it amounts to is that I do not believe their story.'

'I suspect Kit may have the right of it,' Guy said, looking at me thoughtfully, 'but I fear there is nothing we can do about it.'

I held my peace at that, for I saw that they were all looking fearful. Sometimes I feel that players lead very protected lives. Only Guy was likely to understand what I was saying, having spent some time in the hard life of the streets. My service with Walsingham had long ago put an end to my own innocence.

'Come,' Ned said, 'it is time we made our way to the church.'

It was a short service, the funeral of Christopher Marlowe. He had no family here in London, for they were in Canterbury, too far away to be summoned in time for this hasty ceremony. Almost all those present were from the world of the playhouses. The coroner came, as a mark of respect, I suppose, as did one or two of the jurors, those who had not immediately returned to their daily business. Near the front I recognised Sir Thomas Walsingham, whom I had seen a few times at Seething Lane. I did not think he had been at the inquest, but perhaps news had only reached him in time for him to ride over from Scadbury for the funeral.

Robert Poley, Ingram Frizer, and Nicholas Skeres were not present.

After the service we walked out into the bright summer's day and round beside the side of the north tower. The church's sexton had just finished digging the grave, barely deep enough for decency, and stood to one side, leaning on his shovel and wiping his hot face with a large handkerchief. No one had provided money for a coffin, although I suppose Sir Thomas might have done so, had there not been such haste to bury Marlowe the moment the inquest was over. Instead, his shroud-wrapped body was removed from the parish coffin borrowed for pauper funerals, and lowered into the dirty grave. I thought of Marlowe's fine slashed doublets, with their gem-studded buttons, his silk shirts, his velvet breeches. To think that he should come to this. All around the grave the players were unashamedly weeping. Released myself from the angry restraint which had kept me dry eyed until now, I let my own tears fall.

As the vicar spoke the words 'earth to earth, ashes to ashes', a thrush, perched in an ancient yew tree beside the graveyard wall, began to sing, a wonderful flowing melody. It seemed a more fitting epitaph for this singer of verse than the dry words of the funeral service.

The following day I told the sisters in my two wards that I would be obliged to go out at midday, and might be absent for two hours at most. Everything was in hand, the triplets still doing well enough, even the small one, and the other mother's fever abated. Nol had been persuaded not to pick at his bandaged fingers with the promise of more sweetmeats if he was good.

While the hospital midday dinner was being served, I set off across the Bridge to Phelippes's office in the Custom House. I was well known here now, after my time in charge of the intelligence service. My banked down anger propelled me fast up the stairs and along the corridor. Outside Phelippes's door I stopped. I could hear voices within. Phelippes, but others I was not sure of. Not, to my relief, my lord of Essex. I knocked and was bidden in.

There were two men seated with Phelippes. The older man, leaning on a cane, I had met before. Lord Burghley. I bowed deeply. Old he might be now, and clearly growing frail, he was still the most powerful person in the kingdom after the Queen. Beyond him, a slight figure I had only seen at a distance, his younger son, being groomed up to take his place, Sir Robert Cecil. I bowed again, almost as low.

'Kit,' Phelippes said. There was a slight note of surprise in his voice, but not quite as much surprise as I might have expected. I was the one who was surprised. What were the Cecils doing here, with the man who was running the intelligence service of their great rival, the Earl of Essex?

'My Lord,' he said, I believe you have met Dr Alvarez before.'

I bowed again, and Lord Burghley inclined his head.

'Sir Robert, this is Dr Alvarez, a physician at St Thomas's hospital.'

Another bow, another inclination of the head.

'Dr Alvarez needs no introduction,' Sir Robert said. His voice was quite high pitched, but musical. 'We are well aware of Dr Alvarez's services to the Queen and to England.'

I found myself unaccountably blushing. I had come to rant at Phelippes and now found myself seriously wrong footed.

'I wonder why you are here, Kit?' Phelippes's tone was bland.

I might ask the same about these gentlemen I thought. However, I must say something, so I had better say what I had come to say, though perhaps in more moderate language. The three men remained seated and I was not invited to sit, but I preferred to remain standing.

'It is about the killing of Christopher Marlowe,' I said, watching their faces carefully. Phelippes's did not change, but the two Cecils exchanged a glance.

'I believe his death was no accident, but was deliberate murder, deliberately planned.'

None of them said anything, so I recounted briefly what I had overheard at Hampton Court, and the encounter between Poley, Frizer, and Marlowe outside the Rose.

They were all listening intently, not interrupting, so I went on to repeat what I had said to the players after the inquest, about the nature of Marlowe's injury, the fact that he had had no weapon and had apparently been unable to defend himself, even by throwing up his arms.

'I believe he was murdered,' I ended. 'It was no accident.'

There was a moment's silence, then Phelippes said calmly, 'And what do you propose we do about it? The inquest verdict has been given. Are you suggesting that Ingram Frizer should now be arrested for murder? I am no lawyer, but I am not sure that is possible. Not after the coroner's verdict.'

I knew that Phelippes was very well versed in the law, so I ignored that.

'There is no reason Frizer, or either of the other men, should have killed Marlowe for personal reasons. I believe they were paid to do it. As you know very well, Thomas, there has been a most careful attempt to incriminate Marlowe with the charges of heresy and treason, but it could not be proved. It is very *convenient* that he is now dead.'

Inside I was shaking. I knew that by speaking thus I was virtually running my own head into a noose.

Phelippes turned to Burghley. 'What do you say, my lord?'

Burghley cleared his throat, rested both hands on his stick and fixed on me a penetrating glance that had not dimmed with age.

'I am aware that Marlowe was no friend of yours, Dr Alvarez. It is very commendable of you, therefore, to seek justice for him. However, the verdict has been given. To drag this affair through the streets, as it were, would do no good. London trembles on the brink of more riots, even a serious uprising. It would not be wise to add fuel to that fire. You have made an excellent case, and I honour you for it, but we will let the matter rest, and confine ourselves to prayers for the poor young man's soul.'

Halfway across the Bridge, where there is a gap between the houses, I stopped. This was a favourite place of mine, where you can watch the river flowing away to the sea. As it was mid summer, the docks below the Customs House were crowded with vessels from the Low Countries, from Venice, from Constantinople, some perhaps even from the New World, their masts and spars a veritable floating forest. The long ferry was just departing for Gravesend, and the usual scatter of wherries plied back and forth. Over all the river traffic, the grim walls of the Tower rose.

Perhaps it was better for Marlowe to have died quickly in Deptford than to have endured torture in the Tower and a heretic's death by fire in Smithfield. For it might have come to that. I knew beyond a doubt that those great men had planned his secret killing. The Cecils certainly, but perhaps Essex also, the rivals working together for once to rid themselves of a man who knew too much.

There is danger in words.

Marlowe had been a man of words, beautiful words, poetry which sang as sweetly as the thrush had sung over his pauper's grave.

And after all, what is left of such a man, but his words? His paltry crimes, his brawls, even his cruel words to a Portingall refugee – all these would vanish into thin air. His vision, his plays, had dealt too often for me with the dark side of life, but perhaps if we do not confront the dark side we can never come to know the side turned to the light. Watching him in the playhouse, as Faustus cried out in despair, I had felt that he was crying out to me. Or for me.

Marlowe would not be forgotten, however those men, great in worldly power, might have hoped to silence him. He would live through his words.

I had been wrong to try to hold back the passing moment, as Faustus in his despair had tried to do. We cannot give way to the hope that time may cease. Nor should it. Should time stand still, it would be a kind of

271

death. The astronomical clock would continue to mark the passing of time, long after I was gone. The river would continue to flow, ever changing, into the sea, there to be lost, like Faustus's vision of his soul transformed into water drops.

There is danger in words, but there is power too, and an enlargement of man's spirit.

Marlowe's words – like time – would never cease.

Historical Note

The events which took place in London in 1592-3 are historically accurate. They heralded the beginning of troubles which would continue throughout the 1590s, growing worse toward the end of the decade with a series of failed harvests, leading to widespread hunger and starvation.

A number of factors contributed to the unrest. Throughout England, more and more of the landowners, whose incomes had been falling ever since the population crash caused by the Great Pestilence (Black Death), were looking about for ways to improve their financial position. The wool trade had long been a major part of the economy, and had grown even more important once England became famous for high quality finished cloth, as well as its traditional export of fleeces.

For medium and large landowners, turning over their land to grazing for sheep offered a much more attractive and financially viable alternative to collecting rents or service from dozens of small tenants. They began to turn these tenants off their rented farms. Also, for landless families, previously employed on the lord's own farms, the replacement of agricultural labour by sheep-herding meant the disappearance of jobs.

In addition, many overlords began to 'enclose' (that is, take possession of) the common lands on which villagers had the right to graze their stock, and woodlands where they had the right to cut timber for building and to gather firewood.

These practices took place over a much longer period than the later 'clearances' in the Scottish Highlands. And since landholdings were much smaller, the effect was slower and more drawn out, but the results were similar.

These results were two-fold. First, England began to see the homeless country people moving into the towns in search of work, and above all they flocked to London, which could not cope with the numbers – it could not house, feed, or provide employment for the incomers.

Hungry, dispossessed, and without work, these people turned naturally to blaming the foreign refugees who had come to London. Many were skilled craftsmen or professional men, unlikely to fill the kind of jobs needed by the dispossessed, but there is little place for reason in an atmosphere of resentment. All foreigners were hated.

Secondly, the reduction in the acreage of farmland in England dedicated to arable crops meant the beginning of food shortages. When the harvest was poor, there was a serious dearth.

Moreover, ever since the Great Pestilence, the common people had begun to find their own voice. The resulting collapse in the labour force meant that labour became more valuable, one of the factors leading to the Peasants' Revolt of 1381. A readiness to question the authority of the Church and of the nobles led to further disturbances, like the rise of the Lollards and Jack Cade's revolt in the fifteenth century, as well as various disturbances during the sixteenth. Increased literacy, the arrival of printing, publication of the Bible in English, and the opening up of the world through exploration – all of these meant that the restlessness of the common people grew more strident, only to explode in the seventeenth century.

The anti-foreign atmosphere in London was aggravated by Marlowe's play, *The Jew of Malta*, and when the provocative placards began to be posted up on walls throughout the city, reference was made to several of his plays. Was this a crude attempt to implicate Marlowe in the fostering of discontent?

The case of Marlowe's death is one of the great unsolved mysteries. Was he killed by accident or deliberately? Even now many of his activities remain in the shadows. Certainly there are questions to be asked (but probably not answered) about the curious coin forging incident. On more than one occasion Marlowe was protected by the Privy Council or someone in power, even back at the time when Cambridge was ordered to grant him his degree, despite his prolonged absences from the university.

It is possible that more documentary evidence may come to light, but it may have been destroyed long ago. What survives as 'evidence' of Marlowe's heresy was too flimsy to stand up in court at the time. Marlowe was not imprisoned, only required to report daily to the Privy Council. Most men, even on such poor evidence, would have been imprisoned. Kyd, after all, was tortured.

Why wasn't Marlowe?

Was someone protecting him? Yet it looks, from our perspective, as though someone (someone else?) wanted to put a stop to him. He seems to have had dangerous information, and he was clearly a loose cannon.

The inquest brought in a verdict which pardoned that unmitigated scoundrel, Ingram Frizer, declaring he had acted in self defence. This writer, for one, doesn't believe a word of it.

Marlowe was murdered.

The Author

Ann Swinfen spent her childhood partly in England and partly on the east coast of America. She was educated at Somerville College, Oxford, where she read Classics and Mathematics and married a fellow undergraduate, the historian David Swinfen. While bringing up their five children and studying for a postgraduate MSc in Mathematics and a BA and PhD in English Literature, she had a variety of jobs, including university lecturer, translator, freelance journalist and software designer. She served for nine years on the governing council of the Open University and for five years worked as a manager and editor in the technical author division of an international computer company, but gave up her full-time job to concentrate on her writing, while continuing part-time university teaching in English Literature. In 1995 she founded Dundee Book Events, a voluntary organisation promoting books and authors to the general public.

She is the author of the highly acclaimed series, *The Chronicles of Christoval Alvarez*. Set in the late sixteenth century, it features a young Marrano physician recruited as a code-breaker and spy in Walsingham's secret service. In order, the books are: ***The Secret World of Christoval Alvarez***, ***The Enterprise of England***, ***The Portuguese Affair***, ***Bartholomew Fair***, ***Suffer the Little Children***, ***Voyage to Muscovy***, ***The Play's the Thing,*** and ***That Time May Cease***.

Her *Fenland Series* takes place in East Anglia during the seventeenth century. In the first book, ***Flood***, both men and women fight desperately to save their land from greedy and unscrupulous speculators. The second, ***Betrayal***, continues the story of the dangerous search for legal redress and security for the embattled villagers, at a time when few could be trusted.

Her latest series, *Oxford Medieval Mysteries*, is set in the fourteenth century and features bookseller Nicholas Elyot, a young widower with two small children, and his university friend Jordain Brinkylsworth, who are faced with crime in the troubled world following the Black Death. The first book in the series is ***The Bookseller's Tale***, the second is ***The Novice's Tale***.

She has also written two standalone novels. *The Testament of Mariam*, set in the first century, recounts, from an unusual perspective, one of the most famous and yet ambiguous stories in human history, while exploring life under a foreign occupying force, in lands still torn by conflict to this day. *This Rough Ocean* is based on the real-life experiences of the Swinfen family during the 1640s, at the time of the English Civil War, when John Swynfen was imprisoned for opposing the killing of the king, and his wife Anne had to fight for the survival of her children and dependents.

Ann Swinfen now lives on the northeast coast of Scotland, with her husband, formerly vice-principal of the University of Dundee, and a rescue cat called Maxi.
www.annswinfen.com